BEST DEFENSE

This Large Print Book carries the
Seal of Approval of N.A.V.H.

BETH BOWMAN, P.I.

BEST DEFENSE

RANDY RAWLS

THORNDIKE PRESS
A part of Gale, Cengage Learning

GALE
CENGAGE Learning·

Farmington Hills, Mich • San Francisco • New York • Waterville, Maine
Meriden, Conn • Mason, Ohio • Chicago

LIBRARY OF CONGRESS CATALOGING-IN-PUBLICATION DATA

Rawls, Randy, 1938–
    Best defense : Beth Bowman, P.I. / by Randy Rawls. — Large print edition.
      pages ; cm. — (Thorndike Press large print mystery)
    ISBN 978-1-4104-6939-7 (hardcover) — ISBN 1-4104-6939-5 (hardcover)
    1. Women private investigators—Fiction. 2. Murder—Investigation—Fiction. 3. Kidnapping—Investigation—Fiction. 4. Florida—Fiction. I. Title.
PS3618.A967B47 2014
813'.6—dc23   2014005058

Published in 2014 by arrangement with Midnight Ink, an imprint of Llewellyn Publications, Woodbury, MN 55125-2989 (USA).

Printed in Mexico
1 2 3 4 5 6 7 18 17 16 15 14

Best Defense is dedicated to My Honey, Ronnie Bender, who tolerates me well, and to my wonderful children, Theresa (Tracy) Rawls Eilers and David Rawls.

ACKNOWLEDGMENTS

Every author, especially this one, needs others to lean on; to get through a difficult scene, to insure the words say exactly what you mean them to say, and, of course, to help with all those pesky typos and grammar issues. I am fortunate to have some wonderful friends, each of them accomplished authors, to review my material and keep me straight. So, a hearty thanks to Sylvia Dickey Smith, Earl Staggs, Gregg Brickman, Vicki Landis, Stephanie Levine, Rich Hodes, and Ann Meier. Each of you have significant fingerprints on *Best Defense,* and I am fortunate you were there.

ONE

My client, Sabrina Hammonds, lived in one of Broward County's many upscale neighborhoods. Large, single-family homes on lots big enough to stage a rodeo. From the street, I could see the fenced area in the back that surrounded their Olympic-sized pool.

The front yard sprouted the obligatory palm trees and blooming flora. Landscaping blocks divided everything into neat sections. Either Mr. Hammonds was a nature freak, or he used a lawn care service. From what I'd seen of him, probably the latter. His tastes ran more to skanky women.

The wide driveway leading to the three-car garage was empty. Not much of an indicator since it was the same when I first visited Ms. Hammonds. She kept her S-Class Mercedes out of the hot Florida sun. I'd have done the same — if I'd had a garage and a hundred thousand dollar car.

Especially if I had such a luxury ride.

I parked under the porte-cochere, checked my briefcase to make sure I hadn't forgotten the report, then headed for the massive front entrance. As I reached toward the bell, I noticed the door was ajar. Not open, mind you, just a small gap like someone had come out and let the door swing closed behind them. I pushed the button and the chimes of Big Ben sounded. They didn't seem a bit out of context.

While waiting for the echo to die away, I looked around. It was a fancy protected entryway with a half-circle stained glass window above the oversized walnut double doors. The window had the inevitable palm tree etched into it. An air conditioning vent pumped cold air into the semi-enclosed area, making it almost comfortable, despite the ninety-plus degrees temperature a few steps away.

When I was there before, the maid had opened the door, then reported my presence to Ms. Hammonds. I figured she could be in the back of the house — a long way from the front. Since I didn't want to appear pushy, I waited longer than my norm before nudging the bell again. As before, the day ticked away with no response.

I supposed it could be the maid's day off.

Since I'd never had enough money to employ a domestic, I wasn't sure how their workweeks went. If so, Ms. Hammonds might be slow getting to the door. I waited.

After what I considered a suitable time, I rang the bell a third time. Same result.

Could Ms. Hammonds be out, no one home? Always possible and even probable, given the length of time I'd stood there. Yet, the unsecured door beckoned me. Would I be remiss to walk away, leaving the house open? Wouldn't I be doing my civic duty to stick my head in to see if everything was all right? I mean, it was something any good citizen would be expected to do, right? Sure, it would.

I sounded the chimes of Big Ben once more. By this time, my normal personality was kicking in. I have a great deal of difficulty with patience. I realize that might sound incongruent with my working as a PI. My job requires I spend hours waiting for something to happen, whether it be a stakeout on a criminal or waiting for a husband or a wife to make a meet. In those instances, I fidget, I pace, I play mental word and number games. I've taught myself to multiply three digit numbers by three digit numbers while lurking in inconspicuous places.

I checked my watch — for at least the tenth time. No response to the doorbell. Time to see what the story was. I pulled on the door and peeked into the house. The contrast between the outside brightness and the inside dimness made it tough to see.

I stepped across the threshold and hit a switch on the panel beside the door. When the lights came on, I saw two things — the first was closed blinds. The second sent a chill to my soul. In the middle of the foyer, a body sprawled on the floor. From the position of the arms and legs, I knew the person was not napping.

I rushed over, hoping against hope my first impression was wrong. But checking the carotid artery gave truth to my fear — no pulse. With all the blood on her clothing and puddled on the floor around her, I wasn't surprised. The body lay face down, but I was sure I knew her. From the shape and size, it had to be Ms. Hammonds. It looked like her husband got to her before I did. I wanted to roll her over, but knew that would be stupid. The police would not appreciate my messing with their crime scene.

Her husband. Could he still be in the house? I whirled around, my eyes digging into every corner. No one there, but I saw only one of the twenty or so rooms that made up the Hammonds' mansion. I took my pistol out of my purse, then set off to ensure I was alone — or that no one wishing me harm was there.

While searching the lower level, I called nine-one-one and reported my discoveries. The operator told me to meet the police out front, but I ignored her. If someone was in the house, I wanted to know.

In a large pantry off the kitchen, I found the maid. She, too, was dead. From the marks on her neck, my guess was someone had strangled her. As I completed my trip around the downstairs, I heard a noise from the front of the house, then a call of, "Police. Anyone here?" I took a deep breath and started toward the front room.

The cops met me in the hall with the obligatory order to drop my weapon and assume *the position* against the wall. I complied and a young patrolman named Johnson explored areas I preferred not touched by a stranger. However, I understood. I'd have done the same if I had found anyone during my search, and I wouldn't have concerned myself about his or her private parts.

Once he finished, I showed my PI credentials. "Before this goes too far, I suggest you go after the victim's husband. His name is

John Hammonds, and he's an attorney with Hammonds, Perches, and Ballson in Fort Lauderdale."

"And why should I do that?"

"Because," I said, frustration setting in, "she hired me to catch him with one of his women. She was going to divorce him and clean out his bank accounts. From the look of things, he figured it out and took care of the problem."

Johnson said, "Sorry, your hunches aren't enough for me to act on. You'll have to save it for the detectives. They should be here soon. Anyone else in the house?"

"I didn't make it upstairs, but I found another body." I told him about the maid. "She must have seen him, so he killed her also. I'm telling you, the sooner you arrest the husband, the quicker you close the case."

"Like I said, ma'am, that's the detectives' call. Now, if you'll just wait out front with Officer LaBelle, I'll secure the scene." He walked me to the front door.

On the lawn, I repeated my plea to La-Belle. Same results. Someone had given them specific instructions about their duties at a homicide scene, and I assumed they had scored high in that class.

That left me nothing to do but exercise

14

patience — again — so I walked to my car, climbed in, fired it up, and started the air conditioner. Mom always said you don't have to practice to be miserable. Standing in South Florida's blazing sun equaled miserable. Sitting in an air-conditioned car equaled better. No contest.

I took the surveillance report out of my briefcase. A wasted effort. No one now to deliver it to. I spent a few minutes feeling sorry for the lost fee, sorry for myself.

But if I thought my day was bad, it hit rock bottom when the unmarked police car came to a stop behind me. I may have steamed up my rearview mirror when Detectives Dick Bannon and Major Sargent got out. I knew them. They knew me. I had no respect for them. They didn't like me. And those were the parts of our relationship you could mention in mixed company.

They didn't look any different from the first time I saw them — or the last time. They were both six-footers, give or take an inch. Dark blue off-the-rack suits that showed the wear and tear of the street. However, the clothing didn't really matter, they just carried an aura of cop. Maybe it was the squint of their eyes or the way they walked. I couldn't identify it, but they may as well have worn their badges on their foreheads.

Bannon tapped on my window. When I lowered it, he said, "Well, Ms. Bowman, so nice to see you again. I understand we have another homicide with your fingerprints on it."

"Not exactly," I said. "You have a homicide. I'm just the citizen who found the bodies."

"So I heard. Let's find some place we can sit and talk. This sun is too hot for my liking. The M.E. is on the way."

"My favorite skirt-PI," Sargent said from behind Bannon, giving me his *pretty* smile, the one he reserved for use with his most sarcastic remarks. "Somehow I just knew we'd meet again. How many bodies this time? Dispatch said only one, but I figure I misheard. You're better than that."

I wanted to tell him there was one less body than I'd like — his — but decided that wouldn't be smart. Also, I had to admit, he had a point. The last time I saw him and Bannon, the body count would have made a car-bomber proud. Rather than match their attitudes, I went with, "Sorry, it's two. And yes, before you ask, one of them was a client of mine. Sabrina Hammonds, wife of John Hammonds of Hammonds, Perches, and Ballson."

"Looks like you're moving up in society," Bannon said. "And I'm impressed. You even learned the name of your client. Last time we crossed paths, you didn't have a clue about the identity of the woman who hired you."

That elicited a laugh from the two of them and a grimace from me. He was right, but I wasn't there to revisit that situation. Of course, I could have enjoyed telling them I'd solved the case, not them.

They hadn't changed a bit since our last encounter. If forced to talk to them, and they were cops so I had no choice, I preferred Bannon. At least I could catch him in a listening mode once in a while. Sargent, never — always sour, always sarcastic, always a horse's ass.

I said, "If you can drag yourselves out of the past, there's a dead woman in there whose husband killed her. I tried to explain to the two uniforms, but they have heads carved from the same oak tree as yours. Is it a requirement to have a hardwood cranium to be a cop in this town?"

I smiled my most innocent smile while hesitating, then jumped in when I saw a response appear in Sargent's eyes. "Now, listen carefully, and I will explain this to you. Don't worry about taking notes, I will

17

enunciate very slowly. Ms. Hammonds came to me because her loving husband has been sleeping around on her. She planned to divorce him and take every dime he has. He discovered her plot and took care of the problem before it went too far. That's it. End of case. Now, I recommend you put out a BOLO on him before he skips the state."

Bannon looked at Sargent and shook his head. The look in his eyes told me there was a hole in my hypothesis.

"Yeah," Sargent said. "She's hallucinating again. Ma'am, Ms. Private Investigator, Mr. Hammonds is on his way. He should be here any minute. He was in court when we made contact. It took a few minutes for him to get an adjournment, or he'd be here already."

My stomach sailed south. "You sure?"

"Oh no, Ma'am, I'm not sure. I just make up stories like this on the fly. However, I really must get on about my business instead of listening to your fairy tales. But, if you'd like, I'll give you time to explain your crazy theory to him as soon as he arrives. Detective Bannon, if you will please take the *lady's* statement, I'll get things rolling inside."

"Hold up, Major," Bannon said. "That could be Mr. Hammonds turning into the driveway now. Ms. Bowman, please don't leave. I'd better escort Mr. Hammonds. He can't like what he'll see."

I cooled my heels for the next two hours while detectives, uniforms, and the medical examiner did their thing. After an eternity, the bodies were removed. Various groups went into the house with few leaving. I recognized some of the faces, crime scene techs I'd seen on previous jobs. I didn't envy them. The place had at least twenty rooms that would require detailed examination. I hoped they didn't find any more victims.

To save gas — one never knew how much the next tank full would cost — I killed my engine and left the car. The Hammonds had a gazebo in an area of the yard shaded by palm trees so I camped out there. The time gave me a chance to review the bad fortune that placed me in a position to find the bodies.

Ms. Hammonds had hired me to get *the goods* on her husband, John Hammonds, Attorney at Law. She said he was unfaithful, and she wanted a divorce — along with the houses, the cars, his property, and all his money.

Based on her description, he was easy to spot leaving his office. Picture the success-

ful attorney as played by the newest Holly-
wood superstar and that was John Hammonds. Over six feet tall, weight under
control, and black, well-trimmed hair that
bounced with each step — but not too
much — wearing a suit that fit him perfectly.
While he didn't have the Hollywood-scruffy
beard, his five o'clock shadow made his face
swarthy. The kind of man who could make
any girl's heart flutter — handsome by every
definition in every dictionary.

Since I'd planted a GPS tracking device
under his right rear wheel well, following
him was no problem. He drove straight to
an expensive restaurant where he approached a woman sitting alone at a table
in the bar, kissed her on the cheek, and sat
across from her, taking her hand in his. She
didn't fit the image of a floozy, having
passed several years of her prime, but their
actions showed they were close. From my
position across the room, nursing an over-
priced mixed drink, heavy on the water, I
could see familiarity flowing between them.
They were circumspect though, not groping
in public. After a couple of drinks, they went
to dinner while I sat in my car and watched
through the window, munching a stale sandwich.

They took their time as if they were in no

rush to get to the deed. When they left, they went in Mr. Hammonds' car. He drove to a Hilton, let the valet have his car, then walked with her through the lobby. I followed his example and stayed with them until she led him into a room. Enough for me. Case wrapped, time to go home to bed.

The next morning — today — I compiled the report I was anxious to give to Ms. Hammonds. After being unable to reach her on the phone, I drove over. If I didn't deliver it, I'd have to watch Mr. H. again that evening. I could see no point in running up the bill. He was what he was, and I knew what he was.

As I re-thought the day, it was obvious he was a husband who took the easy way out of divorce and losing his riches — he killed his wife. Yeah, I knew the first reaction was to suspect the spouse, but in this case, it made sense. She knew about his philandering ways. She hired me. She wanted a divorce. She wanted all his money and possessions. Solution? Eliminate her. Sounded solid to me. However, perhaps Bannon and Sargent knew something I didn't — or maybe they were being pigheaded again as in the last time we shared an investigation. I ended up doing all the work in that one while they insulted my intellect.

Finally, after I'd gone through my *facts* the forty-eighth time, or so it seemed, Bannon approached me and dropped onto the bench. "Ms. Bowman, thank you for waiting. I'd like to get a statement, if you're willing."

"Willing? What makes you think that? I've been picking up splinters in my butt just to pass the time of day. Anytime you're ready, as long as you make it right now. Otherwise, I'm out of here."

He laid a small recorder on the table. "Do you mind if I tape it?"

"Whatever," I said, fluttering a hand. "It's short and not so sweet. Let me know when to start talking."

He flicked a button, then established the date, time, location, and our identities. "In your own words, Ms. Bowman, explain the events leading up to your discovery of the body and your subsequent actions."

I went through my story, being careful not to leave anything out. I wanted them to know everything I knew — which, in the telling, didn't seem like all that much.

After asking a couple of questions to clarify points he thought I missed, he turned the recorder off. He rubbed his hand over his face, a face that now seemed old and tired. It was like wrinkles had developed since he arrived at the house. "Thank you, Ms. Bowman. We'll be in touch if we need anything else."

"Hold on," I said. "You're not getting off that easy. How'd she die? Are you arresting her husband? How about the maid? Any other bodies in the house?"

He gave me a look filled with fatigue. "The M.E. says two gunshot wounds in the back. Probably one penetrated the heart. No, we're not arresting her husband. No reason to. Third, someone strangled the maid. My best guess is that someone snuck up behind her with some sort of garrote. Ms. Hammonds and the maid appear to be the only victims." He paused. "Now, if you're satisfied, I still have hours of work to do." He started down the steps of the gazebo, then stopped. "I envy you, Ms. Bowman. You can find a body and walk away. Public employees like me have to clean up the mess."

"What about me? Do I have to hang around any longer?"

"No, Ms. Bowman. In fact, I'd feel much better if you left."

A day that started on a high had collapsed into a heap of nothing. My client was dead, and no one except me thought her husband was a likely suspect. Plus, I had Bannon and

Sargent in my life again. All I needed to top it off was one of my mom's phone calls telling me of her premonitions. I climbed into my Toyota and backed out of the driveway.

TWO

I drove aimlessly, nowhere to go, and the rest of the day to get there. The man I adored, Dr. David Rasmussen, was at a medical convention in Los Angeles. Four o'clock in Florida meant one o'clock there. Hours before I could talk to him. Besides, what would I tell him? *Hey, honey, you see it's like this. A wife hired me to follow her husband. I caught him with his honey. But before I could report to her, somebody killed her, and I'm the only one who thinks the husband is the logical suspect. Then it got worse. Bannon and Sargent caught the case. They haven't changed — still don't believe a word I say.*

No, that wouldn't work. David already had doubts about us because of my profession. No need to encourage that attitude. After considering all the options, I figured going home was the best bet. My fridge was looking like a biological warfare lab — lots of green stuff growing, and I don't mean broccoli or any of that other green stuff I had to eat as a child. I could clean it while hoping a new case came along. Or Sly Bergstrom landed a client who needed me.

Sylvester Bergstrom was the senior partner at Bergstrom and Bergowitz. B&B represented major civil cases for insurance companies. I connected to them soon after moving from Dallas to South Florida. A letter of introduction and recommendation from one of the top firms in Texas got my toe in the door, but my job performance kept me there. Sly, as his friends called him, was a solid supporter as long as I developed the information he needed to keep him on top. I did, and he was. He paid a nice retainer that was sufficient to handle my mortgage, but not enough to keep food in the refrigerator and gas in the car. For that, I needed freelance work or for him to land a really big case that would allow me billable hours for days, perhaps weeks.

I pulled into my driveway and turned the engine off. I sat there. If someone had come by, I'd have said I was listening to the radio, but really, I was just killing time. I was in the midst of my own premonition, the one that said if I went into the house, my mother would call. After a few minutes, I shrugged, gave up, and went in.

Sure enough, the phone rang as soon as I opened the door. I scurried through to the kitchen and checked the caller ID. Yep. May as well get it over with.

"Hi, Mom. So good to hear from you."

"What's up? What kind of trouble are you in?"

"None. Everything is fine. Why do you ask something like that?" Like I needed an answer to that one. I couldn't remember any time in my life she hadn't anticipated my problems, or thought she was anticipating them. Even my marriage to Sonny-the-Bunny didn't escape her radar. A week before the ceremony, she told me he'd never be faithful to one woman, least of all, *me.* She figured any woman who dressed as casually as I did could never get a man. Of course, I refused to believe her, married him, and stayed with the jerk for two years, even after suspecting she was right. Walking in on him with one of his lady-*friends* proved it was time to leave.

My mother said, "No real reason. I just had a feeling something was going on there. Are you sure you're okay?"

"Yes, Mom. It's been a quiet day." Inspiration struck. "I spent the day with my head in the refrigerator. I had no idea it needed cleaning so badly. That's probably what caused your feeling. Some of the stuff I pulled out of there might have been toxic. Maybe that's why you thought I was in trouble." I chuckled to reinforce my words, then swallowed it. If I laid it on too thick, she'd be sure to see through it.

"I don't think so," she said, doubt resonating through the line. "It didn't feel like that kind of premonition."

"Well, I can't think of anything else. Maybe it was something you ate."

"Funny. If I've told you once, I've told you a dozen times. Funny, you are not. Now, if you're sure you're all right, I'll hang up. I have to get dressed. I have a date tonight. Bye, dear."

"Good-bye, Mom. Have a nice time." Her words registered with a bang. "A date? Who —" I stopped because I was speaking into a dead phone.

A date? Well, why not? My mother was an attractive woman who stayed single after my father died when I was young. She worked hard to raise my brother and me. Oh, she went out with a few men, but none of them caught her fancy. She'd say, "After your dad, no man measures up." So I was sure that whomever she was dating would soon be history.

The refrigerator put up a hardy fight, but finally succumbed to my superior intellect and power. Well, that and a full bottle of Lysol. When I finished, the green was gone, my refrigerator smelled fresh and clean, and I had burned enough daylight to consider what to have for dinner.

The phone rang. When I checked the caller ID, the number was not familiar. "Hello."

"Ms. Bowman," a man said in a rushed voice. "This is John Hammonds. I need your help."

"Slow down. Who'd you say you are?"

"John Hammonds. You know my wife, Sabrina. That's why I'm calling. I need your help."

I lowered the phone and stared at the earpiece, then put it back into speaking position. "Did you say you need my help?"

"Yes. Can you come over — I mean, right now? Uh, if it's convenient?"

"John Hammonds? As in husband of Sabrina Hammonds?"

"Yes. I told you that. Please, I need to talk to you. Come to my house. I'll make it worth your while."

For the second time that day, I was at the Hammonds' house. No matter how I played it, his phone call made no sense. Why had he summoned me? If it had been the police, I'd have understood, but the husband I suspected of being the murderer? It just didn't add up. However, it was so intriguing I couldn't resist. So, I made a fast sandwich, grabbed a bottle of water, and jumped into my car, eating as I drove.

Hammonds' driveway was wide and long, but I still had to park near the street. There were cop cars everywhere, or so it seemed. A couple of Ford Crown Victorias, a current year black and white that shined like it had just left the showroom, patrol cars that had actually seen patrol duty, even a Dodge Charger. The common factor was each had the cheapest hubcaps money could buy. The one that didn't seem to fit, other than my Toyota, appeared to be a rental.

Lights blazed wherever I looked — front lawn, gazebo, and shining through every window. Before I could get out of my car, a uniform was beside it. "Excuse me. Are you Ms. Bowman?"

"Yes, I am. I —"

"Come with me." He opened my door and ushered me out, then turned and quick-stepped away. As I fell behind, he said, "We'll go through the garage. The front area is still a crime scene."

That part pleased me and not because it was a crime scene. I remembered the foyer from earlier. I didn't care to walk through there.

He punched in a code at the garage door, and it swung upward.

Fluorescent lights glared, giving everything the brightness and harshness of high noon. I flinched as memories of Sabrina's crumpled body flooded me when we passed her Mercedes. My escort rapped on the door to the house.

Another young uniform swung the door inward. From his looks, the two of them could have been in the same class. If so, I assumed the inside officer scored higher — simply because he drew the better duty — inside and air-conditioned.

"Ms. Bowman for Mr. Hammonds," my escort said.

"She's expected."

Their treatment made me feel like some kind of dignitary — or maybe a Miami politician slipping into a *private* meeting with Meyer Lansky during World War II. I started to crack a joke, but decided that might not be smart. The policemen were taking their duties seriously, and I should, too. Instead, I thanked my outside escort and turned toward his compatriot.

"Go through there," he said, pointing into the kitchen. He closed the door, then took up what looked like a guard position.

I frowned, not having a clue to what was going on. But, since no one insisted on frisking me or having me spread-eagle, I felt I must be on the good-guy side of things. I walked through the kitchen to the living room into a gathering of people — three of whom I recognized. Bannon, Sargent, and Hammonds. From the uniforms, I surmised that four were policemen. And from all the trimmings on one of those uniforms, I could tell there was a senior officer present. That probably explained the beat cops' courtesy.

But the last person was the surprise that caused my mouth to flop so far open I felt I should push up on my chin. Hammonds' lady friend from the previous night sat in one of the plush chairs. My first impulse was to stomp over and grab a handful of her dyed hair, but common sense prevailed. Maybe the cops had brought her in for questioning. Maybe she was in cahoots with Hammonds on eliminating his wife. Maybe she . . . I had no idea why she was there, but I was pissed that she was.

I studied her a moment, making sure she saw my glare. She met it with a smile, a small one, but a smile. I realized she did not look as uncomfortable as she would if the cops had hauled her in, yet there was a sadness radiating from her. It was as if she had collapsed into herself. Even with that, she didn't look out of place. She looked like she belonged.

Her hair had the sheen of professional care, and the navy pantsuit she wore screamed expensive. She had on a simple necklace ending in a pendant that box stores could not afford to stock. I flashed to my image of her the previous night and realized she had been well dressed then also. I figured her services must be so good she could overcome age and looks. Not something I chose to give a lot of thought — too gross.

"Ms. Bowman," Hammonds said, coming to his feet. "Thank you for coming. Can we talk a moment?"

I couldn't tear my eyes away from the broad Hammonds had shacked up with, but answered as best I could. "Yeah, I have some things to say to you."

"Let's find a place with some privacy." He waved me forward, then walked down a hall, stopping at an open doorway.

I followed and when I caught up, saw that he was leading me into an office. From the masculine cut of the furniture, I supposed it was his. "I hope they whack your nuts off, then hang you," I said. "A simple ending with a shot of drugs is too good for you."

"Please," he said, moving into the chair behind the desk. "Before you damn me to hell — and worse — have a seat and hear me out. Then, if you're willing, I'd like to hire you."

There my danged mouth went again, flopping open. "Hire me? You have to be crazy. Either that or you've got the biggest pair of balls hung on any man. Which is it?"

"Neither," he said, the sadness on his face reminding me of a bloodhound. "I'm simply a man who lost the woman he loves . . . and more. Will you give me a few minutes of your time? I'll even pay you if it will help. Name your rate."

"Talk. Listening is free. But don't drag it out too long. I have a weak stomach. I'd hate to throw up on your fancy carpet."

"Everything okay in here?" Sargent stood in the doorway.

"Yes," Hammonds said, a bit of snarl in his voice. "I told you I wanted privacy. Now get the hell out of here and close the door behind you. I'll let you know if I need your intervention."

Sargent's expression was priceless. I'd have paid admission to see it. He knew

Hammonds had slammed him, but he was powerless. His lips became a thin line as he pulled the door closed, disappearing behind it.

Hammonds rubbed his hand over his face, and his weariness returned. It was no façade. His reaction to Sargent was the façade.

I studied him, noticing the bloodshot eyes and the puffiness beneath them. I fought my female instinct to feel sorry for him. He looked old and sad and bereft and . . . John Hammonds was a man in pain.

"I need your help," he said. "But I know you won't give it unless I convince you I did *not* kill my wife. Ms. Bowman, I beg you to believe me. I did *not* kill her. I loved her. She and my daughter were my reasons for living. They were everything to me."

THREE

Daughter? Had I heard right? I didn't know they had children. But why should I? I only had the one meeting with Ms. Hammonds. We sat in the living room and talked business. Specifically, her husband's philandering and my fees. She explained she was sure he'd be with one of his *loose* women that night, and she wanted to know. According to her, he ran around on her, telling her he had to work or had meetings or some such. She was tired of it and wanted a divorce. If I could get her the evidence, she'd make it worth my while.

Since I'd heard a variation of the same story many times before from many different wives — and a few husbands — we came to a quick agreement, and I was on my way. The session only lasted an hour or so. She could have had a whole passel of kids hidden all over the house. Not to mention school, daycare, and camps. They could have been lost in the acreage behind the house, and I'd have never known. Kids were not part of my assignment.

That didn't change the jolt I felt, though. "I'm sorry. I didn't know you had a family." I hesitated, wondering if I should continue, then did, "But that doesn't excuse last night."

"That's what I need to explain." Hammonds stopped and rubbed his face again, the rasp of his five o'clock shadow audible through his fingers. "I need to correct your misconception."

The bags under his eyes seemed to grow even as I stared at him, but I kept my face hard and held my tongue. If he wanted to explain, he could do it without any encouragement from me.

He leaned forward and placed his forearms on his desk as if to emphasize his sincerity. "This might come as a surprise, but I know my wife hired you to watch me. The two of you met yesterday morning here at the house. She told you I had a history of picking up women for sex. She asked you to follow me and obtain evidence she could use in court for a divorce. Am I right?"

My mouth dropped open again, or that's how I felt. He knew about his wife hiring me? I expected excuses. I expected explanations. I expected revelations about his wife's frigidity. I expected about anything except what he'd said. I squeaked out, "Yes, but —"

"Ms. Bowman, please understand that I love my wife very much. And, I believe she loves . . . uh, loved me the same. However, she was possessive. Yes, even jealous — something I never gave her reason to be. You're not the first she hired to *get the goods* on me. Over the years, I learned to live with it. Anytime I was out at night, I expected to have someone documenting my activities. Last night, it was you. When I saw you watching me, I thought you might be the one, but having someone like you around was old hat. I knew I was doing nothing wrong."

"Yes, but —"

He held up a hand. "As soon as you left yesterday, Sabrina called to let me know she hired you. She always did that." He hesitated, took a linen handkerchief from the inner pocket of his jacket, and wiped his eyes. "I never understood, but I lived with it. It was as if . . . like she had to punish me — or something. I hope you'll understand that your assignment was just one of many. However, don't fret. I'll pay you. Just send me an invoice."

Tears beat an unwanted path to my eyes as I studied him, but I forced them down. It was a different story than I'd heard before, but no way was I going to buy it. "That's a nice twist," I said, waving my hand to let him know I was unconvinced. "But you had to anticipate I might have a difficult time believing it. Talk's cheap. What else do you have?"

"I understand. How can I convince you?"

"Tell me about last night. Also, explain why your honey's sitting in the front room?"

"Ah. Yes, you did follow us, didn't you? The *honey* I had dinner with, then escorted to her hotel is my sister — my *older* sister by two years. She's in the living room now because I need her here. Her name is Madeline Hammonds. She's in town on business and has a room at The Hilton. She lives in New York and only comes to Florida occasionally. When she does, we have dinner." He leaned back and rested his head on the back of his chair as if those words had exhausted him further.

I went into my dropped chin routine again. However, I recovered with what I knew was the killer question. I leaned forward to put maximum energy into it. "Why wasn't your wife with you if that woman is your sister? Why didn't the three of you go to dinner?"

He looked away, then back at me, and sighed. "Another family secret outed. Nothing mysterious about it. The simple fact is my wife and my sister can't stand one another. It goes back many years, before we married. I doubt either remembers why they decided to hate one another, but that doesn't stop them from keeping as much space between them as possible. If I'd shown up with Sabrina, my sister would have walked out, or vice versa."

I stared at him, my mind in high spin. A lot of husbands — and wives for that matter — had tried to talk their way out of their indiscretions, but Hammonds' story was the most incredible I'd ever heard. So damned incredible, it could be true. He was a top lawyer. Would he come up with such a cockamamie story if it weren't true? Could I trust him? Did I want to trust him? Could I shift him from suspect number one to misunderstood husband? Quite a dilemma, one filled with more questions than I could ever find answers for.

"Look, Ms. Bowman," Hammonds said, his eyes imploring me, "I can see by the look on your face, you don't believe me. I know it sounds strange, but it's the truth. I'd like for you to trust me."

I kept staring.

"I checked you out after Sabrina called yesterday. I know you're on retainer to Bergstrom and Bergowitz. Sly Bergstrom is a golfing partner and close friend. Anyone who's good enough for Sly is good enough for me."

"Excuse me," I said, letting indignation slip into my voice, "but we're not debating whether I'm good enough for you. My debate is whether you're honest enough for me. And with that cock and bull story you spun, I'm not sure you are. It's quite convenient that your wife is not alive to verify what you say."

From the shock and pain in his face, I knew my crudeness had gone too far. "Sorry. That was out of line. But you have to admit, your story is pretty strange," I said with less vehemence than my previous statement.

He waved his hand, as if accepting my apology. "I can call my sister in. She'll verify what I said."

"No need. I believe that woman, sister or not, will support your story. Money can buy more than just a night of ecstasy. Sorry. You'll have to do better than that."

He frowned. "You do have a suspicious mind. However, I understand. It goes with

41

the territory. What kind of PI would you be if you believed everything you heard?" He appeared to think, looking toward the ceiling. "I have it. Call Sly. He knows my wife and her problem. He'll vouch for me."

No way I could argue with that. Sylvester Bergstrom, called Sly by friends, was senior partner in Bergstrom and Bergowitz, one of the most respected law firms in South Florida. When Sly spoke, everyone listened. If he backed up Hammonds' story, that made it fact.

"Look," he said, standing. "I'll leave you alone. Think about what I said. There's the phone. Call Sly if you like. When you make a decision, come get me. Whichever way you decide, I'll try to understand. But, if you believe me, I have something very important to discuss with you." He walked to the door, then turned back, his face questioning. "I hope you're the woman Sly says you are."

I stared at the door as he pulled it closed behind him. I had been confused before, but his performance and story took me to new heights. What gall on his part to wonder if I was the right kind of woman? But, could he be telling the truth? If not, what possible purpose could such a farfetched tale serve? He must know I'd punch holes in it big enough for his Mercedes to race through.

I took out my cell phone and scrolled down to Sly's number, then hesitated. He had made it obvious when I went to work for him that he did not enjoy being bothered at home. His exact words were, "I separate my home life from my business life." However, he added that it was permissible to call in case of an emergency.

I blew my breath up at my bangs, wondering how much of an emergency this was. For me, a big one. For Sly, probably not. Besides, if Hammonds was willing for me to call, it probably meant he was on the level. Or maybe that's what he wanted me to think. If he could sucker me into not calling Sly, it would prove I believed him. Should I trust him? Not a chance — maybe.

To hell with it. I had to know. I could always apologize later and buy Sly a bottle of his favorite scotch. I speed-dialed his number, then counted rings. He picked up after the third.

"Beth, what can I do for you on a Tuesday *evening* when I'm at *home* with my family?"

He might have put some extra emphasis on evening and again on home. I knew I'd better make it good, so I jumped straight to the key question. "How well do you know John Hammonds?"

Sly sighed as if about to address a three-year-old. "Very well. We play golf together and are often at the same social events. Is that why you called, to check up on my social life? I hope you have a better reason."

Uh-oh. Not a good beginning. Quickly, I started from the beginning, but only got as far as finding Ms. Hammonds' body.

Sly jumped in. "Oh my God. John must be devastated. How's Ashley?"

"Who's Ashley?"

"Their daughter. How is she?"

"I don't know. I didn't know they had children until a few minutes ago. Can I finish my story?"

"I'm sorry, Beth. You obviously didn't call just to tell me about Sabrina. What else do you have?"

I finished a quick summary, then said, "I don't know what to think. His story is so farfetched."

There was silence on the line, and I sensed that Sly might be having a quarrel within himself. I waited.

After a moment he said, "I make it a habit to treat what I know about my friends' private lives as a client-attorney situation. But this time, I suppose it's different." He paused. "What John said is true. I've been party to some of her jealous accusations. It got to the point that when he and I attended a meeting at night, I'd take him home and go in with him. Inevitably, she accused him of having been with a woman."

"That's nuts," I said. "Why'd he stay with her?"

"In one word, love. He loved her, and he loved Ashley. He'd never do anything to hurt the marriage. Incidentally, she loved him just as much." He sighed. "Sabrina was an insecure person from a poor background. I guess she could never believe someone like John would want her."

"Damn," I muttered. "You're saying I should believe whatever he tells me. And, if he wants to hire me, I should take the job?"

"Not only that," he said, "but I'll clear your calendar for as long as it takes to help John. You let *me* know when you're available to take on one of our cases."

I only hesitated a split second. "Thanks, Sly. I'm sorry to have bothered you at home."

"Under the circumstances, not a problem this time. Just find the son-of-a-bitch that killed Sabrina." He hung up.

I pondered my phone for about half a moment, then opened the office door. "Mr. Hammonds. Can I see you for a minute?"

He broke off the conversation he was having with the woman he called his sister and looked toward me, then scanned the room. "If you'll excuse me."

As he closed the door behind him, I said, "Sly says I should believe you. But if I discover you're lying to me, I'll dedicate myself to pinning your wife's murder on you."

"Fair enough." He looked relieved. "Can I assume you're ready to work for me?"

"If the situation is right and the money fits, yes."

He took a deep breath amidst a look of sadness. "My five-year-old daughter, Ashley, is missing. It's logical to assume the people who killed my wife kidnapped her. Perhaps my wife put up too much of a fight, or perhaps they were leaving a message. We won't know until we capture them. That's where you come in. I want to hire you to bring my daughter home."

"Me?" Damn, he kept catching me off guard. "You have access to all the cops in the universe. Several of them are in your living room. Why me?"

"Because they have to follow the rules — rules that too often benefit the guilty and impede an investigation. Plus, they are captives of the media. Please understand, I know that world. I'm a defense attorney, and I use those rules to my advantage every day. From what I've heard Sly say, rules and Beth Bowman are not synonymous."

FOUR

Mr. Hammonds had a point. Cops are too often hogtied when it comes to bringing down criminals. The slanted slope causes them to run uphill all the time — in slick-soled shoes. Me, I take a more downhill approach. If there is an advantage to be found, I grab it.

"Maybe you should explain what rules you expect me to break," I said. "I'd look terrible in prison garb."

"Does that mean you'll take the job?"

"Not so fast. I still need to know what you expect."

He stared at me, then rubbed his chin. "I want my daughter home. I don't care what it costs or what it takes, I simply want her home. And, before I have to hear it again, I know the odds of getting her back alive. That doesn't change anything." He choked back a sob. "If the worst should happen, I at least want her buried beside her mother."

I couldn't help myself. I reached across and laid my hand on his arm. "I'll do anything I can to help. I don't know how much that will be, but you'll get the best I have to give."

He opened a desk drawer, took out a tissue, and blew his nose. "That's all I ask."

"Mr. Hammonds, I need a full briefing on what has happened and what's in the process of happening."

"Please, call me John."

"And I'm Beth. But amenities will have to wait. As I'm sure you know, time is short." The *experts* say kidnapped victims who aren't recovered in the first forty-eight hours aren't likely to be found alive. However, I simply couldn't bring myself to mouth the words. Instead, I asked, "Have you heard from the kidnappers yet?"

"No. According to the police, that's bothersome. It could be good news though. It might mean they're still formulating their plans." He stood. "Let's go into the living room. I'm sure they're wondering what we're concocting."

We entered the living room and had the instant attention of everyone there. John walked to a couch and sat, waving me down beside him. The others relaxed, but not much.

John took his time, eyeing each person, then leaned forward. "If anyone here has not met Beth Bowman, let me introduce her." He turned to me. "This is Beth Bowman."

The officer with the most braid on his uniform said, "My pleasure, Ms. Bowman."

Hammonds eyed him. "Beth. This is Chief Elston of the Coral Lakes police."

"I'm familiar with Ms. Bowman," he said. "At least by reputation." He walked over and stuck out his hand. "It's a pleasure to put a face with it. You don't look near as fierce as Bannon and Sargent describe you — or as incompetent."

I took his hand. "Considering the sources, I take that as a compliment. You must be a pretty forgiving fellow if you keep those two on the payroll." I wanted him to know I could play the hard-ass game as well as he.

Hammonds interrupted. "Chief, I want Beth in on everything you're doing. She will be my personal representative in the investigation. I'm hiring her to recover my daughter."

Elston said, "Mr. Hammonds, I'm sure you realize that's not a workable situation. She's nothing more than a private investigator. My people and I owe her nothing."

His words and tone sent several caustic

comments toward my tongue, but before they arrived, Hammonds took over. "Perhaps I'd better clarify a few things. To me, they're obvious, but apparently not to you. First, it was *my* home that was invaded, *my* wife who was murdered, and most important of all, *my* daughter who has disappeared. If Ashley cannot be returned alive, it is I who will mourn her for the rest of my life, even as I mourn the loss of my wife. And, in spite of any priority you might have, mine is the successful recovery of my daughter. Anyone in this room that doesn't concur can leave *now*." He slammed down on the word now.

John sat back and gazed around the room, meeting every eye that would look at him. Bannon and Sargent were two who studied the toes of their shoes, but they held their seats.

John leaned forward again. "Good. Since no one left, I assume you agree with me. So, here's the deal. You go about your investigation of my wife's and Carmina's deaths as you would any other case. Behind the scenes, I want you to monitor Ashley's disappearance as you would with any other kidnapping. But, and here's the difference, you will report everything you find to Beth. If the kidnappers call for a face-to-face, she

will attend, agreeing to whatever require-
ments they demand. At all times and in all
things having to do with my daughter, Beth
and I will make the decisions. I will meet
whatever conditions they impose to save
Ashley. Is that understood?"

Chief Elston returned to his chair and sat.
"Mr. Hammonds, I have the utmost respect
for you and sympathy for your situation.
However, you're not thinking clearly. This is
a police matter. We must handle it. It can
be no other way."

"There are two problems with that," Hammonds said. "First, as a defense attorney, I
live much of my life with criminals, some of
the lowest forms of humanity. I babysit
them, I dress them, I prep them, I dig into
their heads. You arrest them and let the
prosecutor take it from there. Second, if you
don't agree to cooperate as I laid it out, I'll
pick up the phone and call the mayor, the
attorney general, and the governor. I'm sure
they can find some other agency to handle
the case."

"Are you threatening me?" Elston said,
fire in his eyes. "I'll —"

"That's not a threat," Hammonds
growled. "It's a statement of fact. My way
or the highway. Take your pick. I suggest
you quit wasting time and begin Beth's

briefing now. The kidnappers could call at any minute."

The chief and Hammonds glared like two dogs vying for a bone. The only thing missing was they didn't circle one another. Then, as often happens in the pack, one folded.

Elston said, "Bannon, you're the lead detective. Get your team together and tell Ms. Bowman everything we know." He looked at Hammonds. "And I do mean everything. When this blows up, I don't want our host to be able to say we withheld information." He stood, walked to the window, and stared into the night.

Over the next hour, the police briefed me. They said it was everything they knew. I took their word for that as John Hammonds had insisted they not hold anything back. The gist of it was a woman appeared at Ashley's school during the morning with a note ostensibly signed by Ms. Hammonds authorizing her to pick up Ashley. Since everything looked in order, school officials released Ashley into the lady's custody. Both had disappeared, neither seen nor heard from since.

The two school officials who spoke with the woman were at the stationhouse going through mug shots. A sketch artist was creating an image based on descriptions provided by the two women.

"Once we have a sketch and a solid case file, we'll contact FDLE — that's Florida Department of Law Enforcement — and they'll institute an AMBER Alert," Bannon said.

"I'm well aware of FDLE," I said. "You might remember that I worked with them not so long ago."

Bannon blushed, then continued, "Authorities will flash Ashley's picture, the sketch, and details all over Florida by TV, radio, and the interactive signs along the Interstates and toll roads. By tomorrow morning, everyone in the state will be on the lookout for her."

Hammonds spoke for the first time since the briefing began. "No AMBER Alert."

"Excuse me," Bannon said, an incredulous look on his face. "Did you say no AMBER Alert?"

"That's what I said, and that's what I mean. There will be no publicity about Ashley's disappearance."

"Why? We need that. I mean, AMBER Alerts exist for just this kind of situation. It lets everyone know and invites them to call in sightings."

Hammonds flared. "I know all that. Dammit, don't treat me like you do Joe Sixpack. I've already told you, I know these kinds of people. I know more about the people who did this than you do. I know their strengths and their weaknesses. I also know their fears and what causes them to snap. So when I say no AMBER Alert, I damn well mean no AMBER Alert."

"Easy, John," Chief Elston said. The outburst had apparently caught his attention, bringing him back into our group. He swallowed. "Tell us what you're thinking."

"Nothing complicated," Hammonds said. "You seem to forget that I'm a defense attorney. I've defended some of the finest slime in this state. I've spent more time with them than you've ever dreamed about. You spend all your time trying to get inside their heads to catch them. I spend my time getting to know them, really know them. I have to know what triggers them, what causes them to go off." He hesitated, then continued in a softer voice, "What causes them to panic. Most of them don't handle pressure well. You put the pressure on, they react. That reaction is usually to get rid of the evidence. That would doom Ashley."

Hammonds had walked around the room as he spoke. Now he dropped into a chair and buried his hands in his face. "I can't take that chance. That's why no AMBER Alert, no publicity. We must *not* panic them."

"I see," Chief Elston said. "What you say might make sense to you, but it goes against everything I've learned about apprehending criminals. I may not have the authority to do what you want."

"That's how it must be."

Chief Elston walked back to the window and stared out. In a voice perhaps only for himself, he said, "I hate this job. So many times, there is a chasm between following the rules and doing what might work better. This may be one of those times." He clasped his hands behind him and paced, his head down and brow furrowed, as the rest of us watched. After two circuits, he stopped in front of Hammonds. "Friday. I'll give you until Friday. That's three days. If your approach hasn't worked, and I hope to God it does, I'm pulling out all stops."

Hammonds stood. "Fair enough. Friday evening, it is."

"But," the chief continued, "I'm still going to brief all my officers and tell them to be on the watch for Ashley and the woman who took her. That won't create much of a hubbub." He glared at me. "And even that small effort will get more results than Ms. Bowman can produce. You're making a huge mistake, John."

Hammonds appeared to consider the chief's words, then nodded.

Since they'd reached some form of agreement, and it involved me, it was time to join the conversation. "Chief. I hope you didn't give in too fast. Now, can we get back to my briefing?"

Sargent gave me a nasty look, and Chief Elston said, "Yes. I think that's appropriate. Do you have anything else, Detective Bannon?"

"If we're killing the AMBER Alert, there's not much we can do until we hear from the kidnappers. We have recorders attached to every phone that Mr. Hammonds uses here at the house and at his office. We've alerted his cell carrier, and they're ready to co-operate by monitoring incoming calls to him."

"Sounds like you're neck deep into privacy issues," I said. "I hope you got his permission in writing." I smiled, hoping to inject a touch of humor into the somber gathering.

Sargent continued to scowl, Bannon's face remained impassive, and the chief looked like I had tracked doggy doo-doo onto his white carpet.

Hammonds gave a weak look. "Yes. I insisted on it. Sly told me your opinion of lawyers — you're willing to work for them, but you'll never trust one." He went sad again. "I just want Ashley back."

Seeing any man as sad as John was just too tough. The expression *hangdog look* only scratched the surface of his appearance. Misery emanated out of every pore. It took willpower not to sit beside him and lay his head on my shoulder like I've seen so many mothers do to soothe a hurt child.

I tore my eyes away from Hammonds and turned to the chief. "The note from the school. Did you get it?"

"Yes. Looks like a computer printout with a signature at the bottom. Mr. Hammonds gave us samples of his wife's handwriting. We have our people comparing the note to them." He looked at Hammonds whose head now rested in his open hands.

"Keep talking, chief. I'm all in," he mumbled.

"Why don't you lie down?" the chief said. "We have everything under control." He hesitated. "Tomorrow, you'll be faced with a myriad of decisions. Plus, the damned media will probably be all over you."

"I agree, Mr. Hammonds," I said. "You need your rest. Before you go, though, I need a recent picture of Ashley."

Hammonds stood. "I'll get one from my office." He shuffled out of the room.

To the chief, I said, "I need a copy of the sketch and a copy of the note the woman used at the school. Can you arrange that?"

Hammonds returned and handed me an eight by ten of Ashley. "This was taken a couple of weeks ago. Do whatever you need with it. I have other copies."

Chief Elston looked at Bannon. "Check downtown and see if they have a sketch yet. If so, tell them to email it. Make it high res so we can make copies. Also, get a copy of the note for Ms. Bowman."

We sat around looking uncomfortable while Bannon followed orders. The sketch was complete, and soon I had a hard copy in hand. I studied the woman. Shouldn't be too tough to spot her. Red hair, fancy glasses, heavy lipstick. She should be obvious in any crowd.

Standing, I said, "I expect to know the moment anyone contacts Mr. Hammonds and the full content of what they have to say."

Sargent scowled some more, but Hammonds said, "You will. I promise."

"I'll be waiting for info. Now, I'd better hit the street." I started toward the front door, then stopped, picturing my afternoon visit to the foyer. "I'll go through the garage."

FIVE

Once in my car in Hammonds' driveway, I sat, letting the air conditioner fight the mugginess of the evening while I thought about my agreement with Hammonds. What did I know about finding a missing child? Nothing. Exactly nothing. Yet, Hammonds, or John, as he said I should call him, seemed so forlorn, so desperate in his need for an ally. For good reason, I had to agree, he was terrified that a heavy police presence would cause the kidnappers to panic and kill Ashley. No way could I have told him no. So now, I had a commitment — a very important one.

I rested my forehead on the steering wheel, wishing I could talk to David. Of course, I'd get a lecture first. He did not approve of my chosen profession. That was somewhat understandable since we met in the Emergency Room when he treated me for a concussion — the result of being conked on the head with a heavy object. It was my good fortune he was on duty that day. He must have found something he liked about the lump on my head because before long we were dating. Soon thereafter, I added a mate to that lump and his doubts grew — but only temporarily. He still wasn't sold on my being a private investigator, though.

However, after he got past his disapproval, I was sure he'd offer support and wish me luck. He might even volunteer to scrap the conference and fly home. Of course, I'd tell him not to do that. I'd say I was okay, everything was under control. That didn't change my need to talk to him though.

It was only ten o'clock here, seven in California. He would be at dinner with some of his associates. After that, they'd probably stop in the bar for a drink. Neither of those invited interruptions. I'd have to wait until later, no earlier than midnight, my time, and hope he answered.

If I were to have even the smallest chance of success, I needed more eyes than the two God gave me. I knew a group that might help. Digging my cell phone out of my purse, I hit autodial for Bob Sandiford.

Sandiford was the most unique person I had ever met. He owned a bar that turned a profit, yet he stood on the street corner dressed like a bum, selling newspapers. He often slept on a park bench even though he had more than adequate accommodations in rooms behind the bar. He spent his time, energy, and money assisting any homeless person who would allow it. According to Bob, they were all too often afraid to accept help from anyone, even him.

I met Bob as a street person while pursuing another case, and he took me under his wing. Before confessing his true status, he convinced himself I was worth the effort. I would be eternally grateful I had somehow measured up to his standards. He was not only a person I could rely on, but a true friend. David and I had many a nightcap in Bobby's Bar.

"What's up, Beth?" Bob answered. "David still out of town?"

"Yes. He's attending the world's longest medical convention located about as far away as you can go. But that's not why I called. I need your help."

"You know I'll do anything I can. Why don't you come over, and we'll discuss it? Dot, Street, and Blister are here. I'm sure they'll understand if you want to keep it private."

"No. To pull this off, I need everyone we

know — if they have time, of course."

"How long before you can get here? I might be able to round up a few more of the group."

"Forty-five minutes or so. I have to stop by FedEx Office on the way."

I walked into Bobby's Bar and spotted Dot at the bar talking to Judy, the bartender. Judy was one of Bob's reclamation projects. We started off on opposite sides of things, mainly because I doubted Bob. After hearing Bob's heartrending story, I questioned it with Judy and asked her where she fit into things, thinking she might be his young honey.

After giving me hell for my inference, she told me her story. She ran away from home when she was sixteen, and things went straight downhill. Her memories were so bad she wouldn't share them. All she'd say is she did whatever was necessary to stay alive. Then one night, Bob pulled her cold and wet out of a trashy alley and gave her a place to live until she got herself cleaned up. He had literally saved her life, and she was as loyal to him as any *man's best friend.*

I stared, but couldn't see the liquid in Dot's glass. I hoped it was non-alcoholic. She had a history with the hard stuff she didn't need to tempt.

I nodded to Judy, then sidled up to Dot, taking a hard look at her glass. "I'm guessing that's water you're drinking." Actually, it had to be water or some form of clear liquor on the rocks. Since it was a large glass, I went with good old H_2O.

"Hey, Dearie," Dot said. "You know this ain't booze. I'm on the wagon, been there so long I got calluses on my ass from that hard, wooden seat." She cackled, jumped off the bar stool, and gave me a hug.

There had been times in our relationship when hugging Dot would not have been comfortable. I mean, without trying to hurt anyone's feelings, I can say the homeless often smell better from at least an arm's length away. But that night, Dot simply smelled clean.

"You're looking good," I said, meaning it. She did look good. Her clothes were fresh, her hair wasn't frizzy, and the smile she threw my way said she was satisfied with the world.

"Life's good," Dot said. "I got me a job. Ain't much. Just a damn greeter at Walmart, but it's better than I had in a long time. Feels good to get up in the morning and know I got something to do."

"Congratulations. I'm sure you're the best

damn greeter they ever hired. Soon, you'll be the supervisor of *damn* greeters."

She cackled. "Uh-uh. I'd have to pay too many taxes."

I meant what I said. Dot was a character — cantankerous, stubborn, and quick to anger — but I'd trust her with my life. In fact, there was a time my future was in her hands, and she handled it with TLC, turning catastrophe into victory. Dot's history was spotty, at least that's the story she told me. She was a kept woman her entire adult life until she met the man who used her as rental property. Not only did he share her with his friends and clients, he abused her. Things reached a point where she couldn't take it anymore and killed him. That earned her a stint in Lowell Correctional Institution in Ocala, Florida. Under different circumstances, she might have received a life sentence, but when the police arrived, the evidence of his severe abuse was abundant on her body. The pictures they took were defense exhibit A in her trial, and the jury chose compassion.

After her release, she found herself with no place to go and no skill except pleasing a man. In her own words, she was so old and beat up, she couldn't give it away. So she took to the streets, became another homeless statistic. There, she met another in the same straits, a man who called himself Bridge. They formed a bond and became inseparable. She said it was two years before he would tell her his real name and then only if she promised to keep his secret. He never wanted his family to know how far he had fallen.

Bridge gave his life in my defense, and Dot extracted revenge on his killer. Before the police arrived, I hustled her out of the area and covered for her. Something like that tends to create a bond that endures.

Alone again, Dot went on with life, continuing little by little to improve her status in the world. That's why I was so thrilled at her news about the job. To anyone else, it might have been just a demeaning, minimum-wage position, but to me, and I knew to Dot, it was a huge step forward. I gave her a second hug.

"Good to see you, Judy," I said, reaching across to shake her hand. "This place wouldn't be the same without you keeping the bar. How's school going?"

"It's hard, *ma'am,* but I can't let Bob down. He has so much faith in me. I'll get it done."

The ma'am from Judy was a private joke. Well, I hoped it was a joke. She was in her

67

early twenties, but I didn't want her to think I was old enough to be a ma'am to her. "That's the spirit. Speaking of Bob, he said he'd be here."

"He's in the back with some of our people," Dot said. "He told me to wait out here, then bring you back. He put out the word after you called. They're still drifting in." She hopped down and walked toward the rear of the room where there was a door.

I knew that behind the front room were two dormitories, one for men, and one for women. The furnishings were basic, but clean and comfortable. Bob added them in memory of a homeless man who became his best friend during some trying times. Now a bed was available to anyone who needed it, no questions asked.

I followed Dot out of the bar to the men's dorm.

"Woman coming in," she called as she opened the door. "Bob insists we do that," she whispered, then cackled. "As if there's anything in there I'd want to see, or anyone who'd care if I did."

Several scenes came to mind, but I decided to stay away from them. I was happy with Bob's rule.

Bunks, lockers, chairs, and small tables with lamps filled the large room. There was space for ten tenants, each of whom would have his own little area. Bob even included stationery and envelopes — seldom used was my guess. The walls were pale blue and a sturdy-looking carpet covered the floor.

The women's dorm was a twin, except the walls were soft pink and silk flowers adorned the tables.

Bob, Street, Blister, and three others, one of them female sat around a table in the rear of the room. Each nursed a glass of water. Several extra chairs sat nearby. Dot and I pulled over a couple of the empties and joined them.

I looked at the other woman, trying to place her. I was sure we'd met before. Since Bob was my only contact with the homeless, it had to have been through him.

After the normal greetings, Bob said, "Do you know everyone here?" Before I could respond, he added, "I'll run the table just in case."

I wanted to kiss him. He anticipated I might not remember some of the names, and he was right.

He started at his left. "Dot, as if you could forget her."

I gave Dot a high five.

Bob ignored us and kept talking. "Street, Blister, Viaduct, Ralph, Dabba . . . There may be others drifting in, or it might be tomorrow before they answer my page. Whichever, I'm pretty sure there will be others. Your fame has spread among our little circle. We can get started now."

Ralph? That surprised me. No street name. All the men I'd met in Bob's group used them. "Good to see all of you again," I said, and leaned forward, elbows on the table. "Thanks for meeting with me tonight. I need help. I have a new case and it's a tough one. A little girl's life is at stake."

"Keep it simple, Beth," Bob said. "We'll make our decisions after hearing your spiel." He glanced around the circle, then came back to me. "No one is obligated to stay or participate. Let's hear your story. The beginning is always a good place to start. How do you find yourself in a case involving a small child?"

"Thank you, Bob. I understand." I looked at the group. "And I'll understand if everyone of you walks out." I took a deep breath, then told them everything that had happened.

When I finished, I heard, "Them sonsabitches. They gotta die." I looked at Dot, fully expecting that the words came from her.

She shook her head while nodding toward

Dabba, who swiped at her cheek.

Dabba said, "My little girl was five years old when somebody took her. We gonna get your girl back. I ain't gonna let nothing hurt her."

There was iron in Dabba's voice, and when I looked around the table, I saw heads nodding.

"I'm with you," Dot said, "and anybody that walks on this little girl better just keep walking." Her eyes blazed as she surveyed the group. At that moment, I had no doubt she'd follow me to the gates of Hell and smack them open.

"Easy, Dot," Bob said. "You know we don't operate that way. Nobody has to join unless they want to. That's rule number one here."

I jumped in before Dot could reply. I didn't want problems within the group. "There's not much anyone can do until we hear from the kidnappers. In the meantime, I have a picture of Ashley and a sketch of the woman who picked her up at school. If any of you know this woman, my ears are straining to hear you." I opened the FedEx envelope and passed the papers around.

Everyone stared at the pictures, but my only information came from shaking heads.

Silence ruled the group for several minutes. I'd told them all I knew. There was no point in repeating it. If they had a question, I'd either answer it or tell them I didn't know.

At eleven-thirty, Judy came in, told Bob the bar was empty, and asked if she could close up. He told her yes, and she left. The group settled back into silence.

"Have you considered," Ralph said, "that this might be a revenge thing? Maybe they killed the wife and kidnapped the child because they got a hate for this lawyer. Maybe he's a shyster and messed over them."

I sat forward. "No. I haven't considered that. Expand on your meaning."

"Well, suppose somebody out there thinks . . . what's that lawyer's name?"

"John Hammonds," I said.

"Somebody thinks this Hammonds guy botched his case, didn't work hard enough defending him. Maybe the guy went to jail, and he's pissed about it. So he gets out and goes after Hammonds through his family."

I considered what he'd said. "Could happen. Hammonds admitted he defends some pretty scurvy people."

Ralph continued, "That might mean the little girl's already dead and her body hid some place she can't never be found.

Wouldn't that give the guy the best revenge on Hammonds?"

"No way," Dabba said, jumping in hard. "She's alive. I feel it in my bones. She's alive, and I ain't gonna put up with nobody saying no other shit."

"I didn't mean nothin'," Ralph said, leaning away from Dabba. "I was just speculatin'. It don't mean she's dead, but you gotta admit, there's some nasty people getting out of prison every day."

As Dabba took the floor, arguing with each of the others who dared to be pessimistic, I studied her. The woman was a force. Then I remembered her. She walked away from the first case I brought to Bob and his friends, saying it meant nothing to her. Perhaps she had to be emotional to participate. And emotional she was. Her eyes flared, but there was no fear there. If anything, she reflected determination with every gaze, every word. Even Dot deferred to her.

They fell back into silence, then Dot said, "I agree with Dabba. We're gonna find that little girl."

With that, each of the others said they wanted to help.

Bob said, "Okay, we're in agreement then. We're at your disposal, Beth. I suggest everyone stay here tonight and get as much sleep as you can. We have to be ready to roll in the morning, to start looking for this woman." He tapped the sketch. "When the kidnappers make contact, we have to be there for Beth. She'll need eyes in back of her head."

Six

I walked out of Bobby's Bar, feeling like bowling balls sat on both shoulders. No case had ever seemed so impossible. The well-being of a five-year-old depended on me and so far, I had nothing. True, I had gained allies, but without information to feed them, I had little reason to think they could help.

With the future so uncertain, I grabbed a moment for David. I didn't care what he was doing, I needed to talk to him, and talk to him now. I dialed his number.

"Beth. So good to hear from you," he said when he answered. "Aren't you up rather late?"

That sounded like a strange greeting, but I charged on. "I just wanted to hear your voice. I miss you and wish you were here. This is turning into one long week."

"Yeah, me too," he said.

Reality, or what I took to be reality, dawned on me. "Are you with someone?

Can't you talk now? Where are you?"

"I'm in a cab on the way to the hotel. Phil Houston and Herb Warring are with me. We decided to share the tab since we're all staying in the Hilton. A group of us went out to dinner. It was a fascinating day. Some really good lectures."

Rats. Obviously, he was unwilling to talk in front of the other doctors. Guess he didn't want them to know what a romantic he could be. So much for the solace I sought. "I understand. I just wanted to hear your voice and tell you how much I miss you. You go on with your evening. Maybe we can talk tomorrow."

"Beth, I agree in every way. I'll try to call in the morning during a break. You get some sleep and take very good care of my favorite lady. I'll see you this weekend. Good-night."

The phone went dead, leaving me hanging on the thought of a real conversation with him in the a.m. Then Ashley's plight took over again, slamming me back into depression.

Time to check in with Hammonds, even though I had a promise he or the police would contact me with any new information. For all I knew, the authorities might have talked him out of involving me. Besides, if there were no new developments,

I'd have time to slip home, clean up, grab a few winks, and be ready when the kidnappers called. I punched in his number.

After several rings, while I pictured the police starting the recording equipment, a dog-tired voice said, "Hello, Beth. Nothing new here. They haven't made contact yet. I'm going slightly crazy with the waiting."

"You need to grab hold of yourself, John. It's going to be a long and frustrating boat ride. You're the anchor around which we have to work."

"Yeah, I know. The police keep telling me it's not unusual for the kidnappers to delay contact for a day or two — or longer. That doesn't make it any easier though. Do you want to talk to the duty cop?"

"Sure. Put him on. And, John . . . you need rest. You have to force yourself."

A new voice came on the line, causing me to cringe.

"Hey, it's my favorite skirt-PI. Solve the case yet? Can I go home and get some sleep?"

Sargent. Just my luck to catch him with the duty. I knew I had to keep it official, rather than what I really wanted to say. "Anything new?"

"No. My mission is to stand by so I can keep you informed, and I have nothing to report. Is it okay if I don't stand at attention? Do you have anything to share with me?" His sarcasm dripped from his words.

So much for his having gained respect for me. Well, two could play that game. "If I knew anything, I'd call Chief Elston," I said in my most caustic manner. "Just don't forget my phone number." I flipped my cell closed. That man was just too insufferable.

I checked my watch again. One-thirty. I opted to use some time to make myself presentable for whatever the future held. Plus, I had some new hardware I wanted to pick up.

I headed for home where I crawled into the shower, enjoying the sting of the hot water as I thought about what to do the next day. First thing, if the kidnappers had not made contact, would be to go by Ashley's school and conduct some interviews. Maybe I could unearth something the police had missed, or trigger some forgotten detail. After that, I could canvas near the school with the picture, hoping the woman stopped somewhere along the line and would be remembered. Meager plans, but all I had.

After drying my hair, I slipped into a large T-shirt and a pair of men's boxer shorts, my favorite sleeping attire. Not what I'd use if David were there, but he was in California, and I was in South Florida. I might as well be comfortable. A few minutes later, I was in bed, and sleep pushed everything away.

Somewhere far away church bells rang, and the sound irritated me. I wanted to shut them off, to tell them to quit clanging those damn clappers. There they went again. Shrill — too shrill. Not church bells.

My eyes flew open, and I registered the sound again. My bedside phone. I squinted at the caller ID and recognized Mom's number.

"Mom? What is it?"

"I . . . I'm sorry to wake you. I just don't know what else to do, who else I could call. I can't bother Harve. I mean, he has to go to work in the morning. He needs his sleep with that tough job he has. And you know Dolores is no help. She's a sweet daughter-in-law, and she gave me two wonderful grandchildren, but —"

"Mom. You're babbling. What's wrong?"

Harve is my brother, Delores his wife. They are Mom's favorites, even though they live in Wisconsin. And, of course, his job was more important than anything I did. They had two kids while all I had was a failed marriage to Sonny-the-Bunny. The divorce was the reason I was in Florida.

Texas wasn't big enough for the two of us.

Sonny-the-Bunny? I nicknamed him that because of our bedroom encounters. You can fill in the blanks. But that's not why we divorced. I caught him playing his rabbit tricks with a doe other than me. I'm big on monogamy — especially in a husband.

"I misjudged him, Beth. He acted like such a gentleman at first."

"Who, Mom? Slow down and tell me the whole story. Take a deep breath and start at the top."

She inhaled, then exhaled into the mouthpiece, causing me to push the phone away from my ear. "The man I've been dating is sitting in his car outside. We've been out three, no four times. He's nice, fun to be with, but not . . . well, not someone I have that kind of interest in, if you get my drift."

I got her drift. No sex.

"Anyway, tonight he wanted to come inside when he brought me home. I said no. We both knew what he wanted, and I didn't want to play. He got mad and said he wasn't leaving until I *put out.* Now he's parked across the street, a couple of houses down the block. He's been there for three hours."

I looked at the clock — three a.m. That meant he'd been there since eleven, Dallas time. "Call the police. Tell them you have a

80

stalker. They'll flush him out."

"Beth, I'm not a stupid teenager. I did call. They sent a patrol car, but when it came down the street, Lanny drove off. Thirty minutes later, he was back."

"Lanny? That's his name?"

"Yes. Lanny Strudnocker. And don't start on me. It's a perfectly good name."

I muffled a snicker. When this was over, I'd make sure she paid for this one. Imagine, my mother out with a Strudnocker. I'd never let her live it down.

"And he's there now?"

"Yes, and I'm afraid he'll break in. He . . ." She took a deep breath. "He had a bottle in the car. If he's drinking . . . What do I do if he tries to force his way in?"

Time for me to pay better attention. Mom was serious. "Do you still have that .38 revolver in your nightstand?"

"Yes . . . no. It's on top of the nightstand."

I rolled my eyes. Mothers can be so specific. "Good. Make sure it's loaded. Is your bedroom door closed and locked?"

"No. I want —"

"Forget want. Close and lock it now. Put that old straight-backed chair you keep in the bedroom under the doorknob. Then crawl in bed, put the phone in your lap, and listen. If you hear anything at a window or an outside door, call nine-one-one and report an attempted burglary. If he gets in without your hearing him and tries your bedroom door, put a slug through the door, chest high. If that doesn't stop him, wait until he steps into the room and blow him away. Don't hesitate. Just do it."

"But Beth, Lanny is not —"

"No buts. You either put a bullet in him or be ready for rape and maybe worse. I'll call around and see if I can cash some IOU's. There must still be someone on the Dallas force who owes me. As soon as I have something lined up, I'll be back to you. Understand?"

"Yes, but —"

"Don't but me, Mom. Can you do it? I can't get help until I know you can take care of yourself."

"Yes." This time her voice sounded stronger. "If he hits that door, he's a dead man."

"Good. Center of mass, Mom. Aim for center of mass — just like at the shooting range. Hang on. Help is on the way." I hung up and rubbed my eyes, digging out the last vestiges of sleep.

I had tried to sound more confident than I felt. I'd been gone from the Dallas police force for three years and gone from Dallas for two. While I'd had conversations with old friends in the department, they had become more infrequent as time passed. Whom could I call? Whom could I expect to be on duty at two in the morning? And, it didn't help that Mom lived in Richardson, not Dallas proper where I had carried a badge.

I pulled my phone index from my nightstand and flipped through, looking for a name, any name that could help me. Nothing, no one, acquaintances once, strangers now. Then, pay dirt in the L's. Pam LaToya. Yes, Pam was a possibility. She was a detective on the night shift, or was the last time I spoke with her. We'd been pretty tight when I assisted on one of her cases while still a uniform. After I quit the force and became a PI, I trapped an embezzler and handed the collar to her. She owed me.

I dialed the number, hoping she still worked night shift.

SEVEN

"Dallas Police Department, Northeast Operations, Officer Morrison speaking," a voice said into my ear.

At least the number was still current. That was a relief. "This is Beth Bowman. I used to be a uniform on the force. I'm trying to reach Detective LaToya. Is she available?"

"Bowman? Elizabeth Bowman? How the hell are you, Beth? I haven't heard a word about you in two-three years."

Stunned, I tried to recall how the officer had answered the phone. Nothing. I was so intent on Pam I hadn't listened. One of my many failings — not assimilating what I hear. "I'm sorry. I didn't catch your name. Who is this?"

He laughed, a sound that triggered a memory.

"Ike? Ike Morrison, is that you?" He had the most distinctive laugh I ever heard — somewhere between a serious case of the hiccups and a horse's neigh.

"Of course. Who'd you expect? You think the chief answers the phone here?"

Memories flooded in, images of an experienced officer who served as my unofficial mentor when I was a bumbling rookie. Ike Morrison seemed to materialize every time I did something dumb. He'd pat me on the back and say, "Same kinda mistake I made a bunch of years ago. I'll square it with the sergeant." And he would. I might get a lecture, but Ike would stand beside me and help me absorb the wisdom in the words.

"What are you doing there?" I asked. "I thought you'd be retired by now, emptying every fishing hole in Lake Lewisville."

"Naw. I tried it, but only lasted a year. Came crawling back, begging for any position they'd let me have. Since I'm so danged ancient, they gave me a night desk. I'm guessing you didn't call to renew old acquaintances though. Why do you need to contact Pam? You do know she kicked over to computer fraud, don't you?"

"No. I didn't know that." I paused, hoping Ike still felt like stretching out a protective wing. "I'm looking for a favor. I live in Florida now, but my Mom's in Richardson. There's a stalker outside her window, and she's scared out of her wits." I told him about her call, leaving out nothing, including the response to her nine-one-one call. I drew another distinctive laugh when I mentioned the name Strudnocker.

"She really went out with someone with that moniker? Tell her I have several unmarried friends with much better names. If she's anything like you, I can set her up in a heartbeat."

"I'll let her know, but first I have to get her out of this mess. She dated him, now she's terrified of him. Can you do anything to help me?"

There was silence on the line as I pictured him sorting through possibilities. "Best I can think of is for me to clock out and go over and keep an eye on her. I have a patrol car and wear the uniform. It should be enough to encourage him to leave."

"That would be wonderful," I said. "But can you just walk away?"

"Sure. What are they going to do, retire me?" He rolled out the laugh again. "However, young lady, we're only solving her problem for the rest of tonight. Unless the guy does something overt, we can't arrest him or provide protection for your mom. What're you going to do come daylight?"

"I'm working on it. One problem at a time. How soon do you think you can be there? I have her sitting in bed with a gun pointed at the door. I'd like to tell her the cavalry is on the way."

"Yeah," he said, chortling. "Old, out-to-pasture cavalry. Sure hope I don't have to get in a foot race with him. He'd win, hands down."

"Thanks, Ike. I owe you a fishing trip. Come to Florida, and I'll charter you a boat."

"You got it. Here's my cell number. I need yours, your mother's, and her address. I'll call as soon as I'm in place and your stalker has hit the road."

He read off his ten-digit number, and I wrote it down, feeling like the weight of the world was lifting off my shoulders. Then I reciprocated by giving him the info he needed.

"I'll call and let Mom know. What do you think — half hour?"

"I'm standing up right now. If you'll get off the phone, I'll be out of here."

It was my time to chuckle. "I'm gone." I hit the disconnect button, then threw back my head and exhaled, a feeling of *all is well* enveloping me. It felt like I'd been holding my breath forever.

Easy part over. Now I had to call Mom and get her under control. I only hoped there were no bullet holes in her door yet. There was little doubt in my mind that the slightest noise would launch a round down range. Once my mother says she'll do something, it *will* be done.

When she answered, I said, "Mom. Hang on a bit longer. Things are under control."

"Thank you, Beth. I'm so relieved. I don't have to call your brother, Harve."

Thoughts ripped through my head best not repeated in mixed company. "Yes, Mom. Harve can get a good night's sleep." I hesitated, then surged on. "Here's the deal. Ike Morrison, a Dallas policeman from my past will be outside your house in a few minutes. If your boyfriend doesn't leave, I'm sure Ike will come up with a reason to make him very uncomfortable. Ike will stay there as long as he thinks necessary to protect you. Does that work for you?"

"Oh, Beth, that sounds perfect. I had confidence you would come through for me, and this Ike sounds like such a gentleman."

Sure, as long as it didn't inconvenience Harve. "Now, that takes care of tonight. We need a plan for tomorrow and the next nights. Any ideas?"

I grimaced, thankful she couldn't see me, held the phone away from my mouth, and took a deep breath to gather my courage.

Then I said into the mouthpiece, "Maybe you could visit Harve and Delores for a week or so. I'm sure your Snodbucket will grow discouraged with your absence."

"Strudnocker. Strudnocker, not Snodbucket." The line went quiet, then Mom said, "No. That won't work. Last time I visited them, it was awkward. They had to double up the kids in the same bedroom. They only have a three-bedroom house, you know."

Crap. I had played my ace of spades, and she trumped it. Where to go next? "Mom, you have to get out of Dallas. Ike is going out on a limb tonight. I can't ask him to hang around forever."

"Well, you could invite me to Florida. I mean, we never get to spend time together. This would be a perfect opportunity for some mother-daughter time. I could meet your boyfriend. If there's a chance he'll propose, I should really meet him first, don't you think? You remember what a big mistake you made the first time — even after I tried to tell you. I could catch a flight out in the morning."

Damn. Trapped like a salmon charging up stream. I had leapt right into Mom's net. My mind spun like a centrifuge, but no fresh ideas popped out.

"Beth? Are you still there? You *do* want me to come, don't you? You can show me the beach. I have this great new bikini I found on sale a few weeks ago. If you like it, I can give it to you. It's pretty daring. Your boyfriend will love it."

Just what I wanted, seeing my mom in a *daring* bikini — or worse yet, my being in one. I had the perfect drawer I could bury it in. There was only one thing to say so I said it, "That's a great idea, Mom. Book a flight in the morning, then call me with your arrival time. I'll pick you up at the airport."

"That won't be necessary. I prefer to rent a car. I'll need some way to get around while you work your cases. You are working, aren't you?"

My suspicious mind said this might not be spontaneous. It sounded like she had everything worked out in advance. Was there really a Lanny Strudnocker outside her house? Whatever, she was still my mom, and I had to believe she had a problem. "Call with your schedule, then call when you land. I'll meet you here at the house."

"I need your cell number. You've never given it to me."

Crap. Another trap I'd walked into. It's not that I didn't want her to have my number. I just couldn't afford her interrupting a surveillance or other case activity with one of her premonitions. But, like they say, when caught in a blueberry patch with blue lips and a blue tongue, just admit you're stealing blueberries. I gave her the cell number, then hung up with the excuse I expected a call from Ike at any moment.

Everything was coming together. Well, if you can call having my mother as a houseguest for an indeterminate amount of time coming together.

Don't get me wrong. I love her as much as any divorced daughter can love a mother who views marriage and kids as *the* number one priority for her offspring. Harve had not disappointed her. I had, and she let me know at every opportunity. That didn't mean she was one to say, "Get married and have babies." No, she was much more subtle. I would hear things like, "Oh, Harve's children are so perfect. If *only* you could find a man to have babies with — after marriage, of course." As if locating the perfect mate was as simple as shopping on the Internet.

Ouch. I remembered that David would be back Saturday, and there was no way I could keep from exposing him to Mom if she was still visiting. I had no doubt she'd be ready to propose for me and stand in as Matron of Honor or Best Man — or both. Whoopee, my life was taking a turn — straight down.

My phone rang. It was Ike letting me know he was in place, camped out in front of her house. As he had come down the street in his black and white, he saw a car pull away from the curb. Small and white, probably Japanese, was the best he could come up with.

I thanked him, hung up, and called Mom. "Okay, Mom, things are under control. If you look out the window, you'll see —"

"I see it. A police car. It's parked right across the street. It showed up a few minutes ago, and Lanny drove away. Is he going to stay there? Is that Morrisette you told me about?"

Some day, I might get to tell Mom a story without her taking over, but I doubt it. "Not Morrisette, Morrison. The driver's name is Ike Morrison. He's an old friend of mine. He'll stay until he's convinced your boyfriend is not coming back. Does that work for you?"

"I suppose. He won't fall asleep, will he?"

"No, Mom. He won't fall asleep. Now, I have to go. Get some rest. Don't forget to call me with your travel details as soon as you work them out."

I disconnected and turned off my light. I

needed sleep, as much as I could get to prepare for the next day, especially Mom's arrival. Sunrise promised to usher in a humdinger. Then I remembered I still had Ashley's kidnapper to track. Oh boy, that raced past humdinger straight toward madcap. I was heading into a day like no other I'd ever had.

EIGHT

Those church bells again. They couldn't fool me twice in the same night. I knew there was no church nearby. An alarm clock, yes. A church, no. I opened my eyes and stared. Yep. It was my too-reliable clock, and it read seven-thirty. I felt like I'd just fallen asleep, which wasn't far from the truth.

After Ike's phone call and the last conversation with Mom, I spent forever rolling from one side of my bed to the other. The last time I noticed, the clock hands sat at four-thirty. Then, the church bells.

Groaning, I threw back the covers and headed for the kitchen. Coffee. I needed coffee. After that, a shower, a nice *hot* shower — then more coffee. Since neither Hammonds nor the police contacted me during the night, I assumed things remained the same with Ashley's disappearance.

I considered what to wear. I didn't know when I'd next be able to change clothes. It depended on how fast the case moved once the kidnappers made contact. They had control. All I could do was be ready.

I grabbed one item without any deep thought about it. For lack of a better name, I labeled it my gun bra. After a recent case when I found myself unarmed, facing the business end of a thug's pistol, I decided to find a solution. First, I combed the Internet until I found the weapon I wanted, a .22 caliber American Derringer. I chose the .22 to hold the weight down because I knew where I wanted to conceal it, and a derringer to minimize the size.

With the derringer in hand, I bought several full-coverage bras and took them to Mrs. Gonzalez, a seamstress I knew in Fort Lauderdale. Her ability with a needle and thread was mystical. When I showed her the gun and explained what I wanted, using her daughter as a translator, she gave me her *can do* smile, and told me to come back next week.

Upon my return, I found she had modified the bras by reinforcing the center gore and sewing in a snug holster made from a soft material. When I tried the bra on and slipped the derringer in under a T-shirt, I saw no hint of the weapon. Like I said, she could work magic.

I kept the derringer on the top shelf of my closet out of harm's way in a shoebox. The ammo snuggled in the back of my makeup drawer. I'm a great believer in keeping guns and ammunition separate. Make it as difficult as possible for a burglar to arm himself, that's my motto.

I took out the derringer and its ammo and checked both. All looked well so I loaded it, set the safety, and concealed it, then pulled out my usual jeans and a V-neck T-shirt. However, as I stood in front of the mirror, I realized I had no idea what the day might bring. Perhaps a T-shirt was not the best choice. I rummaged through the drawer and came up with a black knit top with a scoop neck. It looked dressy enough to get me into all but the ritziest places in South Florida, but casual enough for Walmart. Definitely a better choice. And the neckline dipped low enough to allow me to reach the derringer. A lightweight black windbreaker finished my ensemble. No way to tell what over-air-conditioned places I might have to visit.

My last chore was to open the box my Walther P99C came in. I wanted the two empty eight-round magazines I kept there. From another box, I retrieved nine-millimeter ammo and filled them. Then I took the Walther out of my purse, ejected the magazine, and checked it. Once convinced everything was in perfect working order, I re-loaded the pistol, chambered a round, and set the safety to the on position.

The sub-compact Walther was also a recent acquisition, bought after the same experience that sent me looking for a bra gun. The Walther didn't measure up to the full-sized Beretta M9 I wanted — too heavy for a purse — but it would do.

Once I filled my bag with the pistol and extra rounds, along with the other paraphernalia I carried, it felt like a weapon itself. And, with its shoulder strap, I could give it a good swing. Anyone who happened to stand in the way would go down, no doubt about it.

I took a last look in the mirror, knowing Mom would have something to say about my ensemble. There'd be lots of words, but the gist of it would be that no man would find me attractive until I learned to dress to make myself attractive — like wearing a *daring* bikini. Oh, brother.

As I walked out of the house, I smiled, picturing the look on a wannabe rapist's face when I reached into my bra and came out with a gun. I suspected his *weapon* would wilt. The same went for any other thug that tried to take me on.

I headed for Hammonds' place, figuring I'd get a briefing on what the police learned overnight, if anything. It wouldn't do any good to hit Ashley's school too early. Plus, there was always the possibility one of my homeless friends would call to say they spotted the woman who took Ashley. Or maybe the kidnapper would make contact. With Sargent on duty, I'd feel better if I were near Hammonds' phone when it rang.

I pulled into Hammonds' driveway, and a uniform stepped out. She wasn't expecting me, so I had to identify myself, then prove it. I guess she accepted that I wasn't the master criminal returning to the scene of the crime because she walked me through the garage and turned me over to an inside cop.

I heard steps coming my way, and Sargent soon faced me.

"Well, my favorite skirt-PI. You're getting better. Found your way in with no help this time."

Jerk, I thought, but bit back the words that formed. "I'm here to see John Hammonds. You, I do *not* need to see."

He laughed. "Shucks, ma'am. I'm right sorry you feel that way. You know I always look forward to being with you." His smirk put the lie to his words. "Mr. Hammonds is in his study. I reckon a smart PI like you can find her way." He turned and walked back the way he'd come.

There were things I wanted to say, things I needed to say, but I wasn't there to fight. I was there to help John Hammonds. I followed Sargent, then abandoned his trail to head toward Hammonds' office.

Stopping in the doorway, I didn't see him. "Mr. Hammonds?" I said. "Are you in here?"

It seemed a stupid question because I could see the entire office — a conversation niche surrounding a coffee table, and his desk with his chair behind it, facing away from me. Of course, the chair back was tall enough and wide enough to hide a man twice his size. I waited a respectable amount of time, then stepped into the room. "Mr. Hammonds? Would you prefer I come back later?"

If he was in the room, he had to be in the chair. If he wasn't, I could only hope Sargent wasn't listening. If so, for the rest of my life — well, his part of it — he'd harass me that I talked to myself.

The chair swiveled.

"Ms. Bowman. Sorry. Guess I was wool gathering."

The chair continued its trip, and Hammonds came into full front view. He had shaved and changed clothes since I last saw him, but it hadn't improved his appearance. His face was vapid, and, if possible, he looked worse than the night before. His eyes were roadmaps to nowhere, all small secondary roads in red.

"Ever think about that old saying?" he said, his expression showing a bit of life. "Wool gathering. They say all colloquialisms have a foundation in fact, but I can't for the life of me figure that one out. I just can't find a connection between daydreaming and sheep shearing, or wherever the term originated." He lapsed into silence, and his face went blank again.

"If this is a bad time, I can come back this afternoon. Would that be better?"

"No, I'm glad you're here. Did you accomplish what you set out to do?"

In the hours I'd been gone, Hammonds had aged years. The skin on his face sagged, and the bags under his eyes were big enough to cost him dearly if he checked them on an airplane.

I walked to the desk, reached across, and touched his arm. "I did as much as I could. We'll see if it pays off today. How are things here?"

Hammonds glanced toward the living

room and let out a heavy sigh before letting his head drop. "Every chance he gets, that cop tells me I'm making a mistake by trusting my daughter to you. I'm tired of hearing it. I told him to give it a rest, but he doesn't."

I stood across from one of the most successful lawyers in South Florida, but no one would have ever known it. His whole demeanor was one of defeat. I had to add another layer.

I lifted his chin. "John, he may be right. They have a lot more resources than I do. I'm just one person. Perhaps you should —"

"I know that, Beth," he flared. "But I've handled enough criminal cases to know amateurs panic at the first sign of the cops. From what I've seen, these people are not pros. A pro would never have committed murder to set up a kidnapping. Murder is a capital offense in Florida, kidnapping is jail time. Now they know if they're caught, they stand a good chance of getting a death sentence. That means we have to approach them easy."

He stared at me. "Don't you know that having cops near a drop site or setting up some kind of sting is the best way I know to

101

ensure Ashley —" He choked and didn't finish.

"I agree, John, but they have the assets. I only have me and a few friends."

"Yeah, but whatever they have, they'll share with you. Like I said before, if they get cute, I'll have the governor down here. I'll cash every IOU I've ever accepted to get Ashley back — and I don't give a damn whose feelings get bruised."

I backed away and took a visitor's chair. "So what's been happening here?"

"Quiet. Too darn quiet. Why don't they make contact?" He rested his face in his hands and his words came out muffled. "They must know I received their message loud and clear. They must know I'll pay anything."

It hurt to see such a proud man reduced to this level, but I tried not to show it. One of us had to project strength. "Pressure, John. It's all about building up the pressure. And I'm sure they're getting a feel for how the police are reacting. They'll have to find some sneaky way to make contact, expecting your phone calls to be recorded."

"How about emails? The police brought in a laptop and are monitoring my inbox. Do you think they'll email me?"

"Possible, if they use a public computer. I

doubt they'd be dumb enough to use a personal one. The library is always a possibility . . . or a FedEx Office or something like that. Hotels, motels. There are business centers everywhere these days, even some coffee shops. Anyone can use them, and setting up a phony account is a snap. When the authorities backtrack the email, the trail ends at the computer that sent it. No way to identify the author. So I'd say email is a distinct possibility."

"I'll take your word for it. All that techy stuff is too much for me. I yearn for the good old days of handwritten words on a legal pad."

"Did your sister leave?" I asked, hoping to get his mind off his daughter.

"No. She said she'll stay until Ashley comes home. She's a rock, one I need. My whole life she's been the one who stood up when courage was needed."

So much for diverting his thoughts with his sister. Another try was in order. "Yeah, I have a brother like that. He's always there for me." It wasn't exactly the truth, but it kept the conversation moving. I went on, embellishing on what had been a pretty normal big brother-little sister relationship. Harve thought I was a pain in the ass, and I thought he was a macho pig. "When my dad died, Mom had to go to work. Harve was the one I came home from school to, the one who made me a snack, helped me with my homework. I think I know what you mean about your sister."

"Harve?"

"His name is Harvey. Mom always kidded that she named him after Harvey the Rabbit from the old movie. Actually, there's been a Harvey on Mom's side of the family every other generation from way back. Harve lives in Wisconsin with his wife, Delores, and two adorable children. Mom loves his kids and tells me all the time I need to give her grandkids. She —"

"Beth. You're babbling. It's not necessary. I'm not going to fall apart."

Caught. What could I do? I smiled. "Hey, does that mean you don't find my family fascinating?"

My cell phone sang its ditty. I stared at the caller ID a moment, wondering if Mom was testing to see if I'd given her the correct number. Didn't matter. She was about to storm into my life.

Throwing Hammonds an apologetic smile, I said into the phone, "Hi, Mom. Did you get a flight?"

"Yes. I fly out of DFW at two. I'll land in Fort Lauderdale at six-fifteen. It's only a three-hour flight, but we lose an hour because of the time zones."

"Great. Call me when you arrive. Do you still want to rent a car? I can pick you up."

"No. I don't want to be stranded. If you have to work, I can always go to the beach or Disney World. Are you working now?"

I chose not to tell her Disney World was over three hours north of me. Texans tend to think that anywhere except their home state is small with everything located close together. I know because I overcame that same tendency — almost.

"Yes. I'm meeting with a client right now, so I need to cut this short." I threw another smile accompanied by a shrug at Hammonds, who appeared to have forgotten I was in the room. "Sorry, but when the opportunity arises, I have to go with it."

"I understand, Beth. You just go on about your business. I know how to take care of myself."

"That's great, Mom, I —"

"You didn't tell me Ike was such a delightful man. We shared a wonderful breakfast. It seemed like the right thing to do after he sat outside all night. Did you know he's a widower? His wife died two years ago."

I sat up straight in my chair, suspecting there was a lot hidden in those words. "Uh, no, I didn't. I never met her. So, where did you go for breakfast — IHOP?"

"No, silly. I fixed it right here. Pancakes, eggs, bacon, grits, the works. I wouldn't ask a man like Ike to go to IHOP . . . well not when we just met." She chuckled. "Maybe next time."

Great. Now I had created a pickle. Good luck, Ike, I thought. My mom is a determined woman.

After giving directions to my house, I got her off the phone. Of course, she said she didn't need the instructions because she had printed them out before she phoned. That's my mom — efficient to the nth degree.

"Sorry, John," I said. "My mom. She has a problem in Dallas so she'll be camping with me for a few days. But she knows she's on her own. Ashley comes first."

"You don't have to convince me. I know you're a pro."

"Well, since nothing is going on here, I'll hit the road. I have a couple of things I want to check. Call me if anything changes."

He stood and extended his hand. "I'll keep you informed. You do the same."

NINE

I headed for Ashley's school, hoping the two women who saw her abductor had information they weren't aware they had. I didn't know whom they talked to at the police station, but if the detective wasn't female, there might be unasked questions. Any time one woman describes another, a woman's touch adds to the construction of the questions. Plus, the police spend every day emptying the gutter, and the hideousness of society hardens them against tragedy. Sometimes, it narrows their field of vision and causes them to miss important details.

Once there, I parked in a visitor's spot and fumbled through my notes. The women I needed to see were Ms. Dimitri and Ms. Sumatra. The former was the school secretary and the latter was Ashley's teacher. I went to the office where an attractive blond lady in her forties sat behind a desk. The nameplate read Ms. Thelma Dimitri,

Secretary."

"Ms. Dimitri, I'm Beth Bowman, a private investigator hired by John Hammonds to look into the abduction of his daughter, Ashley. I understand you saw the lady who took her." I laid a business card in front of her.

She stood, her arms crossed in front of her. "Abduction? I didn't see it that way. Ms. Lowenstein came into the office, gave me a note signed by Ms. Hammonds giving her permission to pick up Ashley. After satisfying myself that the note was legitimate, I asked Ms. Sumatra to bring Ashley to the office. Once they arrived, Ashley went with Ms. Lowenstein, just like she has gone with other people who have picked her up. I had no way of knowing there was anything wrong."

Oops. I had jumped off on the wrong foot. Some quick backtracking was necessary. "I wasn't being accusatory. The police assured me you acted properly in every way, and I'm sure I would have done the same as you. I have no reason to think otherwise. However, the lady in question did kidnap Mr. Hammonds' daughter. I'm sure you're very observant and very conscientious in your duty. I'm hoping you can help me." I stopped, giving her a chance to respond —

in a more positive way, I hoped.

She didn't uncross her arms, but they appeared to relax a bit. "I spent hours with the police. I have better things to do than defend how I perform my job. I have a school to run here. If you have their report, you know everything that I know. I really don't see —"

"My experience is that many times we know things we're not aware of. Especially, with small things that don't seem important. This can be even more true when women talk about other women."

Her arms came unfolded, and she gave me a skeptical look. "What do you mean?"

"I mean things one woman notices about another, but doesn't make a big deal of. Something a man might never think about."

Her look changed to one of thought before she waved me to a chair. "For example?"

"I noticed the sketch doesn't describe her jewelry. Was she wearing any?"

"Of course. I mean . . . I suppose so. Everyone I know wears jewelry."

"I agree. What kind of earrings did she have on?"

She rested a hand across her chin and tapped her forefinger against her lips as if in deep thought. "I don't remember any. Her hair covered her ears . . . I think. It . . .

wait. When she turned toward the door as Ashley entered, her hair lifted and . . ." She went quiet again. "I did see an earring. There was something about it. It didn't look quite right." She looked at me with expectant eyes.

I said nothing. Sometimes the best way to gain information is to show patience and wait for it.

"It was a pink pearl that clashed with her red hair. A stud, not a dangle."

"Size? Expensive? Real?"

"Oh boy. That's tough. Give me a minute."

I took my gaze off her and looked around her office. I didn't want her to feel pressure as she searched her memory bank.

After a moment, she said, "I have to say expensive, but I can't give you a reason. It wasn't particularly large, what I'd call medium-sized. But something about it makes me say a real pearl. Mind you, I only saw the one. And don't ask if they were cultured or saltwater. I don't move in those circles."

"Good observation. So we have pink pearl stud earrings under," I checked my notes, "red hair. Is that correct?"

"Yes. Not a combination I'd recommend," she said.

"Lipstick. What color was it?"

"Oh, my." She ran a forefinger over her lips as her eyes glazed. "Don't hold me to it, but I'm thinking pink. Does that make sense? A redhead wearing bright pink lipstick? It didn't do her any favors. I remember that."

"Possible," I said. "Any other makeup? Her eyes? Blush?"

She thought for a moment, her fingers dancing around her face as if recreating what she'd seen. "No. I'm drawing nothing there. Just the lipstick."

"Amazing what we see without realizing it, isn't it?" I said. "There may be other things."

"I see what you mean about a woman observing another woman," she said. "None of this came up with the police — just the color and style of her hair."

"You're doing great. Now, what was her complexion? Pale, dark?"

"She was . . . she had a warm skin tone. Kind of golden, yet clear." She hesitated, frowning. "Not what I normally associate with redheads."

"Interesting. How about rings, bracelets?"

"Just a minute. There was something else. Give me a moment. Maybe it'll click in."

"Take your time." I waited as she

scrunched her face up as if in deep thought again.

"It was . . . her eyebrows. They didn't fit a redhead. They were dark, almost black." She paused. "You know, I'm beginning to think the red hair was the part that didn't match. Everything else, skin tone, earrings, lipstick, and eyebrows fit."

"A wig?"

"Could have been," she said. "I wish I'd been more observant. But it was a busy time in the office, and I had no reason to examine her."

"I understand. Now, let's move on to the rest of her jewelry."

There was no hesitation. "She wore rings on almost every finger. But the one that caught my eye was a large marquise-cut green stone on her third finger, left hand. It was surrounded by diamonds. I'm betting all of it was real — an emerald big enough to choke an elephant. She wore it with a simple gold band, like a wedding ring."

"Engagement ring?"

"I should be so lucky." She dangled an empty finger. "Whatever it was, there was a genuine sugar-daddy behind it." She thought again. "Yeah. I'd say it was an engagement ring."

I wrote every word in my notebook.

"Bracelets. Any bracelets?"

"You're thorough. I'll give you that." She went into deep thought mode again. "Left wrist. A diamond tennis bracelet in yellow gold. It flopped around her gold watch. I don't know the brand, but I'd give you expensive. In fact, now that I think about it, everything about her was expensive. Maybe that's one reason I accepted the note so readily."

I handed her the police sketch of the woman. "Look at the glasses. Are they accurate?"

"Yes. Why?"

"Tough question coming. Get ready. Expensive or cheap?"

"Expen . . ." Her eyes glazed again, leading me to believe she was analyzing her memory.

I let the clock tick. An idea had formed in my head, but I didn't want to force her to the same conclusion. If I was right, she had to get there by herself. If wrong . . . well, no risk, no gain.

"Ms. . . ." She looked at my business card. "Bowman, this sounds almost too stupid to say. The frames looked cheap, drugstore cheap. Does that make sense? I mean, she was well dressed, wearing all that expensive jewelry. Why would she have cheap glasses?"

"Yeah, makes one wonder, doesn't it?" It was my turn to think, to consider any points I'd skipped. Nothing came to mind. "I've run out of questions. Can you think of anything we missed?"

She thought some more. "No. You've been very thorough. Well, one more thing. Her clothes were nice, they looked expensive, but . . . They seemed old, like they were out of date." She stopped and shook her head. "If I come up with anything else, I'll call you."

"That'll do it then," I said. "And please don't blame yourself. No one would expect a rich woman to be a kidnapper." I closed my notebook. You've been very helpful, and I thank you. The more I learn, the closer I get to finding Ashley."

"Sorry about my attitude when you came in. I really thought I told the police everything I knew."

"You did. At least, you told the police everything that you knew you knew. I only guided you onto some of the things you didn't know you knew." I smiled and shrugged. "Is Ms. Sumatra in today?"

"Yes. Should I call her for you?"

"Please, if it won't disrupt her class."

"She has an assistant who can cover for her." She used the intercom and paged Ms.

Sumatra, who soon appeared.

I went through my questions with her but didn't learn anything new. She said she was only with the woman for a moment. She brought Ashley into the office, shook hands with the lady, and turned Ashley over to her. She did verify the pink lipstick and the profile of well-to-do, though. That alone made the trip worthwhile.

I walked out of the school, feeling like I'd made progress. The woman had apparently thrown on a shallow disguise in the form of a red wig and cheap glasses. Perhaps that's what she wanted remembered. Obviously, she hadn't counted on someone with Ms. Dimitri's photographic memory. It needed a bit of prodding, but when it clicked in, she gave me more than I expected. The ring might be a real clue, something that could identify her if she stepped out of her house. If it was an engagement ring, she probably never took it off.

Of course, I had no idea of her true hair color, meaning whatever shade her hairdresser made it. She could be blond, black, brunette, or any place in between. Maybe I could get the police to come up with a version of each.

I climbed into my car, fired the engine, and started the air conditioner. Once it was blowing cold, I took out my cell and called Hammonds' number.

"Mr. Hammonds' residence," I heard.

"This is Beth Bowman. Who's the detective on duty today?"

"Bannon, and you're talking to him. What's up?"

I told him about my conversations with Ms. Dimitri and Ms. Sumatra and asked if he could match me up with the sketch artist.

"You might be better than I thought. How long will it take you to get here?" Bannon asked.

"No more than fifteen-twenty minutes."

"Good. Our portrait-maker will be right behind you."

I spent two hours with Officer Germaine and his colored pencils. He started with the sketch he'd made the previous day, then made changes as I asked for them. The glasses came off, the lips assumed a brighter pink color, and the eyebrows went dark brown. I decided to gamble that the wig was approximately the same style as the woman's usual hair, so Germaine did three versions for me — blond, black, and brunette. We decided to stick with basic colors. There were simply too many variations to try one of each.

By three o'clock, I was at FedEx Office again, making color copies of the sketches. At four, I was walking into Bobby's Bar after calling Judy to let Bob know I was on the way. He didn't appreciate his phone ringing when he was working his corner. He set the phone on vibrate, but only answered to Judy. She knew not to call unless it was important.

TEN

Street, Dabba, and Dot had been close enough that Bob called them in. They were waiting for me in the men's dorm.

I opened our meeting by saying, "Our kidnapper used a disguise. We've been looking for the wrong woman." I passed around copies of the new sketches. "I'm pretty sure one of these is closer to her real appearance. Do any of them look familiar?"

"Not to me," Dabba said. "I ain't never seen her."

"Is this the best you got?" Dot asked. "Lots of women can fit this picture. I don't know."

I turned my attention to Street, whose eyes appeared glued to the picture. "How about you? Have you ever seen her?"

"I can't be sure," he said. "Maybe she comes by my corner sometimes. Her hair's like this one, but with streaks." He held up the brunette version. "Light-colored streaks."

"Think, Street, think," I said. "A five-year-old's life is at stake."

"I don't know. I never seen her without sunglasses. Everybody in Florida wears them. Can you put a pair on her?"

"Yeah," Dot said. "It ain't like these folks invite us to dinner."

Dabba cackled. "That's a good'un, Dot. I used to have folks come to dinner. That was before they took Linda. Ain't done it since."

There was an awkward silence, so I pulled out a fresh sketch of the brunette and some colored pencils I borrowed from Officer Germaine. With Street guiding me, I drew dark glasses over her eyes. My efforts at streaking her hair were unsuccessful until Bob found a yellow marker. After using that to add highlights, I asked, "Anything else?"

Street took the picture and walked over to one of the lamps. He held it under the bright light and studied it as if he were selecting lottery numbers. "Yep. I'm purty sure I seen somebody looks a lot like this driving on route four-forty-one."

"That's good. Can you remember what kind of car she was in?"

"Give me a minute," Street said. He plopped down on a bunk.

"Take all the time you need." I turned to

the rest of the group. "Let's go into the bar and have a glass of water or something. Give Street some privacy."

Street joined us a few minutes later. "White Lexus, an old one. That's all I remember."

Great. About every third car in South Florida was white, and a lot of those were Lexuses — or so it seemed. I couldn't let Street see my frustration though. "That's more than we had before. Maybe she'll take the same route again, and someone will spot her. If so, we need a license number." As I spoke, I busied myself adding highlights to several of the other copies of the brunette sketch.

Out of the corner of my eye, I saw each of them nodding as they looked at one another, however, no one had anything to add. After a moment, Bob said, "There's still some daylight. Let's spread out and see if we spot anything. Does everyone have pictures?"

More nodding followed his question, then Street, Dot, and Dabba left.

Bob said, "If others come in, I'll brief them. You're welcome to hang around if you like."

"No. I need to move on. There are some places I want to hit before it gets too dark. I'll leave extra copies of the sketches."

■ ■ ■ ■

In the next three hours, I hit six Publix Super Markets and wandered through eight strip malls. The only thing I learned was my sketch didn't help much. With a little imagination, it fit about every fourth woman I encountered.

At eight-fifteen, my cell phone chirped. Caller ID sent a chill down my spine. Mom. I'd completely forgotten she was coming in.

"Hi, Mom. Did you get in okay? How was the flight?"

"The flight was fine, and I made it to your house without mishap." Her words carried an edge to them — meaning I should have met her at the airport or at least called to verify she landed.

"Sorry I didn't check in with you," I said in what I hoped was an apologetic tone, "but I've been busier than a horsefly in a herd of mares today. I have this case —"

"That's all right, my dear. I know you must give priority to your work."

Ouch. That meant I'd pay later. "It's not that, Mom. It's just I've been dashing from place to —"

"I said it was okay. I'm at your house now, and I found things to keep me busy. If you can tell me when you might get home, I'll try to be through cleaning by then. Didn't you say you cleaned the refrigerator recently?"

Double-ouch. I had really stepped into it now. It would take a lot to dig myself out of this one, so I decided to stall. "Uh, how did you get in?"

Mom chuckled. "I know my daughter. I simply looked for a fake rock in the flower bed. Found one just like mine. Popped it open and there was the key."

I was not doing well. I'd forgotten that I bought my fake rock at the same time Mom got hers — many years ago in Texas. Time to take the leap, though. "I'm not real sure when I'll get there. I still have several leads to pursue. There's food —"

"You need not worry. I picked up something on the drive from the airport. I *know* how busy you are. You just follow your leads, and I'll have dinner with the news. You *do* get CNN, don't you?"

That was the clincher. She never watched CNN. Said it was too liberal for her Texas roots. "Okay, Mom. I'll be there as soon as I can. Make yourself comfortable. And don't clean up. I'll take care of it." It wouldn't have done any good to tell her I thought the place was spotless when I left that morning. If she said it needed cleaning, it needed cleaning. "I have to run now. One of my contacts just showed up. Kisses." I punched the off button with a sigh, wondering if all mothers were like mine, or if I just got lucky.

Before I could feel too sorry for myself, the phone rang again. This time, caller ID told me it was Hammonds' number.

"Beth, here."

"Ms. Bowman. This is Detective Bannon. We have an email. Mr. Hammonds requested I let you know."

"I'm on the way. I'll be there in less than thirty minutes."

I hit Hammonds' house in twenty minutes and made my entry through the garage. I still wasn't up to facing the foyer. Inside, I found Hammonds in his office with Sargent and Bannon.

"So, what does the email say?" I asked after settling into a chair.

"Give her a copy," Hammonds snapped. "I told you she gets everything."

"I printed a copy for her," Sargent answered, his face red.

It was obvious the pressure was getting to Hammonds, and he was getting under Sargent's skin. And, while I had no love, or even respect, for Sargent, I thought Hammonds was being a bit heavy-handed. Sargent might be a horse's ass, but he was doing his job.

"Thanks, Sargent," I said, standing and reaching for the paper before Hammonds did. If I could keep peace between the two of them, life would be easier for everyone.

Sargent handed the copy to me, then turned and left the room. His stride was angry, his heels hitting the floor with force. When he closed the door, it didn't slam, but it had a definite slap to it.

I read aloud, "Three a.m. Instructions in center circle of soccer field at Royal Springs and Wiles." I looked at Hammonds.

"Not much to go on, is there?" he said. "What do you think?"

I studied the message. "It's from someone called *IWantMine* at Yahoo.com. I'm betting when the police track it, they'll come up with phony identifying info. But we expected that, didn't we?" I paused. John's eyes had locked on the paper I held. "Looks like I have an early morning date in Coral Lakes." I handed the paper to John and picked up my purse.

"Wait, Ms. Bowman," Bannon said. "We need to lay out a plan. You'll need police backup. We'll need to get the place staked out early. Maybe we can grab someone and sweat him."

I looked from Bannon to Hammonds. "No. This is their first contact. I'm betting they'll have someone nearby with an open phone watching the pickup to make sure we're playing by the rules. If they see anyone extra . . ." I let my voice die off, not wanting to complete the sentence. The last thing I wanted to say was they might take it out on Ashley.

"You're not being smart," Bannon said. "We have a chance at them."

"This is why Mr. Hammonds hired me. You stay here in case they call or send another email. I'll need to know." I hesitated while taking a deep breath, letting it out slowly. "Look. I say we play it exactly how they say. I'll be back as fast as I can. At least, we'll know what they want and how they want it."

Hammonds said, "Beth . . . be careful. Take it as slow and easy as you need to. Whatever it takes to bring Ashley home."

I left the room with John's eyes boring into me. I'm not sure which they carried more of, hope or fear. And I'm not sure which my heart carried more of, fear or hope. There were only a couple of logical scenarios. I was either walking into a trap, or the instructions were there. The first was illogical, but killing Sabrina wasn't the most logical thing they could have done either.

As soon as I stepped out of the house, I flipped open my cell phone and punched in Bob's number. He answered on the first ring.

"Bob, I have a date at the soccer field on the corner of Royal Springs Drive and Wiles Road. If you have anyone in the area, I could sure use an extra pair of eyes."

"What's going down?"

"They emailed and said they'll have instructions in the center circle of the soccer field at three a.m. I'll pick them up, then head back to Hammonds' house. Until then, I'm going home to try to make peace with my mother. She came in today and is not happy I wasn't there to greet her."

Bob said, "I'll see if anyone is close enough to the intersection to help. Be careful."

"Careful is my middle name — Beth Careful Bowman."

"What was that about your mother?"

I gave him the nickel version of her arrival and the reason for it. "Not only was I not home when she arrived, but she says my house is filthy and threatened to clean it."

"Sounds like you're caught in a lose-lose

situation."

"You nailed it. At this moment, I'm her least favorite daughter, and she has no others."

Bob chuckled. "Don't expect any help from me. I'd rather step between a lioness and her cub than get caught between a mother and daughter. If you run fast enough, the lioness will give up and go back to her little one. You can't run fast enough to escape a vengeful mother."

"Yeah, I know. My mother has been outrunning me my whole life."

"So, what now?"

"Grocery stores. There are several between here and my house. You know, a Publix on almost every corner. Maybe our kidnapper likes to shop at night. I'll stop in before heading home to face Mom. That'll lend truth to my white lie. I told her I had leads to follow."

Bob tsked me. *"Oh what a tangled web we weave, when first we practice to deceive.* Sir Walter Scott's famous words."

"Yeah. His and my mother's. It's her mantra. I'm out of here."

I clicked the cell closed, climbed into the car, and backed out of the driveway, heading for Publix, then home. With luck, I would spot the woman, square things with

Mom, and get a couple of hours sleep. And Jiminy Cricket would land on my shoulder to provide me with guidance. Yeah, right.

Driving in the general direction of my house, I stopped at four more Publixes. No luck.

I was tired, frustrated, and nervous about going home. By now, I figured Mom would have herself worked into a real mad. If only I could stay out until she was asleep, I could avoid her until the morning.

I checked my watch again. Eleven o'clock. Bob hadn't called so his people must have come up empty, and he must not have located a backup for me. Nothing left to do but go home and face Mom.

When I pulled into my driveway, I noticed a couple of things. The first was a red Chrysler convertible. It looked like Mom was planning a fun holiday. Or maybe she was entering her second childhood. I parked my Toyota Camry beside the Chrysler.

The second thing I noticed was the house was dark. I sighed in relief. I wouldn't have to face the music tonight.

ELEVEN

Not knowing where Mom was in the house, I slipped in as quietly as I once did when coming home late from a date. No lights and no noise. She slept like a cat — awake at any change in vibrations. I wanted my small travel clock, the one on my nightstand beside my clock radio. It was battery powered, therefore trustworthy when the power went off. As I passed the guestroom, I peeked in and hoped the lump in the bed was my mother. She chose that moment to snort and turn over. Yep, my mom. All was well.

After retrieving and setting the travel clock, I tiptoed back into the living room where I curled up in my recliner, hoping to cop a few Z's. Until the alarm dinged at two a.m., I flipped back and forth. Maybe, I'm not sure, there were a few minutes of unconsciousness during that time.

■ ■ ■ ■

After wiping the sleep from my eyes, I headed out the door, into my car, and stopped at the first 7-Eleven that crossed my path. Coffee was the magic elixir needed to sharpen my mind. I was already awake — wide awake — with anticipation of what the rest of the night would bring.

My driving went on autopilot as my mind wrestled with the situation. What kind of lowlifes could murder a mother and kidnap a five-year-old? Not to mention the needless death of the maid. What did she do to incite such violence? Wrong place at the wrong time? Leave no witnesses? Disgusting.

There was little doubt I was rushing toward a person or, at the minimum, a note telling Hammonds what it would cost to see his daughter again. How could they put a price on the love of a parent? I wanted them, wanted them bad. Where I wanted them was in the sights of my Walther. The judicial system was too good for them.

Of course, I wasn't naïve enough to think they were unique. I remembered some of the reprobates I pursued in Dallas while a cop. No section of the country has a monopoly on scum. But this particular pond in South Florida would be sanitized.

I took University Drive to Wiles, then turned west. Approaching Royal Springs Drive, I scanned the area. On my left was a rectangular, one-story school surrounded by small trees and bushes. The parking lot had no cars. Same with the business beside it that occupied the corner lot. The shadows were dark and deep in the full moon, but there was no obvious lurker.

I turned to the right and pulled into the parking area alongside the soccer field. One lonely streetlight illuminated the darkness, while all others were dark. Saving energy, maybe. I appreciated the city's thrift, but wouldn't have complained if the place looked like high noon.

It was a full-sized playing surface, at least a hundred yards long. The width was sixty to seventy yards, and I had to cross half of it. I parked so my headlights shone across the center circle, but if there was anything there, I couldn't see it. Leaving the engine running, I slid out, careful to make sure the door did not close. I wanted it open in case I needed to make a hasty getaway. Also, the open door and the inside light might deter any bad people. Yeah, right. Folks who would strangle a maid and put two slugs into Ms. Hammonds' back deterred by a small light? Happens every day — not.

I took the Walther from my purse, then slung the bag over my body, crosswise. I didn't want anyone to be able to grab it and run. Bumping my chest with my wrist, I reassured myself the derringer was in place. Okay, I thought. Enough with the stalling. Let's get it over with.

After scanning the area one more time, especially the school and the business across the street, I filled my lungs, then moved into the tough first step, holding the pistol along the seam of my jeans. I set a fast pace, staying on the edge of the beams of the headlights. I wanted to see, not cast a shadow. I couldn't hide, but there was no point in illuminating myself. They already held all the cards except the joker. That was my role.

Approaching the center circle, I saw an envelope laying on the kickoff spot. It appeared to be plain manila, five by seven. My first thought was letter bomb, showing how paranoid I was — and how scared. I fumbled in my purse, found a pair of latex gloves, and slipped them on over my sweaty palms — with difficulty. If there was evidence, I didn't want to ruin it.

With the padded envelope firmly between my fingers, I stepped into the darkness and did a slow pirouette, scanning the area. Nothing. I didn't see a thing that looked human, just the quietness of the middle of the night in a city park.

My eyes kept jumping to the envelope until I finished my scrutiny of my surroundings in a herky-jerky fashion. Then I examined it in the glare of my headlights. No identifying data. No writing of any kind. A metal clasp secured it.

I hotfooted it toward my car, my head spinning in one direction, then another. I won't say I ran, but I didn't bruise the grass as my feet flew over it. If there were any of Bob's people in the area, they'd have a great story to embellish for him. If there were any of the bad guys in the area, they would know they had me spooked. I didn't care.

Once in the car, I raced out of the parking lot with no thought of my speed. My only goal was to clear the area as fast as I could. If I attracted the attention of a policeman, that was fine, too. At that point, I didn't mind what anyone said about my running like a coward. I intended to be around to run another day.

TWELVE

He watched as the woman scrambled away from the center circle of the soccer field, never looking back. *Now, that's an interesting sight. We didn't figure on a woman. Wonder who she is. Probably some lady cop in plain clothes. Shouldn't matter though. She picked up the message, and that's the important part.* His brow furrowed as he again scanned the area, a worried expression plastering his face. *She has to have someone spotting for her. Nobody would send a lone woman for something like this, even a female cop. I'll just sit tight for a while. They'll get tired of waiting and make a move.*

He had been there for over three hours, having arrived at eleven-thirty. Their plan was for him to be in place before the police could put together a plan. That way, he'd be in position to watch the cops swarm in — if they came. He wasn't concerned about anyone spotting him. He figured anything other than a direct flashlight in his face would never detect him. And, if they found him, no big deal. Just another homeless bum sleeping it off. They'd give him a lecture and send him on his way.

Days before, he had scouted the area and selected the location for the drop — some place in the open where the messenger would be in plain view. Over the weekend, he watched youth soccer games on the field, sitting in the bleachers with the proud parents. That gave him ample opportunity to watch his selected hiding place. No one went near it. Even the smaller children who played games among themselves stayed away. He had smiled at how smart his selection was.

He frowned as the woman's car roared to life, and she pulled away, her wheels spinning on the blacktop. At the street, she didn't hesitate, just charged onto Wiles Road.

Chuckling, he mumbled, "It's a good thing we picked a time when there's little traffic. I wouldn't want her in an accident before Hammonds gets the word."

He settled back onto the short, three-legged stool and scanned the area again. *Time to sit quiet. I'll give it forty-five minutes to see if anyone pops up. Ought to have that much time before there's too much light. That broad must have someone covering her back. I can't believe the cops would let her come alone.* He stuck his legs straight out in front of him, flexing his calf muscles to stop a cramping sensation. *Sure wish I'd brought a cushion. I'm stiff as a board, and my butt's killing me.*

He turned away from the field and lit a cigarette, cupping the flame to obscure it. Taking a deep drag, he swiveled on his perch, keeping one hand over the end of the glowing tip as he did a three-sixty of the area. "No way anyone can see anything in here." He stared at the butt. "Nasty habit. Another rotten thing I learned in prison."

Enjoying his smoke, he kept a sharp watch but saw nothing. The soccer field, parking lot, even the business and school across the street stayed quiet. Nothing moved except an occasional car passing on Wiles Road or Royal Springs Drive.

After his self-allotted forty-five minutes, he picked up his stool and edged his way out of his hidey-hole, shaking his head. "I don't understand why she came alone, but if she didn't, they hid too good for me to spot them. I reckon they're gone by now, and I don't want to be here when the sun comes up."

THIRTEEN

The envelope lay on the passenger seat of my car, tugging at my attention like a burning fuse. I tried to focus on the road, but couldn't keep my eyes off the package. I was fortunate traffic was sparse, or I might have plowed into someone.

My cell phone sang its ditty, startling me. I fumbled it out of my purse and answered with a nervous, "Hello."

"Bob here. Are you on your way back to Hammonds with the envelope?"

"Yes. Wait a minute. How did you know I found an envelope?"

"I just got off the phone with one of my people. He was covering you."

"Where was he? I didn't see him." Even though my crisis was over, the knowledge that Bob had my back reassured me.

"Beth, you have to understand the homeless learn fast to be invisible, especially in the middle of the night. There are too many punks out there who think it's good sport to beat up on someone sleeping on a park bench. No way you or anyone else would ever spot him. What's in the envelope?"

"I don't know. I haven't opened it yet. I figure I owe Hammonds the first look."

"Yeah, probably so. Just for your info, my man saw no one in the area. Whoever left the envelope didn't hang around to see if you picked it up. Either that or he was really good. And, before you ask, we're very good at spotting others. It's called survival."

"Thanks, Bob. I should have remembered. Who was it? I'd like to thank him the next time I see him."

"You don't need to know. He prefers to stay in the background. Just pretend he's any homeless person you meet. Treat them with kindness, and he'll be happy."

"You know I will."

Even if I had been lost and never been to Hammonds' house before, the moment I turned onto his street his address would have been obvious. Light blazed across the yard, from the gazebo, and from each window. I pulled into the driveway, coasted close to the garage, and killed the engine.

I felt safer than I had since heading for the soccer field. It was nice to be back in the cocoon of society. I let out a deep breath, my lungs complaining like I'd held it for the past hour.

Before getting out of the car, I picked up the envelope, glad I hadn't removed the latex gloves. Time to get it inside to Hammonds. I got out of the car and walked up the driveway.

The garage door swung upward, startling me.

Sargent stood inside, his eyes bloodshot — from lack of sleep, I assumed. His gaze locked on the package I carried. He had loosened his tie and taken off his jacket. The stubble covering his jaw was black with traces of gray, like his hair.

"Is that what they left?" he asked.

I nodded.

"Well, don't just stand there. Mr. Hammonds is waiting for us."

He turned and headed into the house with me hot on his heels, hitting the garage door button as he went. If chivalry had to depend on him, its reported demise was indeed true. When we reached the hallway, he stopped and pointed. I took that to mean Hammonds was in his office. Apparently, the two of them would not exchange Christmas cards. Two Type A personalities clashing, but Sargent had to back away or risk his career.

I found Hammonds at his desk, sitting in semi-darkness, only a small lamp for illumination. Even under the poor lighting, I could see he looked as tired as Sargent. No, more so, more tired than any person I'd ever seen. If I hadn't known he was only forty-two, I'd have sworn he was in his seventies. The attractive professional I met had deteriorated into an old man filled with grief. My heart went out to him, wishing I could offer peace, but knowing only the return of Ashley could do that — and then, only partially.

His head came up, and he attempted to smile. It didn't work. He still wore the blue polo shirt he had on when I left, but now it looked bedraggled, which pretty much summed up his whole appearance. He reflected a man hovering on the edge of collapse. He stared at me as if I were his last hope — which, as phony as it might sound, I guess I was.

I scanned his desk to see what he was drinking, but saw only a half-filled coffee cup, and that looked cold. As far as I could tell, he had not sought solace in a bottle. That must have taken strength — strength I'm not sure I would have had in the same situation. I'm not much of a drinker, but there are times I crave a smooth scotch. Had I been in Hammonds' position, I might have been reaching for the bottle.

Further scrutiny revealed that everything was in its proper place. The office was spotless, not one loose paperclip. I assumed he spent his time sprucing up the office, burning off the nervous energy that threatened to consume him. My heart went out to him.

Still wearing my gloves, I placed the envelope on the desk. "This is what they left."

"Don't touch that." It was Sargent.

The voice came as a surprise because I hadn't realized he'd followed me. My first thought was he looked different, fresher somehow. Then it registered that he'd put on his suit jacket and tightened his tie.

"We need to have our crime scene techs go over it first," Sargent said. "There could be evidence that'll lead us to the kidnappers. Or," he frowned, his eyes hard, "it could be a bomb. In any case, let me handle it."

I stared at Sargent, knowing he was right. We needed to follow set procedure. On the other hand, we needed to know whatever message it contained — and every minute could be critical. More damned dilemmas.

I swallowed hard, looking at Hammonds.

The uplift I'd seen in his chin when I placed the envelope in front of him was gone. His hands hovered in the air, frozen by Sargent's words. They trembled, and the tiredness had returned to his face. Then, stubbornness moved in. "I have to know what's in here."

"I know, sir," Sargent said, compassion in his tone. "But we can't risk destroying evidence — evidence that might lead us to your daughter."

"Damn —"

"Maybe you could open it," I injected, my comment directed at Sargent. Both of them were right, and the last thing we needed was a pissing contest. "It appears to be sealed with the clasp, no glue. I'm sure you can empty it without messing it up."

Sargent chewed on his bottom lip.

"C'mon," I said. "You know we have to see the contents. Take a chance. Where's your heart?"

Sargent glared at me, then looked at Hammonds. "Alright. But not in here. I'll take it out by the pool — me, just me. You two remain right here. If it's a bomb . . ." His voice drifted away, but a stubborn look claimed his face, reminding me of the stony countenances carved into Mount Rushmore.

"It can't be an explosive," I said. "They

didn't kidnap Ashley to blow somebody away. They want money, probably lots of it."

"I'm not as prescient as you," Sargent said. "One of my many shortcomings." His sarcasm hovered in the air as he pulled a pair of latex gloves from his jacket pocket and worked his hands into them. He picked up the envelope like it held one of the dead sea scrolls — one that had not been deciphered. "Stay here. I'll bring the contents back . . . if I can."

After Sargent left the room, Hammonds rose, came around the desk, and headed for the door. "No way I can sit here and wait. We can at least keep an eye on him."

"We can watch from the patio," I said. "Sargent is right. It's his play, and he's taking a big chance for us. You and I are bystanders until he's ready to show us what's in the envelope." To myself, I added, *Please don't be a bomb.*

When we stepped outside, I pretended to stumble and saved myself by grabbing Hammonds' arm. I feared he'd keep following Sargent. He cut me a look, but stopped. I may or may not have sighed with relief. Part of me said we had to stay back and let Sargent do his job, while the rest yelled for me to stay with him. But I was responsible for Hammonds, and I needed to keep him safe — and under control.

Forcing my emotions down, I said, "We may as well sit," indicating a couple of comfortable-looking lounge chairs. "It's going to be a long day, no matter what he finds." I settled onto the cushion and leaned back. To my surprise, but not to my surprise, my eyelids threatened to close. It had been a long, tough night, and my adrenalin flow had slowed. The thought of sleep came uninvited to my mind.

"I suppose you're right." Hammonds voice sounded as tired as I felt. He sat beside me.

Along the edge of the pool, Sargent knelt and placed the envelope on a snack table. From his briefcase, he took out a recorder and rested it on a chaise lounge a few feet away. He was about thirty feet from us, but I had no problem seeing his every move. Hammonds had enough pool lights to support an Olympic high-diving event.

Sargent removed his suit coat, folded it in half, and lay it beside the recorder. He loosened his tie, then reached into his pants pocket and pulled out a clasp knife. He swiped his forearm across his forehead, opened a blade on the knife, then pushed a button on the recording device.

His lips appeared to form words as he began working on one wing of the clasp, moving at the speed of an arthritic snail. I assumed he chose to record every motion he made, leaving me to wonder if the recorder was bombproof.

The predawn hour wasn't hot. In fact, for South Florida, it was pretty cool, low seventies, maybe. But sweat ran down my cheeks, defying the weather. When I glanced at Hammonds, he wiped his face, his palm coming away wet. The external temperature had nothing to do with our perspiration. Our internal thermostats were registering well above sweat production. We were victims of tension. But only Sargent was in a position to physically feel it, especially if things went bad.

For a long moment, I saw strain on Sargent's face, then he relaxed. He sat back on his haunches and wiped his face again. Several deep breaths later, he walked to the other side of the table and repeated his act on the second wing of the clasp, moving no faster than before. I stared as his lips continued to move, forming words for the recorder. His professionalism and courage forced me to upgrade my opinion of him — but not much. He was still a horse's ass.

After what seemed an eternity, while my

racing heart waited for an explosion, he leaned back and flexed his neck and shoulders. I realized I had been holding my breath, or as close thereto as one can come. My eyes hurt from squinting. I could picture every hair on his fingers. That's how closely I watched as he worked. I imitated his stretching, taking deep breaths, forcing myself to relax. I couldn't imagine the stress he felt, but my neck hurt. Sargent was a better man than I had given him credit for.

Rubbing the back of his head, he stood and circled the table, his eyes glued to the envelope. I hoped he saw whatever he sought. Or maybe I hoped he didn't see it. I wanted the darn thing to be innocent so we could get the message that might be inside.

After three or four trips around the table, Sargent knelt again, grasped the end of the envelope, and gently shook it. Something slid out and he froze, I froze, and I'm sure Hammonds beside me froze. Then Sargent smiled and picked up the object and held it in the air for us to see.

A DVD.

As if it was an omen, the first hint of daybreak peeked at us above the trees bordering Hammonds' back yard. The world looked brighter, in more ways than one.

Fourteen

Sargent refused to let us have the DVD, explaining it could carry fingerprints. After some discussion, and Hammonds' blood pressure rising, Sargent agreed to make a copy. We headed into the office where Hammonds booted his computer, then turned the chair over to Sargent.

Sargent said, "If there's anything on this disk, and I screw it up, the chief will have my ass." There was no accompanying smile.

I understood his thinking. The evidence chain was so tight no policeman dared challenge it. All it took was one foreign print and a good defense counsel would have the whole thing tossed out of court. And in South Florida, judges were quick to look for reasons to side with the accused.

Hammonds' sister walked in, her appearance disheveled. "I couldn't sleep. Will I be in the way?"

I moved aside to make space for her.

"I'm going to make a duplicate," Sargent said. "Then I'll ship the original off to the lab, and you can do whatever you please with the copy. I only hope it's worth the potential cost to my career."

"Don't worry about it," Hammonds said. "No one is going to mess with your life because of this. That, I promise."

While Hammonds and I stood by, Sargent hit the right keys and we listened to the whir of the drives. A moment later, he punched the button on drive number two and handed me the disk. "I'll send one of our uniforms downtown with the original. You guys can see what's on this one."

Sargent stood and left the room.

I heard him say, "Officer Campbell, I want you to get this to our CSU people and don't spare the tires. Tell them I need it analyzed for prints and anything else they can find as fast as they can crank up their magic machines. If they give you any lip, tell them it's Chief Elston's number one priority."

Hammonds slid into the seat in front of his monitor. "I have to know what's on here."

"Give it a moment," I said. "After what Sargent has been through for us, I think he deserves a chance to see it firsthand."

The sister glanced my way, then nodded.

"She's right, John."

Hammonds cut me a look that left little doubt he considered any delay too long to wait, but lifted his fingers from the keyboard. "Tell him to get in here. I don't have time for this crap."

Sargent reentered the room. "Did you check it?"

"Waiting for you," I said, then nodded to Hammonds.

Sargent smiled, his first real smile in my direction since I'd met him. His behavior over the past hour had gained him a seat with us. He camped out over my shoulder while I sat beside Hammonds. We stared at the monitor as the DVD spun up.

The directory opened. There were three .jpg files and one .rtf file. Their names were *Ashley Watches TV, Ashley Eats Pizza, Ashley Naps,* and *Instructions.*

The titles of the files yanked at my heart, but I tried to stay cool and analytical. My investigative mind said, "Open the instructions," but Hammonds was a mouse click ahead of me. In retrospect, I couldn't blame him for going for the pictures first. If Ashley had been my child, I'd have done the same.

The first picture showed Ashley seated on a small chair watching TV. She was clean and wore a smile. Her blond hair reflected the flash of the camera. From every indication, she was happy and enjoying the show.

The second put her in the same chair, but with a table to match in front of her. A piece of pizza with bites missing lay on a plate. There was no sign of stress or abuse, and again, she had a big smile for the photographer.

In the third, she appeared asleep on a single bed with a Mickey Mouse coverlet over her. Her face was serene, a small smile playing on her lips, as she cuddled a Winnie the Pooh stuffed animal. There were no outward signs she realized things were not normal.

Studying the images, I fought tears. The pictures were so innocent, yet showed how much under the kidnappers' thumbs she was. I couldn't control myself. Tears flowed, and I sniffled.

Hammonds grabbed a tissue, then passed the box to me. I dabbed my eyes, blew my nose, and concentrated on the last picture. Ashley was a beautiful blond child with an angelic face. Who on planet earth would want to kidnap her and hold her for ransom? The depravity of some people was simply beyond my comprehension. I had to get her back.

Hammonds stared at the screen as if he

wanted to climb in and hug his daughter. Moisture pooled in his eyes, threatening to form into droplets.

I said in a quiet voice, "She looks okay. They haven't harmed her."

"Yes," he responded, emotion thick in his voice.

"Is that the outfit she wore to school yesterday?"

He blinked, then clicked back to the first picture. "It could be. She has something like that. I was gone when Sabrina . . ." his voice broke, ". . . when Sabrina dressed her." Though he spoke, his demeanor was of one in a stupor.

To keep both of us from getting too morbid, I said, "Let's see the instructions."

He broke out of his trance. "She looks all right, doesn't she? They haven't hurt her."

I swallowed words I really wanted to say — like, it looked like the bastards had her convinced her parents approved of her captivity. "She looks fine, but let's find out what they want."

He clicked on the .rtf file, and it opened in his MS Word program.

Defense Attorney John Hammonds,
    If you, and whoever's with you, are reading this, we have passed the first

stage of our endeavor. I assume you opened the pictures so you know Ashley is fine. No harm has come to her. If you haven't looked yet, I suggest you do so. I'll wait ☺.

Okay, let's move on. But first, just so you know, I am not alone. Be assured that someone is with Ashley at all times — no matter how many of us are otherwise occupied. In other words, if you deviate from the instructions one inch, someone will make sure Ashley gets her due.

Your incompetence cost me ten years of my life. I want restitution. Let's say each year is worth $100,000, not much by modern standards. Your total bill is one million. I know you'll have no problem raising that amount. I know several others that you failed. Each reported he overpaid by an exorbitant amount.

You and those with you can ease off. I'm sure you're plotting how you'll capture me during the exchange. It won't be quite that simple. My plan is basic. You won't see Ashley until seven days after you pay. And, if you do anything I don't like before or during that period, she will be lost to you forever.

You have the rest of today to accumulate four million dollars. Yes, four million. Why? you're thinking. Pretty simple. We'll use four different drop sites, one million at each site. I, and only I, will know which is THE site. The other three will not be serviced. If you're lucky, you will recover those funds. Otherwise . . . Well, that's just something else for you to worry about.

I'm sure you want to know what happens if you don't pay. Again, nothing complicated. Ashley simply disappears. How? you wonder. Keep wondering. You'll have years to live in the agony that I had — years of knowing you're paying for your incompetence.

Last, I have to tell you I am sorry about your wife. All she had to do was cooperate, and she'd be alive to enjoy this with you. Instead, she chose to play heroine. We couldn't allow that, could we? Make sure you don't try to play hero. It won't work any better for you than it did for her. And if you die, what happens to Ashley?

Use your time wisely. The next contact is on my schedule, and I shall expect you to be ready.

The gazebo in Hammonds' front yard drew me after the drama surrounding the DVD and its contents. I needed fresh air and solitude, and I suspected John Hammonds could use some time alone, also. If I left, maybe Sargent and Hammonds' sister would get the hint and clear out, too.

The octagonal structure measured about thirty feet across — large enough for a living room in most houses, but not out of place on the Hammonds' lawn. It had five tables with separate cushioned benches. I suspected the tables locked together, creating an area for a large buffet. The construction of the building and its contents was with rich-looking wood, perhaps teak. In other words, it radiated luxury and good taste. The thought crossed my mind to ask Sly if he had partied there.

I sat at the center table. In front of me lay a printout of the message from the kidnapper and the three pictures he included. I stared at the words, trying to squeeze more from them. There had to be something that would tell us who was behind the murders and kidnapping. Something that would help me see between the lines.

I decided to take it apart, but my cell phone interrupted before I could begin. I fumbled it out of my purse and looked at the number. Bob Sandiford. "Hey, Bob, what's up?"

"Just wanted to let you know we have a dozen people on the street with the picture and sketch. They range from Fort Lauderdale up here to Boca. That's not a lot, but if they see anything, they'll let me know, and I'll pass the word to you."

"Thanks, Bob. I really appreciate this."

"I expect we'll get more volunteers as the day wears on. Communications is not what we do best. But each of these people can identify with tragedy. They'll step up as soon as they find out what happened. Hang in, Beth. If that woman puts her nose outside, we have a chance of spotting her."

"Terrific."

"What was in the envelope? Have you opened it yet?"

"Sorry. I'm so tired my mind isn't functioning like it should." I told him about getting back to Hammonds' place, the contest with Sargent, and the contents of the envelope. I finished with, "There was a DVD containing the kidnapper's demands."

"Was there anything that helps?"

"Yes . . . and no. We know Ashley is okay

— well, was okay. He sent pictures showing her in normal situations. I was about to take the note apart when you called, hoping to find something between the lines. In the meantime, we sit and wait."

"Good luck with your read. If there's anything there, I'm confident you'll find it."

"Thanks."

"Call me if I can do anything else. If we come up with the woman, I'll let you know." He rang off.

It made me feel better knowing Bob was on the team. With his network of homeless people, we stood a chance of spotting the female who picked up Ashley from school. I hoped she'd have to go to Publix or Winn-Dixie or somewhere to restock the refrigerator.

FIFTEEN

I rubbed my eyes, then stood and walked around the table in the gazebo, wondering if I could grab a power nap somewhere. Exhaustion threatened to overtake me. That and the sadness and hopelessness I felt. My eyes fell on the kidnapper's note. I picked it up, sat, and began to read.

If you, and whoever's with you, are reading this, we have passed the first stage of our endeavor. I assume you opened the pictures so you know Ashley is fine. No harm has come to her. If you haven't looked yet, I suggest you do so. I'll wait ☺.

The smiley face bugged me. Ransom notes were no place for humor — even bad humor. The bum could save that crap for another day.

First stage. Did that mean he lumped the

murders of Carmina and Sabrina, the kidnapping of Ashley, and the staging of this message as only the first phase? If so, I shuddered, wondering what would constitute the second phase. Or maybe I didn't want to know.

Okay, let's move on. But first, just so you know, I am not alone. Be assured that someone is with Ashley at all times — no matter how many of us are otherwise occupied. In other words, if you deviate from the instructions one inch, someone will make sure Ashley gets her due.

This bothered me even though I hadn't expected to be dealing with a single person. Kidnapping was difficult for a lone individual to pull off. At a minimum, someone had to watch the victim while another made a pickup. But this time, he wrote *many of us.* Did that mean three, five, ten? Of course, the more of them there were, the worse our chances of bringing them down and rescuing Ashley. Not a pleasant thought, but one I needed to plan for. And what could he mean by *Ashley gets her due*? A strange choice of words that nagged at me.

Your incompetence cost me ten years of my life. I want restitution. Let's say each year is worth $100,000, not much by modern standards. Your total bill is one million. I know you'll have no problem raising that amount. I know several others that you failed. Each reported he overpaid by an exorbitant amount.

The paragraph intrigued me. Had his braggadocio given us a clue that could help us identify him? Our kidnapper said he lost ten years. That could mean he went to prison when Hammonds' efforts were unsuccessful in his defense. Allowing for pretrial confinement, that meant he hired Hammonds eleven or twelve years ago. Or, allowing for the snail's pace of the judicial system, call the window eleven to fifteen years ago. Since John's success rate was high — he didn't lose many — the number that went against him during that time couldn't have been substantial. A small lead, but the first of the case.

A hundred thousand a year. Was there significance to that amount? Could that be what he paid Hammonds? It could just be a convenient way for him to arrive at one million for a ransom amount. The letter continued.

You and those with you can ease off. I'm sure you're plotting how you'll capture me during the exchange. It won't be quite that simple. My plan is basic. You won't see Ashley until seven days after you pay. And, if you do anything I don't like before or during that period, she will be lost to you forever.

All I read from that was he was a diabolical bastard. Smart, but diabolical. Seven days from the ransom collection could take him almost any place on the planet. He was trying to tie our hands while he made his getaway. However, if he released Ashley a week after receiving payment, someone would have to stay in the area to do it, and that would be stupid. Fat chance.

You have the rest of today to accumulate four million dollars. Yes, four million. Why? you're thinking. Pretty simple. We'll use four different drop sites, one million at each site. I, and only I, will know which is THE site. The other three will not be serviced. If you're lucky, you will recover those funds. Otherwise . . .

Well, that's just something else for you to worry about.

Did he really think Hammonds could put together four million dollars in one day? Could anybody do that? And the use of four drop sites, with one to be *serviced* by the kidnapper? What was that all about? Perhaps he thought he could split our forces. That made no sense. He must know we'd turn out as many people as we needed to watch four sites — or forty-four sites. Strange. Very strange. He must have some special places in mind.

I'm sure you want to know what happens if you don't pay. Again, nothing complicated. Ashley simply disappears. How, you wonder. Keep wondering. You'll have years to live in the agony that I had — years of knowing you're paying for your incompetence.

No threat to kill Ashley. Wasn't that supposed to be the ultimate convincer in a kidnapping? Pay up or your friend/mate/child dies. Often, from what I'd read, there was the additional threat of dismemberment. Could he mean he'd simply keep Ashley? Did he mean he'd dispose of her in a way her body would never be found? I hoped the former. It wouldn't be the first time kidnappers grabbed young people and kept them. However, I couldn't recall any voluntarily released.

There was the Elizabeth Smart disappearance — kidnapped and held for nine months before someone recognized her on the street. The guy who did that was enough of a nut case that he almost got away with it. Fortunately, it was one of those times the justice system worked, and the kidnappers got what they deserved. But I didn't remember there being a call for ransom. Not the same as Ashley's situation. My man was smart and sane enough to come up with a foolproof plan — at least on the surface.

It felt like a snake crawled over my stomach as I remembered Jaycee Dugard. She spent eighteen years as a backyard captive of a scumbag who was an unimpeachable argument for abortion. His mother failed the world by carrying him to full-term. I could simply pray Ashley had not fallen into the hands of such a creature.

There were other examples of young people disappearing, then reappearing years later. Thinking hard, I couldn't remember any based on revenge. But that didn't mean it couldn't happen.

Last, I have to tell you I am sorry about your wife. All she had to do was cooperate, and she'd be alive to enjoy this with you. Instead, she chose to play heroine. I couldn't allow that, could I? Make sure you don't try to play hero. It won't work any better for you than it did for her. And if you die, what happens to Ashley?

He apologized for killing Sabrina, then blamed her that it happened? Then he threatened Hammonds. That flummoxed me. What kind of sicko could he be?

I reread the note. Possibly, he was a former client, and he had lost. He blamed Hammonds. Of course, he didn't say if he was guilty. He appeared to have a decent education. No street jargon, not even any prison jargon, although the impression he left was he spent ten years in prison. Probably a white-collar criminal. My first thought was that would narrow the suspects. Then I remembered I was in South Florida. No shortage of white-collar crime. Elected officials, lobbyists, and business executives doing the perp walk no longer make the front page of the local newspapers. Voters just yawned and elected the next set.

Ten years in prison. That didn't really

help. It meant he received a sentence of from ten to ninety years. With the revolving door in our prison system, all he had to do was play nice, and they would let him out, no matter what the judge had said.

I shoved the paper aside, my mind numb. I forced his note from my consciousness and reflected on the morning. Whether it was taking my mind off the problem for a moment or what, I don't know. But, I realized the answer might be in Hammonds' office. I checked my watch — seven-thirty — and got up and headed into the house.

My intent was to get a fresh cup of coffee, then talk to Hammonds and Sargent. As I approached the kitchen, I heard a voice I recognized as Bannon. "So, how'd she do? Is she the loose cannon we think she is? How bad is she screwing this up?"

I stopped, then turned to head back outside. Not something I needed to hear. I had enough problems without having my life dissected.

"I'm reevaluating," Sargent said, then paused.

What could I do? I stopped to see what he would say next.

"So far, she's been straight arrow. Her actions last night were on the nose. I don't envy her. This is going to get tougher. But, you know, I have a gut feeling she can handle it."

I almost choked, not sure my ears had registered his words correctly. What a change. I'd have to remember to be nicer to him — well, maybe. I didn't want to hear anymore. I walked outside, then circled the house to come in from the rear. I still wanted the coffee.

Sargent and Bannon were still in the kitchen. "Where've you been?" Sargent said, suspicion in his voice.

"Getting my bearings in the gazebo. Mostly thinking about the ransom note. I have an idea if you two are interested."

"Of course we're interested," Sargent said. "We value our jobs, and the chief says you're calling the shots."

Bannon just stared over the top of his cup.

While refilling my coffee, I said, "I think our perp is an old client of Hammonds. I'm guessing he has him in his files. Maybe you could take him downtown and let him dig back ten to fifteen years for clients he didn't get off. Might be one of them."

Sargent looked at Bannon, pursing his lips. "Yeah, that's what we were talking about before you came in. You want to mention it to Hammonds or should we?"

"You do it. I'm too tired. I'm headed back

to the gazebo to rest my head."

"Yeah," Bannon said, his first comment since I walked in. "You look like you need some rest. We'll take it from here."

I smiled and walked out. Let them take the credit. After the way Hammonds had kicked them around, they deserved it. I dropped onto the bench in the gazebo, the pictures and the message in front of me.

Not long afterwards, Bannon and Hammonds left, headed for Hammonds' downtown office and his files. Sargent left to get some rest so he'd be fresh when he took over later.

I picked up the picture of Ashley watching TV. She was beautiful, and the expression on her face was priceless. She looked so innocent it was hard to believe she was in the hands of unscrupulous thugs, who had already killed two people. No matter how well-written the note, only gutter-slime would do what they did.

As I lay the picture down, I felt more anger flood into me, a bitter taste filling my mouth, bile flaming my throat. My hands hurt, and I discovered I had clinched my fingers so tightly the nails dug into my palms. I grabbed the note and read it again, taking deep breaths to keep from ripping it into shreds. The bastard apologized for killing Sabrina, but made no mention of Carmina, the maid. What was wrong with me that I hadn't noticed it before? That set off a whole new chain of thought. What kind of man would do that? Did he live in a world where hired help meant nothing, where they were non-persons? Maybe some poor little rich boy? I filed it away to mention to Hammonds later. Perhaps it would trigger a memory of a particular client.

"May I bother you a moment?"

I jerked, then spun to my left. Standing outside the gazebo was Hammonds' sister. "Come on in," I said. "I'd appreciate the company."

"I brought some coffee. From what I'm hearing, you were up most of the night."

"Wonderful." More coffee sounded great. I'd had a couple of cups, but another was welcome. Besides, I did want to talk to the sister. Straining, I tried to remember her name. Something with an M.

"I'm Maddy Hammonds, John's sister." She set the coffee on the table along with two packets of Sweet 'n Low and a couple of creamers. "I didn't know how you like it so I tried to come prepared. Now I realize you might prefer sugar."

"No, this is fine."

She sat across from me, wearing jeans,

167

sandals, a loose top, and little or no makeup, her blond hair pulled back with a butterfly clip. She had changed since we stood shoulder to shoulder reviewing the ransom note. I placed her age in mid to late forties — unless she'd had a great cosmetic surgeon. Then she could be in her nineties.

"I appreciate what you're doing for my brother. If he loses Ashley, I don't know how far he'll fall. She and Sabrina were his whole world."

"I'm doing what I can, but we have a long way to go." I busied myself preparing my coffee. "He said you and Sabrina hated one another. Is that right?"

She dipped her head, then sipped from her cup. "Hate is a little strong — at least for me. Let's just say I didn't enjoy being around her, and she returned the feeling."

"Why?" I tasted, then nodded at her. "Excellent coffee. Thanks."

"It's the least I could do. John is very important to me."

"So why the bad blood between you and Sabrina?"

"Is it important? Will it bring Ashley home?"

I forced a smile at her duck of my question, then stifled a yawn. I realized how tired I was. If I didn't get a few hours' sleep soon,

I might fall off the bench. "Sorry. Since it's not a situation I run into every day, my natural curiosity leapt up."

She squinted. "If it reaches a point where it will help John and Ashley for you to know, I'll tell you. Otherwise, it's more personal than I want to share."

I studied her. The crow's-feet at the edge of her eyes said she squinted a lot. "Are you nearsighted?"

"That's a strange question," she said through a smile. "It'll take me awhile to figure how it fits into your investigation. However, since I refused your other question, I'll answer you. Yes. I wear contacts to correct it, but haven't put them in yet."

"Sorry," I said. "I suppose it's the investigator in me. I'm always looking for identifying features. One of yours is the way you're forcing your eyes to focus from across the table." I sipped my coffee, wondering if she had a reason for joining me.

"It was a good observation. Now, may I ask you something?"

"Sure. Same rules as you used. If I don't like it, I won't answer."

"Why are you a private investigator? You're attractive. You seem intelligent. Why would you put yourself in such a position?"

I sipped my coffee as I considered her

question. It opened a painful window that I didn't often let anyone through. But suddenly, I wanted to talk about it. Anything to get my mind off Ashley.

"When I was twelve, my father was murdered. We lived in Addison, Texas, at the time, Dad, Mom, my older brother, and me. One night after I had gone to bed, something woke me, noise coming from the front of the house. Sounded like two people wrestling. I got up and crept up the hall, and looked into the living room. My father was wrestling with someone wearing a ski mask. As I started to yell, a shot rang out, and my father fell to the floor. I stood mute, my voice having deserted me. The shooter saw me, snapped off a shot in my direction, then turned and ran out the front door. He missed me, but Dad was mortally wounded."

"I'm sorry," Maddy said. "That must have been tough."

"It was. But even worse was the fact the police never caught the shooter. As far as I know, he has lived to a ripe old age."

"So, that made you want to be a private investigator?"

"Not exactly. That made me decide to become a cop. Being a cop made me decide to go private."

"I don't understand."

"Political correctness and sympathy for the criminals. I became a cop in Dallas and loved it. But every arrest was a battle with the system. I watched so many guilty bastards walk free because the arresting officer didn't dot an I or cross a T exactly right. I don't mean on important matters. I mean on some BS that some ACLU type dreamed up and convinced a judge to okay. A couple of those were mine. I decided I'd have more freedom if I went private. I have not regretted my decision. Does that answer your question?"

She fiddled with the pink package I had crumpled after sweetening my coffee. She laid it down and smoothed out the wrinkles, then began to fold it. I waited, assuming she'd get there at her own speed.

She took a deep breath and looked straight into my face. "Thank you for telling me, but I'm afraid it doesn't change my opinion. In my business circles, I'm known as a straight-shooter because I don't sugarcoat what I think. Tact has never been my strong suit, and I can't force it now. In your case, I think John made a big mistake. I cannot believe you are some super investigator with a fail-safe technique for rescuing kidnap victims. Instead of pushing the authorities

171

aside and giving you the power, John should have used every agency and every kind of publicity available to spread the story. I believe that would get Ashley home sooner and safer than you ever can. In fact, I don't think you have a clue what you're doing. I sincerely hope his mistake doesn't lead to tragedy."

She set her cup down and stared into my face. "There, I've said what I came to say, and I stand behind my feelings. Can you give me a reason you're a better choice than the police? Can you make me feel better about you?"

I followed her example with my cup and locked my fingers in front of me. In my head, I counted to ten, not wanting to alienate her completely.

"First, I have no inclination to make you feel better about me. You've already formed your opinion, and, frankly, I don't give a rat's ass what it is. Now, under different circumstances, I'd throw your bony ass out of here. But, John is your brother and Ashley is your niece. I assume you and John are close. He and I have a verbal contract. Nowhere in our agreement is there any mention of his sister." I stopped to let the words sink in, then added, "You're not the only one not known for tact and diplomacy."

The look of surprise that spread across her face was satisfying.

I continued, "Since you describe yourself as a straight-shooter, I'll reciprocate. Hindsight is always twenty-twenty. If this thing goes sour, you'll be right by default, and you'll be able to needle your brother for the rest of his life — if you so choose. Me, I'll be upset by the loss of Ashley — and my *failure* — but it won't take over my life. Odds are heavy you'll have the opportunity to remind John that you disagreed. The *experts* say we'll never see Ashley alive. But that has nothing to do with his decision. That's simply the way it is in kidnappings. The victim seldom survives."

"Then why —"

"Don't interrupt. I'm not finished." I hesitated a quick moment as she went mum, then plowed on. "I learned a long time ago to defer to those who know more than I. He says he's an expert on the criminal mind because he spends so much time with such a variety of them. That sounds logical to me. So when he says a heavy police presence could cause them to panic and kill Ashley, who am I to argue? He wants me on the job. I agreed to take the job. Period. And that's about as much as I want to say about the subject. You may think what you please." I finished my speech by picking up my cup and raising it to my lips.

The look of shock on her face faded into a smile. "Thank you for your honesty. I suppose we'll have to agree to disagree. But even though it doesn't matter, I had to let you know my feelings. John made his decision, and that's how it is. We're both stuck with it." She held out her hand.

I stared at the hand. My first impulse was to slap it away. How dare she invade my privacy to remind me I wasn't qualified? To hell with her and her New York attitude. But even as that popped into my mind, I was overcome by the realization I had met an honest woman. That, alone, made the conversation worthwhile. In my life, I met far too few of them. I rose and shook her hand. "I appreciate your opinion," I said, meaning it. I didn't know whether we could be friends, but I could honor her integrity.

"And I appreciate yours. Let me add that contrary to how I may sound, I do hope John made the right decision." She walked around the table toward the exit from the gazebo. "Maybe when this is over, we can have a lunch together. Who knows? We might learn to like each other. Now I suggest you get some sleep. You look like hell."

"Yeah." No witty comments came to mind. Too tired.

Sixteen

I sat again at the table in the gazebo and picked up the message. The letters blurred as my eyes closed, making me realize how stupid I was acting. I was beat, and this might be my best chance to get some rest for the near future. Who knew when the lid might blow off? I slid the paper and the pictures into my briefcase and stepped out of the gazebo. My plan was to locate a sofa in a quiet corner and grab some shuteye.

But first, I wanted a shower. A cleansing and a nap might solve my zombie state. Hammonds was at his office downtown, but I didn't need his permission or for him to point me in the right direction. I had no doubt he'd prefer a clean PI representing him. As for where to find a shower, that shouldn't be a problem in a house like Hammonds'. Each bedroom probably had a full bath attached.

I headed toward the front door, my mind

feeling heavy. Before I arrived, Providence intervened in the form of my cell phone.

Oh, no. Mom. In the excitement of the soccer field run, I forgot she was in town. Feeling a lecture coming, I answered, "Mom. How are you this morning?"

"Don't give me that. If you really wanted to know, you'd have come home last night — or at least called. What kind of life are you leading?"

I guess there was no need telling her I spent a couple of uncomfortable hours flopping from one side of my recliner to the other. She'd accuse me of making it up. "It's a tough case, Mom. Look, I was on my way home to grab a shower. I'll explain when I get there."

"Are you sure? I hear something in your voice like when you were a teenager and up to some devilment."

What is it about mothers? Or is it only mine? I could never put anything over on her. "Well, I need to clean up, and my shower isn't that far away. I promise to tell you the whole story."

"Okay. I'll fix something to eat. Have you taken the time for a proper meal? You know breakfast is the most important meal of the day."

"That sounds great. I'll be there in less

than a half hour." I hit the end button. So much for checking Hammonds' fancy digs.

Twenty-five minutes later, I walked through my front door. The delicious smell of frying bacon greeted me. In the kitchen, I saw Mom at the stove. Not only was there bacon in a pan, but a pot of grits bubbled on a back burner. With that, I realized how hungry I really was. Thinking back, I couldn't remember anything except coffee since . . . well, I couldn't remember.

"I'll be in and out of the shower in fifteen minutes," I said. "That smells so good I can hardly wait."

Mom turned. "I didn't hear you come in, dear. You go ahead and shower. I'll hold the eggs until you're ready. Want two or three? And how many slices of toast? Will three be enough?"

"More than enough," I said. "And two eggs. But you better make it about half a pound of bacon. You know I can't resist it."

Over enough food to feed several of Bob's homeless friends, I filled Mom in on the case. When I finished, there were tears in her eyes.

"You do whatever you need to do," she said. "And don't even think about me and my problems. That little girl's more important than anything else right now. I'll just call Ike and ask him if he can come for a visit. He said you promised him a fishing charter."

"Ike?" Oh, my. What had I started? What had they discussed over that breakfast in Dallas? "Do you really think he'll come? Can he break away from his job?"

She chuckled. "He says it's more of a hobby than a job. They kinda humor him and pay him for coming in. All he has to do is let them know he won't be there."

Figuring I was in a no-win situation, I said, "That's a great idea. If Ike was in the area, I wouldn't feel so guilty about leaving you alone." After a second thought, I added, "Uh . . . where will he stay?"

"Oh, I'm sure he'll get a room in a hotel. That would be much more convenient for him. And . . . well, if we decided to stay out late, we wouldn't disturb you if you were resting."

I rolled my eyes, deciding not to go there. There are some things a daughter should not pursue with her mother.

After a few more words, we lapsed into silence. The good news was, Mom was taken care of. The bad news was, I hadn't made any inroads on finding Ashley. But, after the night I'd had and the thousand calorie breakfast I'd consumed, I couldn't hold my eyes open.

"I'm going to bed down for a bit," I said. "I'll set the alarm, but just in case, give me a good shaking about two."

"No problem."

I followed through with my plan and felt much better when the alarm woke me at one fifty-nine. Mom was through the door a few seconds later.

"Rise and shine. Crime awaits," she said, giving me the same smile she used when I was a child.

Seeing her in the doorway and hearing her words again made me realize how much I missed her. Yeah, although she badgered me about grandchildren, she was still the same wonderful woman who sacrificed her youth to raise me. Giving a long luxurious stretch, I felt twelve years old. Crime busting had not been my objective then. Timmy, who played quarterback in high school and lived down the block, was. But that was then, and now was now. Time to move it.

"I'm awake, Mom. Thanks." I rolled out of bed and adjusted my clothes, then slipped on my sneakers. As I holstered my bragun, Mom stuck her head back into the door.

"What are you doing? What is that?"

Busted. This might take more explaining than I wanted to do. How could I tell my mother I needed to carry a concealed — and I do mean concealed — firearm? I couldn't. "Sorry, Mom. Gotta run. Kisses." I dashed past her, out of the room, and out of the house.

Once in the car, I headed north. Only when I was three blocks away did I pull into a 7-Eleven. I needed gas, but I also needed to consider my next step — and a cup of coffee would help with that.

After filling the tank, I parked in a spot beside the station and called Bob. If I were lucky enough to win the lottery, one of his people would be standing there with the name and address of my mystery woman.

"Hi, Beth. What's happening?"

"I was about to ask you the same thing. I took a few hours to catch forty winks. Since no one woke me, I'm guessing things remain the same."

"I wish I had good news, but I don't. Maybe when people drift in later, someone will have something. Time will tell."

"Okay. I'm going to hit some more of the strip malls near the school. If miracles are real, she stopped in on her way to kidnap Ashley, and I'll find someone who knows her. That's about where I am — waiting for my good fairy to alight and point me in the right direction."

Bob chuckled. "Remember, we're never too old to believe. Don't give up. Ninety percent of any miracle is hard work. Or, in your case, shoe leather."

We promised to keep one another up-to-date, then rung off. My next stop was FedEx Office for more copies of my sketches. But before then, I wanted to check in at the Hammonds house.

Officer Winthrop answered the phone. "Hammonds residence."

"It's me, Beth Bowman. Has Mr. Hammonds called in? Has anything new happened?"

"No, everything is quiet. Nothing, and I do mean nothing, all day. Well, a few media calls, but no one worthwhile."

His comment told me what he thought of the fourth estate. Couldn't say I disagreed with him much. "Give me a call the moment something happens — anything happens. Do you have my cell?"

"Yes, Ms. Bowman. Chief Elston threatened to tattoo it on the back of my hand if I forgot it. Can you hold? I have another call coming in."

"Sure." I didn't have anything else to say to him, but I was curious about who was on the other line.

"Ms. Bowman." He was back. "That was

182

Detective Bannon. He told me to tell you to hang up and keep the line open. Mr. Hammonds wants to talk to you."

I followed instructions and the phone rang. "John," I said into the phone. "What do you have?"

"Five people, four men, one woman. I defended them eight to fifteen years ago and lost. Each of them received sentences that would keep them in jail a minimum of ten years."

"Great," I exclaimed. "Were they white-collar? Well-educated?"

"Yes. Two lobbyists and two county commissioners. The fifth embezzled from an assisted living facility."

"That fits," I said. "Can you bring their files to the house?"

"We're on the way. Bannon alerted the chief, and they're digging for their records, too. Of course, that might take longer. These were pre-computerization and they archived old closed cases in a warehouse in the southwest end of the county."

"We'll take what we can get," I said, pushing my hair out of my eyes. "At least we'll have something to start with. How long before you get there?"

"Maybe thirty minutes — unless I convince Bannon to use the siren."

"Tell him Beth will tell the chief if he doesn't," I said, hoping Bannon would find it humorous. Or maybe he'd cooperate. "If not, I'll be at your house before you arrive."

Seventeen

I arrived at Hammonds' house first and camped out in the gazebo again, loving the fresh air. The temperature was in the nineties, but that was pretty standard for South Florida. I could handle it as long as I didn't have to be in the direct sun. Shade, any shade, reduced the heat to a bearable degree.

Another reason I didn't go in was I had no desire to face Maddy Hammonds. She had told me what she thought, and I didn't need any more of that. And, by being outside, I would be closer when Hammonds arrived. He said five possibilities. Five to find and investigate, and little time to do it. But that was better than no leads at all. Of course, we had to keep our fingers crossed, hoping the kidnapper was one of the five. Hammonds said Bannon gave the names to the chief, and the police were checking them. With perfect luck, we'd find four of them still in jail, leaving the fifth as the logical kidnapper. However, I couldn't recall any time in my life I'd had perfect luck — well, other than meeting David. He was three thousand miles away, though, diluting that good luck. Nothing to do but wait for Hammonds and wish for the best.

My cell phone rang, and I yanked it out of my bag. Maybe it was Hammonds saying they were almost home. That would be great, meaning we could get serious about finding the kidnappers. The call was even better.

"David," I exclaimed. "It's so good to hear from you. God, I miss you. I wish you were here."

"Good to hear your voice, too, and I miss you just as much. I only have a moment — slipped out of a session — but I had to talk to you. Sorry about last night, but I could just hear those two characters ragging me if I said what I wanted to say."

"And what did you want to say?" I asked, cutting in.

David chuckled. "I said it. I miss you. I'm learning that I miss you very much. You have really gotten under my skin in areas I can't scratch in public."

"So, it's all about sex? Is that it?" I said it with what I hoped was a smile in my voice, not wanting David to misunderstand.

"Not at all. You mean much more to me than that. I guess I'd better change the subject before I get into deeper trouble."

"Really? I prefer you keep talking. Get yourself in deeper trouble."

He hesitated, and I refused to rescue him. Let him sweat.

"Okay, I'd much rather be wrinkling the sheets with you than listening to these boring lectures. Is that enough trouble for you?"

I laughed. "The feeling is mutual."

"How are you?" he asked in his serious voice. "Or maybe I should ask, what are you up to, and have you been injured yet?"

I smiled, recognizing he couldn't keep his sense of humor down. We first met because of a bonk on the head I received. A few days later, my cranium took another blow, making him wonder if that was my normal course in life. He never missed an opportunity to make a joke about my proclivity for getting banged around.

In a microsecond, I decided to tell David everything. Maybe it would clear my head to put it into words. After all, he'd almost said he loved me. He'd support me and give me guidance. "I have a new case. Someone kidnapped a five-year-old child after killing the mother. It doesn't look good for the little girl."

"That's terrible. Do you think you can help? Isn't this something for the police?"

"Do you know John Hammonds, the defense lawyer?"

"I've heard of him. Fortunately, I haven't needed his services. How does he fit in?"

"He's my client, and when he speaks, folks listen." I launched into an explanation of why Hammonds wanted me to front the investigation, instead of the police, leaving out nothing. It felt good to talk to someone not involved. Maybe David's clinical analysis was what I needed.

"Wow," he said. "Quite a story. Hammonds is lucky it's you and not me. I wouldn't know what to do. Good luck on getting his daughter home. I'm sure you'll make the right decisions. And Hammonds lived up to his reputation of being brilliant. He hired the best." His voice softened. "The very best."

It wasn't the clinical analysis I had hoped for, but it would have to do. "Thanks, I —"

A plain wrapper police car pulled into the driveway. I bounced from my seat and stepped outside the gazebo. It had to be Hammonds and Bannon. Great. Now I'd finally have something to sink my teeth into other than frustration.

"Sorry, sweetheart," I said. "I have to run. John Hammonds just arrived. He might be carrying the break we've been hoping for."

"I understand. I'll be home Saturday or Sunday. The conference ends Friday night, but they're making some arrangements for the weekend. They've announced an optional visitation for Saturday afternoon. Professionally, I need to attend, but my heart is tugging me home. Please be careful. And . . . well, good luck. I wish I were there to help — or at least give moral support."

"I understand, my love. Running." I clicked off as I started toward the police vehicle, which had stopped at the garage door. I had my fingers crossed, hoping they had names and pictures I could feed to Bob and his people. There was always the chance someone would get careless when there was no one around except a derelict. Since most people have no eyes for the homeless, they often see things no policeman has a chance to observe.

I ran to the passenger side of the sedan. "Do you have the pictures?"

"Pictures?" Hammonds said, opening the door and stepping out. "No pictures, just my files. I'm hoping the police will come up with mug shots. Of course, much of my

189

experience says any similarity between appearance in booking photos and how a person looks in real life is purely coincidental. Plus, they are at least ten years older, but they can age enhance them. Maybe we'll get lucky, and they'll be recognizable."

Disappointed, I said, "Let's get inside and see what you have. Time is slipping by."

EIGHTEEN

Dabba sat in the middle of the city bus, no one beside her or in the rows to her front and back. The combination of her appearance and her constant muttering kept everyone at bay. She didn't care. She didn't need them. She didn't need anyone — anyone except her daughter.

A solitary tear rolled down Dabba's cheek as an image of the last time she saw Linda filled her mind. She mumbled, "So cute. I fixed her pretty blond hair special that day. I did it in banana curls like Shirley Temple in *Rebecca of Sunnybrook Farm*. It was somebody's birthday, and her kindergarten class was having a party." She hesitated. "Whose party was it?" She strained to remember. Her head popped up and an angry look filled her face. In a loud voice, she said, "I can't remember? I want to remember. I must remember everything about my daughter."

The other passengers on the bus squeezed into their seats, as far from her as they could get. The driver glanced over his shoulder, a worried look on his face. That woman wouldn't be the first crazy he'd had on his bus. Seemed like it happened more and more often though. He wondered if he should call for police support.

Dabba quieted, then her muttering returned. "Sally. The party was for little Sally Jenkins. She was turning five years old. Linda told me she was so proud to be the same age as the others. Now they wouldn't call her baby anymore."

Dabba's eyes took on a faraway look, a curtain of tears covering them. "Pink. A pretty pink dress. A new one. Linda wore her new pink dress for the party. And pink shoes. Pink shoes, pink socks, pink dress, and a pink ribbon in her hair. My sweetie was a princess in pink."

Dabba sniffled, looking around the bus. "Where am I? Who are these people? They ain't parents from Linda's school." Her eyes fluttered, and she blinked. *Tired. Always so tired. Sleepy.*

She dozed, an empty smile on her face, a bit of drool slipping from the corner of her mouth.

■ ■ ■ ■

Hammonds, Bannon, Winthrop, and I sat at the dining room table, the five files in front of Hammonds.

Hammonds tapped the stack. "I don't lose many cases. That's not a brag, just a statement of fact. These are five I lost, mostly because they were too guilty for a believable defense." He pointed to the first. "Donald Kenneth Simonson. He was a Broward County commissioner nailed in an FBI sting for soliciting bribes. They had so much on him about all I could do was plead in mitigation. He didn't agree with me then, and I'm sure he wouldn't now, but he got off lucky — only fifteen years. After the trial, he put on a big show in front of the media by firing me and hiring Horace Rheingold. Last I heard, Horace had quit him. Simonson was dirty, too dirty to rescue."

"And he got elected?" I said. "I don't find it difficult to believe he was a criminal, but why would anyone vote for him?"

"Chalk it up to Broward County politics," Hammonds said. "Like Chicago, influence peddling and bribery are part of the county's heritage. Kind of like neutral wallpaper in an attorney's office — seldom noticed.

Speaking of which, look at Sheila Lively-Wesler? She might not have been as obvious as Simonson, but she racked up enough under-the-table cash to buy a resort island, a large one. She was immensely popular and served for years. Every four years, she swept into office on a landslide. One of those things that makes no sense is people don't look at results, they just react to what the politician says."

He hesitated while shaking his head. "Anyway, I had folks volunteering day and night, wanting to testify for her, and I mean some high-powered ones — judges, local athletes, other elected officials. I used as many as I thought the case would tolerate. Too many and the jury tunes out, sometimes going the other way. It was a good trial, but the prosecution simply had more than I could counter. They had the goods on her ex-husband, and he turned on her. He pled out and threw her to the wolves. She got twenty years. She asked me to appeal, but I told her I couldn't continue to take her money." He paused, appearing to think. "Let's say I learned things that left me cold and leave it there."

"Anything that makes you think either of them could be the kidnapper?" I asked.

He stared at the ceiling. "Either or neither.

Both thought they were above the law and thought I failed them. Their egos were out of control. Both of them said things I could interpret as threats. On the other hand, I can't picture either of them doing anything as violent as this. They were quick to bully the weak, but shied away from the strong."

"Interesting," I said.

Bannon tapped the files. "How about the others?"

Hammonds flipped open another folder. "Esteban Edwardo Sabastion. This guy was a lobbyist brought down by his success. In twenty years of working the hallways of Broward County and the city governments, he probably influenced more projects than anyone else in the state. He gave out a lot of gifts and paid for tons of dinners. I still can't say with certainty that he bribed anyone. Did he buy influence? Yes. But, doesn't the big contributor to any campaign buy influence? I mean, how many use their thousands to get someone elected without expecting something in return? My experience says between none and zero.

"Our problem at trial was the prosecutor trotted out several elected and appointed officials who were under suspicion on their own. They told believable stories, saying Sabastion attempted to bribe them. There were never any witnesses, but the sheer number of repetitions overwhelmed the jury — or that was my take. The old *where there's smoke, there's fire* gambit. And I couldn't deny his attempts to influence elected officials. That was his job, and he did it well. Plus, the newspapers blamed him for every over-budget contract in the county forever. In the end, I couldn't counter the negatives. He went down hard — twenty-five years."

"I remember him," Bannon said. "I didn't work the case, but I was glad when he went down. Of course, all I had were the newspapers and office scuttlebutt. Are you saying he wasn't as bad as I heard?"

"About all I can say," Hammonds answered, "is I've defended worse, who either got off or received shorter sentences."

Before Bannon could rebut, I said, "How about this file? Tell us about Mankosky."

Hammonds leaned back in his chair, looked toward the ceiling, and sighed. "Not one of my prouder moments. Herbert Lowery Mankosky." He tapped the folder, a look of regret on his face. "I heard about his arrest, but didn't pay much attention. As far as I could tell from the newspaper reports, he was just another smalltime conman who got himself into a position to embezzle.

Everyday occurrence in South Florida. When he initially contacted me, I ignored him. Later, I wished I had stuck with my first reaction. However, he bushwhacked me in a restaurant one night. I couldn't cause a scene by having him thrown out, so I listened." Hammonds chuckled and shook his head. "Calling him a conman is not giving him enough credit. After he'd spoken for ten minutes, I was on his team. No way could he be guilty. Without going into details, I agreed to represent him."

"And?" I said when he paused.

Again the chuckle and shake of the head. "Later I found out he was one of the dirtiest I ever defended. By the time we got to mitigation, I was ready to abandon him and the courtroom. I even gave it some thought. Quit mid-trial. However, I knew that would destroy me as a defense attorney so I swallowed hard and did my best for him. My efforts earned him thirty years, and we parted company. I haven't heard a word from him since the day of his sentencing and consider myself lucky for it."

"Sounds like he could be our kidnapper," I said.

"Possible, but somehow I doubt it. The man was gutless. He worked in the shadows or against little old ladies. My wife could have ripped him apart. Of course, prison does strange things to people. Maybe he developed a backbone."

"Okay, last one," I said. "Stevenson?"

He opened the file and flipped the pages for a moment. "Daniel Kelso Stevenson. He was different. He walked into my office and asked if the attorney-client relationship began the moment he opened his mouth. I said yes, and he replied, 'Good. I'm guilty, and I want you to defend me.' That was startling. Now, don't get me wrong. I defend a lot of folks guilty as charged. The police don't make near as many mistakes as the media want you to believe. But it's seldom I have someone admit it — especially up front."

"If you knew he was guilty, why'd you take him on?" I asked. "I'd have run for the hills."

"There was something about him. I could say he was likeable, but it was more than that. Yeah, he was smooth. You expect *savoir-faire* in a lobbyist. It's part of the job description. But he was so danged honest — or seemed to be. No matter what I asked him, his response convinced me he was telling the truth — even when he confessed to his worst crimes. Everything about him was a dichotomy. He was a family man who loved his wife and children and put them

198

first. Yet he had no qualms about partying all night with a customer, setting him up with prostitutes, and partaking of their pleasures, if asked. If he had someone who liked to gamble, Stevenson knew the places with games. As he told me, he did whatever it took to make the *sale*. When we were in trial, the audience and the jury loved him. But the evidence was too much. The only possible verdict was guilty, and you could see the remorse on the jurors' faces as the judge read it. Stevenson could have gotten seventy years. The judge gave him fifteen. That was the kind of person Dan was. Everyone loved him. Before you ask, no, I don't think he's the kidnapper. In fact, of the five, I'd put him on the bottom of the list."

I looked at the notes I took while Hammonds spoke. Five convicted criminals, all white-collar, all well-educated, one of them, maybe, a murderer and a kidnapper. Which one? After adding random question marks across a fresh page, I turned to Bannon. "The police are running the whereabouts of these five, right?"

"Yes. Chief Elston is personally honchoing it. It's more than just running names through the computer, though. He said he was going to touch base with a real person to determine if they're where the records say they are. So, if they're still in prison, he's going to speak to the warden. And, if they're on parole, he'll track down the P.O. The chief isn't happy about Mr. Hammonds' decision to cut us out, but he's downright pissed at whoever perpetrated these crimes in his back yard. He'll call as soon as he has something. If it's good, he just might come out here."

"I know. I'm not doubting him. I only wish he could hurry." I looked back at my notes. "Okay, let's fill the time, John. As a group, you know these people better than anyone else here. Rate them for me. Use a scale of one to five, with five being the most unlikely. Put them in order."

Hammonds stared at me, then at the folders. "Difficult, but I'll give it a try. As I said, Stevenson is last." He picked up Stevenson's folder and laid it aside, then spread the others in front of him. "Lively-Wesler?" He rocked back in his chair and stared at the ceiling. "She had a quality I can't quite identify. Not ruthlessness, but not gentleness either. Selfish, greedy. That's about as close as I can come. Let's say she placed herself before all others. Put her in the middle of the pack, number three."

"Fine." I wrote a three beside her name,

then added a five beside Stevenson. "We're left with one, two, and four."

More thinking from Hammonds, more shifting of the files. "Sabastion, number four. Not as harmless as Stevenson, but close."

I wrote a four by Sabastion's name. "Now the tough ones. One and two. Those most likely to murder and kidnap."

"Yeah," Hammonds said. "Mankosky and Simonson. Two jewels. Let's list them that way. Put Mankosky at number one and Simonson at number two. That's as good as I can do."

"If that's what your gut says, we'll go with it. I have it as Mankosky, Simonson, Lively-Wesler, Sabastion, and last, Stevenson. Let's see if Chief Elston's research supports our ranking." I paused. "Sure wish he'd call."

I should have become a prophet. The phone rang.

NINETEEN

The bus stopped at the corner of Royal Ridge and Wiles. Dabba stood and made her way to the front, then paused in the doorway and turned toward the driver. "Next time I ride on here, maybe you could miss a few of the bumps. Bad for my rheumatiz." As his mouth fell open, she dragged her bag down the two steps.

She looked at the street signs, then scratched her frizzled head. "Ain't no soccer fields around here. Ain't nothing but gas stations and drug stores. Same as every corner." She looked east on Wiles, then west, then back at the names of the streets. "Maybe it wasn't Royal Ridge." She thought hard, squeezing her eyes shut with the effort. "Royal something. Dang folks name all the roads the same. But I'm sure Bob said Royal something and Wiles."

A car stopped alongside her, the female driver waiting for the traffic light.

"Hey, you," Dabba yelled, waving her hand.

The woman lowered her window a couple of inches and stuck out a dollar.

"I don't want your money," Dabba said, grabbing the bill. "Is there another street around here called Royal something?"

The window came down another tentative inch. "What did you say?"

Dabba repeated her question and added, "I'm looking for a soccer field on the corner of Royal something and Wiles. It ain't here. Do you know it?"

"Must be Royal Springs," the woman said. "It's that way." She pointed east along Wiles. The light changed, and the woman zoomed away like she thought Dabba was a carjacker.

"Uppity bitch coulda give me a ride," Dabba said. "Acted like I got the measles or some kind of fancy flu."

She raised a hand and crossed the street, paying no attention to the traffic signal. Brake lights flashed, fingers flew, and words were hurled, but she made it across without getting hit. "This way, that woman said. It's this way I'm gonna go. Shortest way to Linda."

She started life as Deborah Livingstone,

born to lower middle-class parents in Hartford, Connecticut, one of two children. Her father was a plumber with a small business that kept food on the table, clothes on their backs, and a roof over their heads, but provided few luxuries. At an early age, Deborah and her younger brother learned to appreciate the value of a dollar.

Like others of that generation, her parents expected Deborah to grow up, marry, and carry on the Livingstone heritage of being a good wife and mother. That's what she did.

At nineteen, with her father's help, she purchased her first car. The salesman was Morgan Burton, Jr., son of the owner of the dealership. While it wasn't love at first sight, it was close enough that they were married a year later. Another year passed and Linda was born.

Deborah settled into her role as mother and housewife, never questioning that it was her destiny. Morgan worked long hours, learning the business from the ground up with the expectation he would take over when his father retired. Linda was a happy baby who grew into a chortling toddler. Life was good in the Burton household.

Linda was her father's daughter following him everywhere when he was at home — first, with her eyes, then crawling, then toddling. He retaliated by treating her like a princess and Deborah like a queen. As Linda began to form words, she tried to emulate Morgan, but Deborah was too tough for her to pronounce. It came out Dabba, and Dabba it stayed. Soon, Morgan used Dabba, also. It became Deborah's new name, one that never failed to make her smile when she remembered its origin.

Dabba and Morgan took on the mantle of respectable middle class. She joined a sewing circle, became a Red Cross worker, and volunteered at many activities. On Wednesday afternoons, she played party bridge with friends, swapping recipes, and catching up on gossip. Morgan joined the Rotarians and in his fourth year, became president of the local chapter. If there was a social or civic event within their range, one or both were involved. Burton Auto Mart thrived, and Morgan rose to Vice-President.

When Linda turned five, she started kindergarten and distinguished herself with her quick learning and bubbling personality. Her teachers doted on her, sending notes home to Dabba and Morgan extolling Linda, saying how much they enjoyed having her in their classes.

Morgan and Dabba wanted another child — Dabba because she loved being a mother and Morgan because he yearned for a son. He remembered the joys of following behind his father and wanted to share the same experiences with his son. But for reasons no doctor could explain, Dabba did not become pregnant. Even as they told one another they had years to conceive, they spoke in a tentative way about adopting a boy.

Then the nightmare began, the nightmare that turned Dabba's world upside down. It started the morning Dabba dressed Linda all in pink and dropped her off at kindergarten.

When Dabba went to the school to pick Linda up, the teachers were surprised. They had seen Linda get in a car with a woman they thought was Dabba. They looked so much alike, it was uncanny — or so they said. Dabba was furious, saying they didn't protect her daughter. Morgan was slower to blame the school, expecting the police to have Linda home soon. His expectations went for naught.

Dabba spent each day driving the streets of the city, looking for Linda. She was likely to slow and stare intently at any little girl with blond curls, especially if she wore pink. Dabba's car became known to authorities as anxious mothers called in complaints of stalking.

Morgan buried his emotions in work and civic activities. His father retired, urged to do so by Morgan, and he became President of Morgan Auto Mart. Sales doubled, then tripled under his whip-cracking leadership.

Conversations between Dabba and Morgan became tinged with anger and blame, then ceased. All thoughts of adoption disappeared into the pink haze of Linda's disappearance.

As the police lost interest in the case because of time, lack of leads, and other priorities, Dabba's search area widened. Soon, she spent days away from home, looking in the nearby countryside, cities, and towns. The house on Utah Street was more and more unoccupied as Morgan slept at the office, and Dabba slept in her car or any motel that happened to be handy. No longer did they share a home.

While Morgan hid in his work, becoming more successful because of it, Dabba's behavior branded her more vagabond. She neglected her hair, her complexion, and her clothing. A quick shower when she remembered and redressing in the same clothes became her trademark. As the odometer on her car rolled up the miles, she turned more grungy, driven by her last image of Linda.

Divorce was inevitable, and it happened five years after the disappearance — without one solid lead to Linda's whereabouts. No ransom demands. No verified sightings. The usual bogus information submitted by people seeking attention, but nothing that helped find Linda.

Although the divorce was fair, Dabba took no interest in the money and ignored the advice of her lawyer on how best to manage it. Her natural thriftiness was the only guide she used, writing occasional checks without considering the dwindling balance. Morgan had agreed, even insisted, on providing her with dependable transportation, but she barely noticed. She drove whatever car he made available. She had only one interest — finding Linda.

Years passed, and Dabba's fanaticism grew while her sanity wobbled. There were periods when she couldn't separate real life from the fantasy of recovering Linda. She spent time in jail for accosting people, accusing them of taking her child. Police escorted her to the city limits and advised her not to return. Everyone was sympathetic, but no one had an answer for her. No one had Linda.

Twenty years after the disappearance, Dabba arrived in Boca Raton, still looking, drifting further and further from reality. When her car died, she left it and walked away with only the clothes on her back and her checkbook. Funds ran out soon afterward, and she took to the street, becoming one of the many homeless who had begun their journeys in the north.

Under a bridge one night, as she huddled against the wind and rain of monsoon season, she met Dot. Dot introduced her to Bob Sandiford, who accepted her without questions and gave her a clean bed whenever she wanted one. She came, she went, she looked for a five-year-old girl dressed all in pink with blond hair and banana curls.

Then Beth walked into Bobby's Bar and announced she was looking for a kidnapped five-year-old girl. Dabba could hardly believe her ears. After all these years, she had an ally, someone who would understand about Linda, someone who would help her. She thought of calling Morgan, letting him know there was new hope. But she couldn't, she didn't know how to reach him. She realized it had been so long. She couldn't remember the last time she spoke to her husband — or was he her ex-husband? So many things were fuzzy in her mind — only Linda in her pink dress, pink shoes, and banana curls was clear.

But now, she had a lifeline. Beth was an investigator who was looking for a five-year-old. That five-year-old had to be Linda. Dabba would help Beth, and that would help Dabba.

Dabba stood on the street corner staring at the soccer field. "That's gotta be it. That's the place Beth found the message. Maybe I'll look around a bit. Linda might have been here."

She walked the fence line until she reached an opening, then stopped. "Mighty big park. Wonder what's down that way." She continued, passing baseball fields, a skateboard park, basketball courts, picnic areas, and a playground for tots.

She sat on a bench and watched the children at play. "Don't see Linda out there. Not one little girl in a pink dress. Most of 'em have on shorts. Ain't no fittin' way to dress a girl." She sighed. "I wish Linda was here." Dabba smiled, her eyes reflecting memories of long ago. "She'd love this place. Swings, slides, seesaws, sandboxes, 'bout everything she likes. When Beth and I find her, I might bring her here." Her smile grew wider. "Yes, that's what I'll do. She'll be so happy."

After a half hour, she stood, stretched, and

continued her trip around the complex, then entered where she'd begun — at the soccer field. The playing surface stretched in front of her, tucked into a corner of the park. It was green, the color of well-watered grass, except in front of the goals. That consisted of bare dirt, worn from the many struggles that took place there. Two sides were fenced, the ones bounded by streets. The third had a parking lot and a baseball diamond.

The fourth, actually an end, approached the Sawgrass Expressway. Dabba saw tall growth that looked like the boundary separating the highway property and the city park. A large, well-manicured ficus hedge blocked the hillside of the elevated roadway from view. Only the cars whizzing by above were visible. She walked toward it, mumbling, "Betcha there's plenty of cubbyholes in there. Bet I could hide, and nobody'd ever find me."

She stopped and measured it with her eyes. "Must be ten-feet-tall. I'd hate to have the job of cutting it. Must have some mighty tall gardeners. Probably basketball players." She giggled at her joke. "And thick. I can't even see light on the other side. Now, let me see. There's gotta be a hole in here a person can scoot right into."

Dabba walked along the hedge, keeping her eyes glued to the ground. "Yep, just like I thought. There's a way in." She knelt and peered into the shadowed interior. "Uh-huh. Perfect." She crawled in, dragging her large bag behind her.

Once inside, she hunkered down and looked around. "There's been somebody else here, and it ain't long ago." She sniffed. "Cigarette smoke. Somebody was in here smoking." She pulled a leaf up to her nose and sniffed again. "Can't fool an old ex-smoker like me. I can smell the stink a block away. And some bad perfume . . . no, after-shave. A man was here last night. Wonder where he bedded down."

She crawled on all fours, examining the ground. "Ought to be some sign of a bed-roll." She ran her fingers along the surface. "Oh, what's this?" She felt a small round depression with her fingers. "Could it be? Maybe he didn't come here to sleep." She continued exploring. "Yep, here's a second one." A moment later, she found a third. "A three-legged stool. Some man was in here with a three-legged stool. Twarn't homeless neither, not with that perfume smell. I be damned." She peered through the hedge toward the field where the center circle was in her line of sight. "He sat right here smok-

212

ing and watched Beth get the message. And I bet she never knowed it. Don't that beat all?"

She sat a moment, her face screwed up in thought. "Think I'll just hang around to see if he comes back. If he does, I can grab him and find out where he hid Linda. Not here though. This is his place. I'll go down the line a bit." She exited the hole and began another search. Twenty feet away, she found a small opening and crawled in. There was enough space for her and her bag. Perfect.

She took out a soiled space blanket, one side dark green and the other silver. "With all this shade to keep me cool, nice place to take a nap." She rolled herself in the emergency sleeping bag and soon slept.

TWENTY

He stood in the doorway, scratching his neck. "There must have been five thousand mosquitoes at that soccer field last night. Had to be because about two thousand drank my blood like Kool-Aid. The rest spent their time buzzing my ears and flying up my nose." He walked to the once-upscale sofa, dropped onto it, and yawned as he rubbed his hairy belly. His chest glowed with tattoos, many of them prison tats. At six-two, two hundred seventy-five pounds, his stomach protruded like a medicine ball, hanging over a pair of dirty shorts. His shoulder length hair hung in wild disarray.

"Did the package get picked up?" The voice came from a recliner facing a picture window. Heavy curtains hung over the opening, shadowing the person.

The furnishings had the look of expensive — years ago. Now they showed the signs of age, cigarette burns, and moisture circles scarring the coffee and end tables. The lampshades bore a yellowish tinge as if nicotine had swirled around them for too long.

"Yeah. Some broad showed up. You should have seen her — so scared she couldn't wait to grab and run." He shook a cigarette free from a pack on the table, lit it, and took a deep drag. "If that's the best they got, the money's ours." Smoke pulsed out with the words.

"Maybe. But until I have John Hammonds' cash in my pocket, I'll keep expecting a trick. Sleazy lawyers like him aren't likely to give up that kind of capital without a fight. Bank balance is all those people understand."

He sucked another drag on the cigarette and blew smoke toward the recliner. "I'll take your word for it. Ain't never been around such rich cats — well, except when they was putting me in jail. What's next?"

"For you? Quit blowing smoke over here, then take a shower. You reek. Sometimes I wonder how you stand yourself."

"Hell, I smelled a lot worse in prison, and them around me smelled worse than me. Besides, it weren't no picnic setting on that stool last night with them lizards and bugs running around. You wouldn't believe the size of them things. Don't give me no shit about smoking or nothing else. I'm the one taking the chances. I'll smoke where I please and shower when I get damned-well-ready."

The voice from the recliner took on a more serious tone. "Then ready better be about now. The way you stink you'll scare the kid so bad we won't be able to control her."

"You want to give me a clue what you're thinking? When do we collect?"

"Get cleaned up. Don't make me tell you again. This job can be done just as well without you."

"Don't try to be so damn bossy. There's no way you can drop me. And knock off talking like I'm some kind of servant. You just remember, if I walk, you're stuck with the kid." He pulled on the cigarette again, then crushed it in an overflowing ashtray.

"Yeah? Well I can blow your damn head off, and you won't have to worry about it." There was the distinctive click of the hammer of a revolver. "Then what do you have?"

"Alright, I'm going. Where's your sense of humor?" He rose and sauntered from the room in an *I'm in no hurry* shuffle.

Forty-five minutes later, he reentered. "So now I'm clean and smelling good. What's next?" He wore different shorts, cleaner but no less wrinkled. His hair looked better, but he had not shaved.

The recliner turned toward him. "Clean? Maybe. Smelling good? That's a laugh. You must buy that cologne by the gallon. In any lesser amounts, they'd have to pay to get rid of it. They can smell you downtown. Go scrub some of it off. And while you're back there, shave and put on some decent clothes. I need you to go out in public."

He glared. "Once I get dressed, maybe you'll get down off your high horse and let me know the plan." He stomped from the room.

When he next entered, he was clean-shaven, had combed his hair, and his pants and shirt were suitable for South Florida. Sandals adorned his feet. He pirouetted. "Do I pass inspection?"

"I suppose. My eyes aren't watering from the smell anymore."

"What's my assignment?"

"I've been thinking about that woman who made the pickup. Not a cop. I'm pretty sure they wouldn't use a cop without backup. They just wouldn't take that chance. Police are like wolves, travel in a pack. Are you sure there were no police around the area?"

"I already explained that. I was there three

hours before she arrived, and I stayed an extra hour after she took the package. I didn't see a soul except the woman."

"That brings us back to who she was. Find out. That's your assignment."

"And just how do I do that?"

"I don't know. You say you're an expert. Hell, ask a cop for all I care."

When the phone rang, Hammonds, Bannon, Maddy, and I jumped. I can't speak for them, but I'm pretty sure I quit breathing. The chief or the kidnappers? Either could be good — or bad. We waited until Officer Winthrop stuck his head in the doorway. "Chief's on the line. Wants everybody to listen."

We exhaled, and John punched the conference button.

"We're here, chief," he said. "Beth, Detective Bannon, my sister, and me. What did you find out?"

"Not as much as I wish. It'll take awhile to track three of them. But we can scratch two off the list."

"Which two?" I asked.

"Mankosky and Simonson. They're both dead. Died in prison. Mankosky didn't have a lot of friends. One of his non-friends slipped a homemade knife between his ribs.

He must have tried to con the wrong guy. That was two years ago." The chief paused.

"And Simonson?" I asked, impatience creeping into my voice. "What happened to him?"

"Slow down, Beth. I'm getting to him." I heard the flipping of papers. "He was a heavy smoker. Lung cancer took him out last year."

"That fits," Hammonds said. "He drove me nuts, always having to rush outside for a cigarette. I told him those things would kill him. He just laughed at me."

"Yeah? Well, the cigarettes had the last laugh. He died in the prison hospital."

I looked at my list. "That accounts for numbers one and two. How about three, four, and five?"

"What's with the numbers?" the chief asked.

"Beth had Mr. Hammonds rate them in order of probability," Bannon said. "Mankosky was one and Simonson two."

"Good idea, Beth. Who's your three?"

"Sheila Lively-Wesler. Anything on her?"

"She's out of prison. Gone back to her old neighborhood to live with her family. Far as I could get on short notice, she's clean. Keeping her nose out of politics and enjoying her freedom. But I've got her parole officer coming in tomorrow. I'll interview him, then ask him to keep a close eye on her. Your number four?"

"Esteban Edwardo Sabastion."

More papers flipping. "He got out a year ago on parole. I'm trying to reach his P.O. to see where he is now. Put him on the later list."

"Last is Daniel Kelso Stevenson."

"He got out and rumors say he skipped the country. Again, I'm trying to verify."

"So we have three active possibles, Lively-Wesler, Stevenson, and Sabastion." I underlined their names. "The other two are dead. Are you sure about the dead ones?"

"I'm told they have death certificates. Does that help? But before you doubt me, I have a call in for the warden at Marion. I'll find out for sure." He sighed. "Sorry, but that's the best I could do with the time I had. We just have to hope it's one of the three. They're our best shot for solving this mess. I'll keep working the phones and email."

In a heavy voice, Hammonds said, "I know you're doing your best, chief. No one expected you to have a crystal ball."

"So, how are your preparations coming?" Chief Elston asked. "Any problems raising the money?"

"Problems? Four million dollars on short notice? Chief, you obviously think I'm worth a lot more than I am. I'm calling in every IOU I ever collected. And if that doesn't work, I'll steal it." He smiled a sad smile. "Anything to get Ashley back."

"I don't suppose there's been any more contact."

"No," I answered, looking at Hammonds who had collapsed into his chair. "The note said they'd give us today, so I suppose they're lying low until the sun sets."

"Yeah," the chief said. "Let me get back to work. I'll be in touch."

"Wait," I said. "Do you have pictures? I need something my sources can show around."

"Sure, if you want their mug shots from years ago. I'll have them emailed to you. And, if I can get anything more current, I'll ship those, too."

"Good. Can you have them age enhanced? That might help."

"Will do. Now, if you don't have anything else, I'm out of here."

Before I could think, there was a click on the line. I reached over and hit the off button. Palpable sadness filled the room.

Maddy said, "I wish he'd show more sense

of urgency. Doesn't he know how serious this is?"

"He knows," Bannon said in a defensive tone. "The chief is —"

"Maddy, we have to trust him," I said. "He's pushing every button he can find. If there's anything to be discovered about them, he'll get it."

"Well, you can sit on your ass, but not me. I'm going to do something — even if it's only drive the streets. Ashley's out there somewhere." She rose and stalked from the room.

I watched her go, then turned toward John and Bannon. John still looked lost, and Bannon looked pissed.

I patted Bannon on the arm. "Civilians. They don't understand things like us *professionals.*" I gave him my best grin to let him know I shared his angst.

Quietness settled over the room. I could guess what Hammonds had on his mind. Bannon, not a clue. Perhaps he was wishing he was on the street doing what he did best — tracking down criminals. Maybe he was thinking how he'd be handling the case if things were different. Or maybe he had Maddy in his imaginary gun sights.

I kept sorting through the chief's words, looking for more than I'd heard. As far as I could tell, it wasn't there. The simple fact was that all we'd managed to do so far was eliminate two possibilities. That left three from John's list — plus the rest of the population of South Florida.

After another few minutes, I said, "Do you have addresses for Sabastion, Stevenson, and Lively-Wesler?"

"Yes," Hammonds said. "But they're the ones from when I represented them. They may be way out of date, plus the chief says their whereabouts are unknown."

"True, but checking them out will give me something to do. Maybe they're hiding in plain sight."

He flipped papers in two of the folders, then turned the pages toward me. "Here's where they used to live."

After copying the addresses, I said, "Excuse me. I need to relay what we have to the folks who are helping me." I stood and left the room, dialing as I walked.

Five minutes later, I paced in the gazebo after updating Bob on the three suspects. I promised pictures as soon as they were available. In return, he said he'd pass the info to his homeless friends and see who was willing to check their houses. He warned me not to expect much. He doubted any of his people had ever moved in the same super-rich circles as Lively-Wesler, Sabastion, and Stevenson.

I continued pacing. Couldn't think of anything else to do. Then Mom came to mind making me feel guilty. I grimaced and pushed her out.

TWENTY-ONE

An hour later, I still waited for the chief. An hour in which he did not call and the pictures did not arrive. My lack of patience had me bubbling. I had to move, to do something. As I stood in the gazebo and brushed off the seat of my jeans, Maddy pulled into the driveway.

She stopped the car, got out and walked toward me, wearing an apologetic smile. When she was close enough to talk, she said, "Guess I came across like a horse's ass when we talked last."

Those were hardly the words I expected to hear. However, if she wanted to talk, listening was better than doing nothing. "Yeah. You did."

"I'm sorry. It's just that the police seem so much more qualified than you. Even Chief Elston told John he was making a mistake. And those two detectives — Bannon and Sargent — they keep saying the police should be handling it. I didn't mean to hurt your feelings, but —"

"You don't need to apologize or explain to me," I exploded at her, forgetting my desire to listen first. "However, you do owe Bannon, Sargent, and the chief an apology — the sooner the better. They're working their asses off for John and Ashley under guidelines John imposed. Do you think they enjoy sitting around and waiting while the kidnappers dictate? Do you think they enjoyed having John tell them they had to provide me with any information that comes their way? That they do nothing without clearing it with me? I don't think so. If he hadn't intervened, they'd have announcements and posters all over the place by now — TV, roadside, radio, every restaurant, and gas station in South Florida. Every cop in the state would have Ashley's picture and statistics in his pocket. Your brother called them off, and they're living with it."

I mentally grabbed myself, trying to rein in my emotions. After several deep breaths, I said, "If you don't have any more canvassing to do to solve the case, I suggest you get your skinny butt inside and tell whoever is on duty you were out of line. I've known females like you all my life. You're spoiled, selfish, and have no grasp of real society.

You've lived in your own little world of privilege, a world where everything is fun and games. I don't need your apologies, the police do."

She glared at me, her cheeks flushing red. With apparent effort, she studied her fire truck-red fingernails while taking several deep breaths. I was ready for her to lash back at me or storm into the house, but instead, she said, "I accept what you said."

She stopped talking, and I stayed ready for an assault. I figured she was not a woman to allow another to belittle her and get away with it. She fooled me again. "What are you going to do? Can I go with you?"

I'm sure surprise showed on my face as my adrenaline flow returned to near normal. "No. If you really want to help — both me and the cops — take care of John. He needs you more than I do. I'm afraid he's about to unravel. And we just cannot allow that to happen."

"You're right. I should do that. I *can* do that. I *will* do that."

Maddy headed for the house, and I sat and stewed. Inaction was driving me nuts. When I considered the way I attacked Maddy, I wasn't proud of myself. There had to be something productive I could do.

Maybe I should team up with Dot and hit the neighborhoods where the three survivors had lived. I could at least discover if their families were still in the area. And, if I were double-down lucky, someone might come forward who saw something out of the ordinary, a witness who had seen Ashley.

I took out my phone and called Bobby's Bar. Yes, Dot was there and would be ready to roll when I arrived. I smiled. Already I felt more relaxed.

He drove down Hammonds' street, not sure how he would learn the identity of the woman he saw at the soccer field. If he didn't come up with her name, he'd never hear the end of it. His partner was not one to take *I don't know* as an answer.

He pulled to the curb, lowered the windows, and killed the engine. *Maybe I'll get lucky and she'll come by. I sure don't know any place else to look.* He settled down in the seat, his eyes on Hammonds' house.

A white car sat in the driveway along with what appeared to be an unmarked police car. There were human-shaped shadows in the gazebo, but he couldn't make out any details because of the distance.

A woman left the gazebo and walked at a quick pace toward the house. Not the one

228

from the soccer field. Taller, thinner, and the hair was longer. He squinted. There was still a person there — could be another woman.

A moment later, someone else walked out of the gazebo and headed toward the white car. He grabbed a pair of binoculars laying on the passenger seat. *That could be her. Size, hair, the way she walks. Yep, that has to be her.*

She entered the white car and backed from the driveway.

He started the engine, then allowed her to open space in front of him before falling in behind. *I'll just follow along and see what she's up to. A lot better than going home with empty hands.*

The light in the upstairs window went out, leaving the house in darkness, except for the external illumination. There was enough of that to discourage a platoon of infantry. A sure sign of a woman living alone.

"She's gone to bed," Mom said. "Is that it? Can we leave now? We've been sitting here for close to an hour. What did you learn?"

I stalled by pretending to study my watch. Eleven-thirty. "Dot should be about ready for a pick up. I need to move the car."

"This sure isn't what I expected," Mom said. "Are all your cases this boring?"

She'd been jabbering for the past four hours, asking the same dumb questions over and over again. Things like, "Is this all you do? Let's go bang on the door. What do you do when you need the bathroom? Why don't you just tell the police what you suspect?" And several variations with the same theme. At least my conscience was no longer nagging me. In fact, I felt like nagging it for convincing me I needed to pick up Mom and take her with me while I cased the three houses.

After calling Dot, finding her at the bar, and telling her I'd like her help, I swung by, and she climbed into the car with me. On the way to the Lively-Wesler neighborhood, I came up with the bright idea of inviting Mom along, telling myself she'd enjoy the adventure. No one ever said I was a harvest moon on a dark night. It turned out to be the dumb idea I mentioned above. Chatter, chatter, chatter when quiet, quiet, quiet would have pleased me.

We hit the first neighborhood about six-thirty, cruised around the block a couple of times, then parked a few houses away and stared. What we saw was an upscale neighborhood and a well-maintained house and grounds. A few people passed, walking dogs of various sizes. The smallest, a red, mini-Pomeranian couldn't have weighed more than five pounds. The biggest, a black and brown Rottweiler, easily outweighed the lady who held his leash. When they passed the car, the dog stared at me — eye to eye — as if memorizing my features for a lineup. It might have been the only time Mom stopped talking. And yes, I cringed. Couldn't help myself.

Dot asked my plan.

"Well, I thought I'd knock on a few doors. Ask which house belongs to the Lively-Wesler's. Maybe that'll open the door to a couple more questions, like has anyone seen a new five-year-old girl in the neighborhood. Basically, I'll play it by ear and hope for a break."

"Uh-huh."

Dot's response was as tepid as mine had been. The bottom line was I had no plan, and she recognized it. In fact, I didn't have a clue. "What would you do?" I addressed that to Dot, but at the last moment, tried to include Mom.

Mom's answer came fast. "I'd kick the door in and see if the kid's there. If she is, I'd call the cops. Case closed."

"And if she isn't?" I said. "She'll be the

one hitting nine-one-one, and we'll all be comforted with the county's hospitality for the night before meeting a judge in the morning. Not a good plan."

Dot had stayed quiet while Mom and I blathered. When I looked at her, she appeared deep in thought. "Dot? Do you have an idea?"

"Your idea's not bad, not bad at all. The problem is everybody's gonna remember you asking questions. You're too proper, too easy to remember. If she is the kidnapper, it could go bad for the kid. Take me a couple of blocks away and drop me off. Let me work the neighborhood. Nobody pays no attention to us homeless people. They act like looking us in the face will make them one of us. They just hand out money to get rid of us as fast as they can. But I seen the insides of plenty of houses while the woman runs around looking for her purse."

No one said anything for a moment. Even Mom kept her lips zipped. I had to admit Dot's idea was better than mine. Even if someone remembered a homeless woman at her front door, no way they'd recall enough to identify her. With me, it could be the opposite, and that could be trouble. "Okay, Dot, you're on. Assume your undercover look."

I let her out two blocks away, then returned to a spot where I could watch the house. The only thing I saw that added to what I knew was Dot working her way down the street. She had adopted a whole different persona — defeated, stooped from the waist. Her frizzled hair flew in every direction. Her blouse was out, hanging over the top of her pants. A second look revealed the buttons were misaligned, giving the shirt a skewed look. All she was missing was a shopping cart. She already had a sack hanging over her shoulder. I didn't want to guess where she'd found that. Every step sang *homeless, helpless, and faceless.*

As she said, no one would remember what she looked like. She'd be safe from the police.

TWENTY-TWO

We repeated the routine twice more in the neighborhoods where Sabastion and Stevenson lived prior to incarceration. The bad news was we discovered nothing that helped resolve the kidnapping.

With the way things went, Dot was the big winner. She was fifty bucks richer.

When Dot crawled in the back seat after our last surveillance, she said, "I've about had it. Maybe you should take your mom home, then take me back to Bob's."

I glanced at her, and she cut her eyes toward Mom. Dot was up to something, but I had no idea what it was. So, I did what I do best — played dumb and went along with her.

Dropping Mom off at my house was not as easy as it should have been.

"Now, Beth, don't be stubborn. I'm not a bit tired. I'll just stay with you while you take Dot home, then we can come back here. You know it's not safe for a woman to be running around alone this late at night. When we get back, you can get a good night's rest. You need it. The way you look now, no man would ever come near you, much less ask you for a date."

"No, Mom. It's best if I go without you." Her expression sent me searching for inspiration and it struck. "I don't know how long I'll be at Bob's, I have to see if he has anything for me. Then I'm headed for Hammonds' place to catch up on developments there. I have no idea how late I'll be. If I get too tired, I'll just camp out in one of Hammonds' many bedrooms."

That did it. She rolled her eyes at me, gave in, and went into the house. I pulled out of the driveway, pointing the car toward Boca Raton. "Okay, Dot, what did you mean with the eye roll? Do you have something you need to tell me?"

"Find some place to stop. I got me a idea."

I followed her suggestion and pulled into the first strip mall we came to. Once parked, I said, "Okay, let me hear it."

Dot's mouth opened, but my cell phone cut off whatever she intended to say. Hoping it was someone with info on Ashley, I held up a finger and checked the caller ID. Mom.

"Yes, Mom. Something happen?"

"He's here — parked right across the street. He's —"

"Whoa, slow down." She was rushing off like a greyhound after a plastic rabbit, her words coming out staccato style. "Who's where?"

"Lanny. You remember Lanny — my friend from Texas. Well, he was my friend. Now, he's . . . well, he's here, parked out on the street, staring at the house. What am I going to do?"

"Hold it," I said, perhaps louder than I should. "I don't know any Lanny."

"Of course you do. I told you about him. Lanny Strudnocker from Dallas, the man I dated. That's why I'm visiting. Remember?"

"Oh." Yes, I did remember. It was because of his stalking that I had Mom to entertain. "You must be mistaken. He's back in Texas. He has no idea where you are or where I live."

"Uh, he might. I might have mentioned your address to him. I might even have mentioned that I hoped to visit you soon. If he went to my house and found me gone, maybe he . . ."

I let her stew for a moment, fighting what I really wanted to say. I was brought up *not* to talk to my mother that way. I looked at

236

Dot whose face was a series of question marks. "Give me a moment. Make sure the windows and doors are locked, then turn off all the inside lights. I'll call as soon as I come up with something. It will only be a few minutes."

"Oh, hurry, Beth. He scares me."

I disconnected, then told Dot what Mom said.

She gave a look — similar to the ones I'd gotten from Mom my whole life. "Well, git this car rollin'. We gotta hep her."

As we drove, we formulated a plan. Actually, doing it with Dot sounded like fun. Nothing like busting a guy's chops in the middle of the night.

I dropped Dot a couple of blocks from my house, then drove past. There was a current year car parked across the street with a man in it. It was plain enough to be a rental, and, if so, the man would be Lanny Strudnocker. The thought made me smile. I still couldn't buy the name Strudnocker.

I continued along the street and around the corner where I parked. I opened my glove box and took out something all smart South Floridians keep in their vehicles — a small steel hammer for breaking a window if I drive into a canal. Exiting, I worked my way toward my house on foot, being careful to stay in the shadows. About fifty yards from his car, I stopped under a tree and waited.

The wait was short-lived. Dot came down the sidewalk toward me, pushing a beat-up shopping cart. I wasn't surprised even a little bit she'd found the cart, or the stuff piled in it. She was still the most inventive person I ever met.

She acted so nonchalant, I hoped she hadn't forgotten our plan. As she came alongside, she peered into the car, then tapped on the window. When she got no response, she slapped the window with an open hand, and yelled, "Hey. I'm talking to you."

Strudnocker's head turned toward her.

He must have hit the window-down button, because I heard Dot say, "That's more like it. You gotta coupla dollars for a old woman? I could shore use —"

Apparently, he closed the window because she stopped in mid-speech. She backed the shopping cart away, circled to the other side, then without hesitating, rammed into the passenger door. Not too hard, but with enough noise to get his attention.

I grimaced, hoping it was a plastic shopping cart. Otherwise, Mr. *Stalker du jour* would have a nice dent to explain to the rental agency.

"Hey, you old bitch," he screamed as the window went down. "What do you think you're doing?"

That was my cue to move. In a crouch, I raced toward the back of his vehicle, hoping he was so engrossed with calling Dot names he wouldn't see me coming. I came up in his blind spot, still in a crouch.

"I asked real nice for a dollar," Dot said. "You ain't got no reason to be mean to me."

"Get away from my car before I come out there and kick your ass." He popped his door open.

That was as far as he got because I was at his back door by then. I swung the hammer, and his rear window shattered. His head swiveled toward the racket, and his eyes went huge. But he didn't appear to be too concerned about the window. His gaze had locked onto my other hand, the one holding my Walther.

"Unlock the doors," I said. "You have a problem." I let him see the inside of my pistol, from the business end, and heard the click of the locks.

His door began to swing open, and a leg came out. Too slow. By then, Dot had slid into the passenger seat. "Uh-uh, dearie," she said, clamping onto his shoulder. "You just stay right inside. Miss Beth wants to talk to you."

Dot released her hold on him with her left hand while her right produced my old .38, the one I *lent* her weeks before. "I hope you do what she says. She's mean as a python what ain't et for weeks when folks don't do right by her." She cackled, adding a more terrifying element to the moment. "And she ain't *near* as mean as me."

Strudnocker's eyes stared at her gun as he pulled his leg in and closed the door.

While that was going on, I crawled in behind him and planted the barrel of the Walther at the base of his skull. "You just keep your eyes to the front. All you're going to do is nod your head so I know your ears aren't clogged. Understand?"

He nodded, his head jumping up and down like a bobblehead doll.

"Easy. Don't sprain anything." I hesitated, allowing him a moment to consider his situation. When I figured he'd had enough time to see no way out, I said, "Here's the deal, Snodbucket." I hesitated, then continued, "That is your name, isn't it?"

"Strudnocker," he said in a barely audible voice. "It's Strudnocker, not Snodbucket."

"Wrong," I said, giving him a nudge with

the Walther. "I changed it. It's Snodbucket now. Agree?"

In the rearview mirror, I saw his mouth open, but before he could speak, Dot cut in, "You better say yes. I done told you she's mean. I don't want to get your brains all over me. And I know for shore she'll blow your head off. I seen her do it before."

Strudnocker nodded.

"Good," I said. "Now, Snodbucket, here's the deal. My name is Beth Bowman. My mother is Sandra Bowman. As you know, she's inside my house, visiting with me. She came to Florida because you were stalking her in Texas. Now you're here." I paused. "Am I right about you stalking her?"

"Uh . . ."

Another nudge with the Walther.

"I . . . ah . . . I . . ."

He seemed to have lost his voice so I decided to help him. "Stalking. Mom calls it stalking. I call it stalking. Dot calls it stalking." I looked toward Dot.

"Beth and her mama's right. When you follow a woman around, it's stalking. Ain't no argument about that."

"See, Snodbucket, we're all in agreement here. It's time to nod."

He nodded.

I dug the barrel into his C3 vertebra. "I'm

sure you noticed what happened to your window. Instead of shooting you, suppose I just crack you with my little hammer hard enough to shatter you right here." I nudged the vertebra again. "Probably wouldn't kill you, but you'd be a vegetable. Right?"

After only a brief hesitancy, his head went up and down.

"Good. I think you're getting the message. Now, we're nearing the end of the trail. In a few minutes, Dot and I will get out of the car, and you will drive away. You'll go straight to the airport, turn in your rental, and fly home to Texas. Upon arrival, you'll forget where the city of Richardson is and that you ever heard of my mother. Do you understand?"

The nod came faster that time.

"Give me your driver's license. But do it real, real slow. The sweat on my trigger finger is making things slippery here."

He moved with the speed of a sloth and produced his wallet, which he held over the seat back.

"No. Take out the license. Don't want you to think I'd take your money or credit cards."

"I would," Dot said. "I could use a new do. How much ya got?"

"Now, Dot," I said. "No fair. This is a not-for-profit operation. It's only to help a stalker before he gets himself hurt."

Strudnocker produced his license and handed it over.

"I see you live in Greenville," I said, keeping the pistol tight against his hairline. "If you lived in Richardson, you'd have a new problem."

He didn't respond. Probably because I was imprinting circles on the back of his neck.

I continued, "With the housing market as bad as it is these days, I'd hate for you to have to sell your house." I sighed. "Greenville's not as far from Richardson as I'd like, but I bet you know the roads good enough to go anyplace you want without ever crossing into Richardson. If you have to go north, you'll bypass my mother's town. Right?" I nudged.

He nodded.

"Fine. We're almost finished here. Last words. If I hear that you have bothered my mother again, I will come to Texas, track you down, and kill you. But first, I will castrate you and watch you bleed out. When they bury you, there'll be no proof you're a man. You can spend purgatory looking for what you men pride the most."

"He ain't no man, honey," Dot said. "He

might carry the equipment, but a real man don't stalk women."

"Good point, Dot. What say you, Snodbucket?"

"I'll be travelin' with her," Dot said. "Ain't no way I'd miss a show like that."

"Judging from your color, Snodbucket, you seem to have grasped my seriousness." The rearview mirror reflected a man whose face resembled the fungus that too often grows in my refrigerator.

"Yeah, he's looking awful green," Dot said. "He better not throw up on me."

"He wouldn't dare. Would you, Snodbucket?"

Head shake.

I copied his address, then dropped his license over his shoulder. "You'll need this at the airport. Don't lose it. But remember what we talked about. I know *where you live.*" For emphasis, I gave him a sharp rap on the head with the barrel of my pistol, just enough for a headache to reinforce what I'd said. "When you turn this car in, you might want to tell them you found it like this when you got back to it in a parking lot. Happens all the time in Florida. You can even make a few bucks by coming up with a list of stolen property."

I slipped out the back door as Dot exited

the front. When I tapped on his front window, he spun my way. I gave him a big smile and a *wind-it-up* motion. He didn't need a second encouragement. He was gone in a squeal of tires.

Dot and I giggled like two teenagers as we made our way to my car.

"That was one scared dude," Dot said. "I swear I never seen nobody can turn mean like you. When you git that way, you even scare me."

"It's an act, only an act. Actually, I'm just a harmless putty-tat."

"Uh-huh."

"And speaking of which, I'd better let Mom know everything is all right. She'll be wondering what happened to us." I started toward my house.

"Uh, Beth," Dot said. "You really want to go up there. She just gonna want to come with us again. I mean, I still got that idea, and it don't call for her to be with us. And, it can't wait, it needs to be done now."

"Um, good point," I said. "I love her, but she can be a bit . . . uh . . ."

"I unnerstand. She's your mother, and mothers love their daughters. But she needs to know 'bout Snodbucket. You can call her."

"That's what I'll do. I'll ring her as soon

as we get out of here. I don't think it could happen, but Snodbucket might recover his courage and call the cops."

"Ain't much chance of that. That man might be halfway to Texas by now. Bet he can't make his foot let up on that gas pedal. Pro'bly forgot all about the airport."

We enjoyed another laugh at his expense as I dug out my cell phone and dialed Mom.

When I said I'd call her, I expected a frantic woman to answer the phone. I expected a mother filled with admiration for her daughter who had rescued her from evil. I expected a woman released from fear. Guess I should have called someone else.

"Oh, that's good," Mom said when I told her she could relax because her stalker was on his way to Texas and out of her life forever. "I knew you'd take care of him. And even if you couldn't, Ike would. He'll be here tomorrow, you know?"

"Tomorrow?" I echoed like a parrot. It was news to me.

"Oh, yes. I called him a bit ago. He said he had a ticket. He's taking the same flight I took." She went on in a more hesitant voice. "If you don't need my help anymore — I mean, Dot can help you, can't she — Ike and I are going to Orlando. We want to spend a few days hitting the theme parks —

Disney, Universal Studios, Epcot. It'll be such fun to share them with someone my age." Her voice had grown in confidence as she got closer to the *my age* part.

Several questions popped into my mind, but I decided to leave them there. After all, she was old enough to live her own life. Things like sleeping arrangements were none of my business.

"You and Ike go and have fun with my blessings," I said. "I hope I can see him before he leaves Florida though."

TWENTY-THREE

He dropped onto the couch in the living room, leaned his head back, and blew out a long breath. "I'm tired. It's tough following people around all night and not getting caught."

"It wasn't all night. It was only a few hours. What did you discover?"

"There were three of them, all women. Two stayed in the car while one worked the street and knocked on doors. She was a weird-looking bitch. Like something out of a movie about bums and hoboes. The driver was the same person I saw at the soccer field picking up the envelope. I'm sure of that. Never got a good look at the other one. Far as I could tell, they didn't have a plan. Just moved from neighborhood to neighborhood. Three stops along the way."

He held out a piece of paper. "The top line is the license number of the car she drove. Below that is the address where the third woman got out. About all I could tell was she had some mileage on her. I don't mean old-old, but no spring chicken, either."

"Where'd they go after dropping her off?"

"Beats me. Far as I could tell, they hadn't made me. I figured I should leave well enough alone and head back here. Can you run the plate and the address?"

"Not a problem. You did a good job tonight. Get some rest. By the time you get up in the morning I'll know everything there is to know about her. If she ever bought a pair of shoes on the Internet, I'll have her shoe size. And I'll know the same about whoever lives at that address. Cyberspace is a wonderful place — unless you want to stay hidden."

He chuckled. "You sure are a whiz with the keyboard. Yeah, I think I will get some rest. Been a long day. Soon's I get a beer, I'm headed for bed." He stood and arched his back in a big stretch. "How's the kid?"

"Asking when her folks are coming home. I told her they should pick her up next week. She seemed to accept that. Guess she's been left with babysitters before."

"Did she ask about school — why she's not going?"

"Yeah, but I told her it was out this week

— teachers' holiday."

He smiled. "That could happen. See you in the morning." He headed toward the kitchen.

While I spoke to Mom on the phone, Dot and I reached my car and crawled in. I felt good, good that Mom would be out of my hair for a few days and good that I'd been able to solve her problem. I sure wasn't making any headway on mine — finding Ashley. Then I remembered Dot mentioning an idea. "Okay, let's hear it. What's the brainstorm you came up with?"

Dot twisted in the seat to face me. "You might not like it, but it's a good way to find out if that little girl is in one of them houses. That's what you want, ain't it?"

"Yes," I said, wondering where she was heading. We'd already spent a couple of hours with each house and come up empty.

"I know how to find out. It can't miss, works ev'ry time."

I stared at her, not doubting her, but trying to guess her plan. When nothing surfaced, I said, "How?"

"Garbage. Ev'rything you ever need to know about a house is in the trash. All I got to do —"

"You're talking about dumpster-diving,

250

aren't you?" I was so incredulous my voice had jumped into falsetto. "I don't want to do that."

"Why not?" Dot said, defiance in her eyes. "I done a whole lot worse. And who said anythang about you? You just drive. I wouldn't expect you to mess up your *purdy* manicure. Hell, you could even break a nail or get one stinky."

Oops, I'd crossed a line, and it was time to hop back over. "I'm sorry, Dot. I didn't mean it that way." I hesitated. "I just meant, is this something we really want to do?"

"I told you," Dot said, her voice still not normal. "Just drive the dang car, and I'll do the diving. The answer's in the garbage."

"That's not what I mean." I could see Dot's back was up and probably wasn't coming down anytime soon. More discussion followed, but Dot was determined. The more she talked and the more I listened, the more convinced I became she was right. If there was a five-year-old in the house, the garbage held the evidence. However, there was no way I could let Dot go by herself. If someone called the cops, she'd be in hand-cuffs in a flash. If I were along, my PI license would cut us some slack — maybe. It might slow the police down long enough for me to tell them I worked for Chief Elston. And throwing John Hammonds' name around should carry some weight, too.

It took another ten minutes before Dot gave in and agreed I could go with her — as long as I did exactly what she said. What she said was, "You better be damn careful 'round the back of them houses. Don't go knockin' no cans over or bangin' 'em togther. Ain't no way nobody will think it's cats." She said it with a great deal of reluctance in her voice, but I might have seen a smile try to creep through.

I vowed to make up for her hurt feelings later. In the meantime, I thought her rule was perfect. My dumpster-diving experience was nil. I'd raided a few paper recycling bins, but never searched a garbage can. It was her show.

Three hours later, I drove toward Bobby's Bar. Dot's thoroughness had given me a whole new appreciation for those who man the garbage trucks every day. In my newfound appreciation, they were unsung heroes on a level with soldiers, police officers, firemen, teachers, and others who go above and beyond. I vowed to call them Sanitation Engineers from that day forth. They deserved a special title.

It only took one experience for me to learn

not to have my head over the can when I yanked the lid off. That single burst of South Florida sun-baked garbage stench almost knocked me off my feet while Dot stood by and laughed. From then on, it was reach as far as I could, keep my head turned, hold my breath, and lift. I supposed it was something I could use on my resume if I got desperate enough. However, I never intended to get that desperate. I might admire the Sanitation Engineers, but I had no intention of ever joining them.

Other than the education, though, it was a wasted effort. If one of the houses held a five-year-old girl, the garbage didn't reflect it. No pizza boxes, no juice cartons, no macaroni and cheese containers. Not even a chocolate chip cookie box.

On the way to the bar, both of us were quiet. I don't know what was in Dot's mind, but mine was numb. I had been so sure one of the three — Lively-Wesler, Sabastion, or Stevenson — was the kidnapper. During the drive, I accepted that I had nothing to hang that notion on except simply wishing it. But I had hung my expectations on it, and they were smashed.

There was always the possibility I was right and the guilty person had Ashley stashed some other place. If so, he or she would have to go back and forth. I perked up a bit. Maybe I could get some of my homeless friends to keep an eye on the houses. It might be one of them yet.

Dot suggested, and I concurred, that I stay in Bob's dorm the rest of the night. I was down and dog-tired, but wired, like I'd spent the night at Starbucks instead of absorbing garbage smells. I didn't want to go home and face Mom. I had had enough failures in one twenty-four-hour period — well, if you didn't count my encounter with Strudnocker. In spite of how I felt, I smiled, remembering his hasty departure.

After showering long enough to get the South Florida water police after me, I crammed the clothes I'd worn into a plastic bag, tied it tight, then put that one into another bag. I hadn't decided whether to try to clean them or find a fire hot enough to incinerate them. Of course, the latter could get the EPA regulators after me for polluting the atmosphere.

I assumed Dot was as exhausted as I when I lay on the cot next to her. There was time for a few hours sleep before I needed to head back to Hammonds' with the hopes that something new — and good — had happened.

I closed my eyes. A garbage can appeared,

and I smelled its unique aroma. My eyes popped open. I closed them again. Strudnocker's fear-filled face appeared. My eyes popped open. The third time produced a picture of Ashley, holding out her arms. I sat up. No way I could sleep.

"Somethin' wrong?" Dot said.

"Sorry. I didn't mean to wake you."

"Wake me? Dearie, I ain't been asleep. My head just refuses to shut down. All I can think of is that sweet little girl out there with them nasty people. Nah, ain't no sleep in me."

"Me either. Dot, I feel like I'm in a dark room and can't find the light switch. I know it's there, but I can't even touch a wall."

"You thinking too hard. Prob'ly need to get your mind off it for a while. You be surprised what you can think of when you ain't thinking about it."

"Huh?"

"Oh, you know what I mean."

There didn't seem to be anything to say to that so I didn't say anything. Neither did Dot.

Dot's bed squeaked, and I sensed she had turned toward me. When her lamp came on, I saw I was right.

"I meant to ask you earlier. Did you have somebody backin' you last night?"

"Huh?" Damn, not understanding was getting to be a habit. "What do you mean? I didn't have anyone except you — well, and Mom."

"Shit. I might be wrong, but I shore thought I saw somebody."

That sat me up. "Who? When?" My mind flew to Bannon and Sargent. Had those bastards put someone on my tail in spite of the warnings from Hammonds.

Dot swung around and put her feet on the floor. "I can't be shore. It was after I did the third house. As I made my way back to where you parked, I saw a car about a block behind you. It had dark windows, and I don't know but my gut said there was a man in the front seat all scrunched down. As I thought about it, my mind remembered there might have been a car at the second house, too. Nothing that really stood out, just a feeling — if you know what I mean."

"What about the first house?"

Dot shrugged. "No idea. I squeezed on it, but there was nothing about the first stop I remember."

"So, why didn't you mention it then?"

"I was going to, but when I got to the car, your mom was talkin' a mile a minute, and it slipped my mind. Then we got all wrapped around with her boyfriend, and it went plumb away. I reckon getting my head off it caused it to come back. Like I said before, not remembering is sometimes the best way to remember."

I mulled her last statement. "I think I understand. What kind of car was it? Was it an unmarked police car?"

Dot shook her head. "Dearie, I don't know. Like I said, it was more a feeling than something I really saw. Now you got me worried, though. If it wasn't somebody on your side, it coulda been . . ." Her voice trailed away and her brow furrowed.

"Yeah," I said. "It could have been part of the kidnapping team keeping tabs on me. They might have picked me up at the soccer field last night. Damn. How could I have been so careless?"

That thought quieted us and a moment later, Dot turned off the lamp. I lay in the darkness hoping it was Bannon and Sargent, not the bad guys. If I hadn't feared waking Hammonds, who needed all the sleep he could get, I'd have called the house then. Instead, I vowed to call after the sun came up. That's the last thing I remember. Exhaustion defeated worry, and I slept.

TWENTY-FOUR

In spite of how late — or early, depending on your point of view — it was when I fell asleep, the sun awoke right on time. And so did Dot. I guess sleeping on or under park benches and bridges taught her to hit the street as soon as *Old Sol* did. Probably saved some rude awakenings.

Dot finished dressing, then asked, "How do I look? Will I pass muster as the best *damn* greeter at Walmart today? My shift starts at nine. I get off at six if you need help tonight. I don't work tomorrow so we can sneak around all night."

"You look great," I said. And she did. Living on the street had kept her in trim athletic shape, not an ounce of flab anywhere. *Pinch an inch* did not apply to her. I was envious. And her *greeter outfit,* as she called it, fit like it was tailored for her. She had the kind of body that off-the-rack clothes fit to a T. The Dot who prowled with me the previous night and the Dot prancing in front of me were as different as peanut butter and mayonnaise. I loved both of them.

I continued, "As for tonight, since I don't know what I'll be doing, I don't know if I'll need help or not. Tell you what, though. I'll leave word here at the bar."

"Works for me," she said, sneaking another look in the full-length mirror. "Now, let's see if there's any coffee in this place."

We headed into the front area where Bob sat in a booth with Street, Blister, and Ralph. When we entered, Bob called, "Java behind the bar. Help yourselves, then join us. Fill us in on last night."

I poured a cup of coffee and handed it to Dot. As I began to fill a cup for me, my stomach growled. That gave me a better idea. I walked to the booth. "Instead of sipping bar *swill,* why don't we go to Denny's?" I punctuated the word swill with a smile to let Bob know I was kidding. "I'll treat everyone to a full course breakfast with all the trimmings. I talk better on a full stomach."

"Sounds right to me," Dot said.

Bob looked around the table and received nods from everyone. "Looks like you're on, Beth. Hope your credit card has room for all these hungry bellies."

"Yeah," Street said, laughing. "A couple or three classic combos will do me."

"You eat, I'll buy," I said, then sealed the deal with a fist bump.

The waitress doubling as hostess did a double take when we walked in. Bob had on his street corner attire while Blister, Street, and Ralph were dressed like . . . well, like the homeless people they were. I've already described Dot. I wore a set of the backup clothes I kept in my car — black slacks, a light blue top, and flats. While none of us would pass for rich, we reflected several levels of society. However, to give the waitress credit, she recovered in a heartbeat and seated us as if we were visiting celebrities.

No one pigged out, although everyone cleaned his or her plate — including me. Guess I was hungrier than I thought. While eating, we chatted like old friends who met around the breakfast table all the time. Blister told stories of the street, some of the things that happened to him on a frequent basis. The one that got the biggest chuckle was one about a woman in a limo who invited him to her place for a *special* treat. Better than money, she told him.

When I asked if he went with her, he said,

"A gentleman never tells." However, his lascivious grin finished the story. Between bursts of laughter around the table, I said, "You should write a book. *Normal* people would get quite an education."

"Nah," he answered. "What would I do with all that money?"

That produced more laughter as two sets of hands belonging to Dot and Street jumped out, palms up.

When Blister ran out of stories and quieted, Bob turned to me. "Okay, tell us about last night. Did you discover anything?"

"Only if negatives help," I said. "We pretty well determined Ashley is not in one of the three houses belonging to Lively-Wesler, Stevenson, and Sabastion. Doesn't mean one of them isn't guilty. Just means we didn't come up with any evidence of her presence. At this point, I'm a bit flummoxed. We need a break, and it needs to come soon. If anyone has any ideas, my ears are wide open."

I looked around the table and received a series of shrugs until I reached Ralph. His brow was furrowed, and his face appeared pinched. "Ralph, do you have something for me?"

"If I may," he said. "I have a theory I'd like to share."

I realized he had stayed quiet during Blister's exploits, apparently deep in thought. "Please. Anything you have is better than what I'm sitting on."

"I been thinking about the whole situation — the murder of Ms. Hammonds, the kidnapping, the note they sent, and the five people on your suspect list. Maybe it's a case of the forest versus the trees thing. You been thinking so much about everything, you might be missing the small thing. Hammonds failed them, so they went to prison. You spent your time concentrating on the three that are still alive and loose in the world somewhere. Maybe that's not where it's at."

"Oh?" I said. "You think one of the dead guys did it?"

"No, no." Ralph chuckled, as did the others around the table. "I'm not into ghost-avengers. Well, not yet anyway. But there are other possibilities. Do you have time for a story?"

"I'm always up for a good story. Just ask Dot. I listen to her outrageous tales all the time. And some of hers are . . . whooee."

"Every one of them is true," Dot said.

"Oh, sure," I said. "Any day I expect to hear about the time Martians gave you a handout." I laughed to make sure she knew

I was kidding.

"Humph," Dot said. "If you got something to say that will help Beth, you just let fly, Ralph."

"That will be her call," Ralph said. "I think it might."

Dabba threw back her space blanket, sat up, and swept her hand along the ground where she'd lain. "There it is." She picked up a pebble and tossed it aside. "Funny how something so little can dig so deep in you." She rolled her shoulders, then stretched. "May as well go find some coffee. Ain't no need hangin' around here. If he didn't come back last night, he won't be here during the day." She crouched in her hidey-hole in the hedge and looked across the soccer field. "Good, it's clear. Hate to go through all them weeds on the other side again. Full of bugs."

She folded her covering, crammed it into her bag, then inched her way out of the hedge. When she could, she stood to full height and repeated her stretching routine, accompanied by various pops and cracks as her joints responded. "I'll be back," she said into the hole. "Hmm, maybe I oughta take a look at the hole he used. I reckon I could've slept right through his comin' and goin'."

She walked along the hedge about twenty feet and peeked in through a small tunnel, took a deep breath, exhaled, then sniffed a couple of times. "Nope. Don't smell like he's been back. He will though. I just feel it in my bones. And when he does, I'll stomp the truth out of 'em. He'll tell me where my Linda is."

She ambled across the field.

Ralph's face puckered as if he was looking deep into the past. "About thirty years ago, there was a man named Ralph Spagnolli. He led a life filled with luck, but he was too damn dumb to know it. He had a beautiful wife, who was expecting their first child. In fact, you could say Spagnolli had the best of everything going for him — loving wife, a child coming, a good job, and a bright future. But he didn't have enough sense to stay home and live the good life. He hung out in a local beer hall where he fell in with some bad people. Now, don't get me wrong, he knew they were bad weather on a clear spring day. When a couple of them asked him to be their driver for a burglary, he knew he shouldn't. He knew it was not the right thing to do. But, like I said, he wasn't too smart, figured what the heck, it'd be fun. The burglary collapsed, and the three of them ended up in handcuffs.

"Because he had no previous record, Spagnolli only got five years. His friends went down harder. They'd been in and out of the slammer many times. That wasn't the tough part, though. When the judge announced the sentence, Spagnolli's wife collapsed. While he was en route to prison, she was in the hospital losing the baby."

"That's terrible," Dot said. "That man —"

"That's not all," Ralph said. "Let me finish. Spagnolli's time in prison was hell on earth. Since he was young and good-looking, you can figure what happened to him. The good part of that was protection came with the *boyfriends*. So, four years later, when he went out on parole, he still had his health. But he had aged many times the four years he'd been away."

"What about his wife?" I asked. "What did she do after she lost the baby?"

"I'm getting to that." He paused, appearing to reflect again on the past, his face sad and forlorn. "I'll stick to the nickel version. Short and sweet, she took to the bottle. Nursed it like a baby on a full tit. She made the trip to the prison once a month, but after the first six months, Spagnolli never saw her sober again. Many times she arrived so sloppy drunk the guards wouldn't let her in. Finally, just before his release, she went into the hospital — alcohol poisoning. She died there. When he got out, there was only her grave to visit.

"He spent a lot of time crying over that grave, cursing his fate. It took him another year before he figured out it was all his fault. He and only he made the decision to go in on the robbery. That decision cost him his baby and his wife. No matter how hard he looked for someone else to blame, the finger pointed straight back at him. Spagnolli took to the street and ran from the past."

"Sad," Bob said, touching Ralph on the arm. "He shouldn't feel so bad though. Unfortunately, there are many stories like that." He paused and stared into Ralph's face. "I never asked before, but I'm guessing your last name is Spagnolli — Ralph Spagnolli. It's not important to any of us. Only you as you are today are important. I'm curious. Is that why you don't have a street name? Because you don't want to escape the past?"

"That's some of it," Ralph said. "I don't want any excuse to forget I killed my baby and the woman I loved. That she took my downfall so hard she destroyed herself. That she couldn't live with what I did. When they bury me, the only things I want on my tombstone are my name and *Stupid beyond hope.*"

Silence descended on the table like a shroud over a corpse. Each person went quiet, as if he or she were alone. My mind took off spinning, wondering why Ralph had shared his sad story, his painful past. What did his history have to do with me and finding Ashley? Then it hit me. He was telling me how dumb I'd been.

"Ralph," I said in a hushed voice. "You think the kidnapper might be one of the spouses left behind, don't you? Any one of them could be seeking revenge for the loss of ten years." Something clicked in my head. "Or the death of a husband. Mankosky or Simonson. They both died in prison. The ultimate loss. Is that what you're thinking?"

"I know how much pain a criminal leaves in his wake. The victims take several forms. If one of those victims shifts the guilt to the lawyer, believing he didn't do his best, well . . ."

"Anything can happen," I finished for him. "Thanks, Ralph. I hurt for what you've been through, but I appreciate your telling your story. I might never have bought the idea without hearing about you, your wife, and your baby. Also, know that helping find Ashley will go a long way toward squaring the board for you. I'm sure your wife would be thrilled."

I waved for the waitress. "If you good folks will excuse me, I'll pay the bill, then get to work. Ralph has given me a whole new approach to pursue. Stay as long as you like." I threw cash on the table for a substantial tip, figuring the waitress had earned it and would keep the coffee coming.

Dot stood beside me. "Yeah, I gotta go, too. Gotta put my *greeter* face on before I go to work."

The waitress dropped the ticket into my hand, and I headed for the checkout register, credit card in my other hand.

I walked back to Bobby's Bar, my cell phone glued to my ear. The first call went to Hammonds' house. Just my luck, Sargent had the duty. "Did you have anyone following me last night?"

"Huh? Every time I think you're making progress, you go buggo on me again. What? You think I'd risk my career on this case? You know the rules Hammonds and the chief forced on me. It's your show. I'm just a phone-sitter."

"Strange as it may sound, I was hoping for a different answer. There may have been a car on my tail."

"And I'm guessing you got nothing but a hunch — no plate, no make or model, and certainly no description of the driver."

I swallowed my embarrassment at having to admit he was right, then admitted he was right. "I had other things on my mind at the time. But that's not the important part right now. I have a whole new trail we need to follow."

I gave him a rundown on Ralph's idea — without identifying Ralph. It wasn't that I didn't want to give Ralph credit, I just didn't want to hear Sargent's laughter if I said a homeless guy suggested it.

He promised to locate the whereabouts of the spouses, and we rang off.

My next call went to Mom to let her know I was on my way home, and maybe we could do lunch. Of course, breakfast still sat heavy on my stomach, but I needed to spend some time with her. Our moments together, other than last night, had been rare. And last night didn't count for much. I was preoccupied, and she jabbered.

As often happens though, my plan had to change. My cell phone rang. When I answered, I had Sargent in my ear.

"You better get over here. We have an email."

TWENTY-FIVE

He glanced around and seeing no one, entered the house and walked into the front room. "Okay, the email's on its way. I did like you told me. Used a library in Boca this time. Phony name, the whole bit. I'd feel better though if you did it. I ain't as comfortable around computers as you."

"You know I have to stay with the kid. She's scared of you. She's never been around anyone as big and ugly as you."

"Yeah. Well, I just hope I didn't do nothing wrong. Nothing that'll bring the cops to your door."

"If you followed my instructions, you didn't. Sit down, and let's talk about tonight. My guess is they'll send that PI, Beth Bowman, to pick up the message again. If so, I think it's time we let her know she's in over her head, and let Hammonds know we're onto his crap. I want you to grab her, spook her some, then turn her loose. I want her to know we're serious. That way, she'll not only take the instructions back to Hammonds, but she'll reinforce them with her fear. A few bruises might help her on her way."

He flopped onto the sofa, a big smile on his face. "Piece of cake. Should be fun. But if she's jumpy like the last pickup, I'll never get near her. I mean, she grabbed that envelope and ran like a deer on the second day of hunting season."

"Not to worry. I thought of that. I'm fixing it so she walks right into your hands. You just be ready. That doesn't mean I want her getting a good look at you, though. We'll go with disguise B."

I called Mom to let her know my plan had changed, that something important had come up on the kidnapping. I told her I wouldn't be able to go home until later — maybe. She didn't exactly threaten to write me out of her will, but her tone said it was a possibility. Story of my life, disappointing my mother.

After running the police gauntlet in Hammonds' front yard, I was inside with Hammonds, Maddy, and Sargent.

"What's in the email?" I asked. "Did they give us the drops and exchange info?"

"No such luck," Sargent said. "They're still playing cute. I'll read it to you. It says, Same time, same place. Follow the instructions in the zip lock. Three a.m. sharp. Come alone. If you involve the police, your daughter will pay."

I looked at Hammonds. "Sounds like another DVD coming. Are you ready for what it might contain?"

"I'm more than ready to get Ashley home, if that's what you mean. I hope they're ready to release her."

Maddy's stony expression said she agreed with him.

Sargent asked, "Are you up for another trip to the soccer field? This time, we might be able to nail them."

"Oh, no," Hammonds said. "I've already told you we play it however the kidnappers say. No deviations. I will not risk Ashley's life."

"But —"

"No buts," Hammonds said, raising his voice. "What does it take to get through to you people? I don't give a damn about the money. I don't give a damn about the kidnappers. All I want is my daughter. Don't make me call Chief Elston." The glare he gave Sargent raised the temperature in the room by several degrees.

Maddy laid her hand on her brother's arm. "Easy, John. Maybe you should listen to the experts a bit more and the amateurs a bit less."

I bit my tongue to keep it from flapping and making a bad situation worse. This was between John and Maddy. I shouldn't even have been there.

"As I've told you before, Maddy," John said. "I'm doing it the way I think best. It's not that I don't trust the police. It's just that I have to follow my instincts. Those instincts say no publicity and no police presence."

Sargent looked at me, then Hammonds. "I understand, sir. But you're asking Ms. Bowman to take one helluva chance. She got away with it once. She might not —"

As Maddy nodded, Hammonds cut in. "Beth? Do you have a problem with this?"

"None whatsoever," I said, then grinned. "That's why you're paying me the big bucks." My attempt at levity fell flat as the faces of Sargent and Hammonds stayed ugly, and Maddy continued to frown.

Sargent broke first. "I don't agree. Everything I know says this is wrong. But I recognize when I'm whipped. We operate same as before." He rose and turned toward the door.

"Wait," I said. "If it's another CD or DVD or thumb drive or whatever, can you have a team ready to get us into it?" His eyes flashed, so I added, "You were great on the first one, but we did lose an hour or so. We might not have that luxury this time."

Hammonds nodded, and both of us looked at Sargent.

"Bowman, you're a real pain in the ass." He paused and sighed. "I'll have a team here. We'll be prepared for whatever you deliver." He started out of the room, but stopped in the doorway. "Be careful. I'd hate to lose my favorite skirt-PI."

He grinned, spun, and clomped down the hall.

"Damn," I said. "I don't know whether to be insulted or complimented."

"From him, hard to say," Hammonds said. "Whichever though, I echo his words. Be careful. You're my best bet for getting Ashley home."

"Good luck," Maddy said. "Ashley is depending on you." Her tone said a lot more, something like, *You're so out of your league.*

After calling Bob to bring him up to date and ask if one of his *invisible* people could keep an eye on me, I headed for my house.

My hope was things would stay quiet for the afternoon, and I could enjoy some time with Mom. It did, and it was nice. We spent the afternoon mall-crawling, sipping lattes at Starbucks, and just being Mother and Daughter. As with mothers everywhere, she forgave me for neglecting her. As for me, it was a pleasure being with her.

I knew better than to tell her about my early morning rendezvous at the soccer field. She'd tell me it was too dangerous, then insist on going with me. The first I didn't need to hear, and the second was out of the question. Instead, I told her I would stay at the Hammonds' residence that night. We had hopes of a break in the kidnapping.

At five, I took her to my house where she picked up her rental and headed for the airport to meet Ike. I wanted to go with her, but she insisted I go about my business. So, with a kiss on her cheek, I sent her off on her latest conquest. I had little doubt Ike would love her. How could he not? I did.

I showered and dressed in clothing more suitable for a middle of the night soccer field rendezvous — jeans, T-shirt with a scoop neck, and tennis shoes. Yes, I wore a gun bra with my derringer safely tucked away. My purse didn't change, continuing to weigh in heavy enough for a solid weapon if swung by its shoulder strap. I settled at the kitchen table with a cup of coffee and my guns and gave them a close inspection. After satisfying myself they were in perfect working order, I put the Walther in my purse and holstered the derringer. Taking a last look around, I sighed and walked out the front door.

My mind buzzed with doubts about the situation. Was I right in backing Hammonds about keeping the police away? Were my stubbornness and my bias against Sargent and Bannon swaying my judgment? Would a stakeout give us the best opportunity to grab one of the kidnappers, then rescue Ashley? Maybe if I moved in early, I could spot whoever put the package on the field. Doubts. Doubts. Filled with doubts. If something bad happened to Ashley, could I live with myself?

No. The note said show up at three a.m. sharp and come alone. It warned about involving the police. Hammonds' call was the right one. It was up to me. No police, no backup. Well, except Bob's people — I hoped.

It was two-forty-five, and I cruised Royal Springs Drive at about twenty miles per hour, my eyes glued to the soccer field. All I saw was darkness. If anyone or anything was out there, I couldn't see it. I continued north under the Sawgrass Expressway, then U-turned a few blocks later. I wanted another look at my target before having to do the walk at the top of the hour.

At the intersection with Wiles Road, I turned left and examined as much of the field as was visible. Wasted effort.

I U-turned again, then stopped in a right-turn lane. There was no other traffic, so I used it as a parking space while my watch ticked toward the appointed hour. A couple of minutes before three, I pulled out and hit the soccer field parking lot on time, hoping the kidnappers gave points for punctuality.

As I lowered the windows, the pounding in my chest smothered any outside noises. I put my hand over my heart, willing the sound to lessen so I could listen. No luck with the thump-thump-thump, but the feel of my derringer brought a degree of confidence. I quickly squelched it, no time for overconfidence. There was a job to do. Taking a deep breath, I pulled on a pair of latex gloves. I climbed out of the car and looked around. There were scattered clouds hiding a three-quarters moon. When the moon found a hole, it cast enough light to see a few feet, but when it went away, everything was black.

As on my previous visit, I left the engine running, headlights on, and car door open, ready for a quick exit. I took the Walther from my purse and clenched it in my fingers. In my left, I carried a small flashlight. Taking a deep breath and closing my eyes, I took a first step toward the field. When I opened them, I had crossed the sideline. Good. I was on my way. Staying out of the beams cast by my car, I shined my light left and right, then toward the center circle. Around me, I saw nothing, but there was a reflection from the middle of the field. That was my target.

My heart continued its loud thumping, seeming to accelerate with each step. I dared not hesitate, or I might bolt from the field. I shuddered, realizing this was worse than my first trip. It must have been the knowledge of the unparalleled cruelty the kidnappers were capable of that caused it. Cold sweat coated my forehead.

After an eternity, I reached my target. A clear plastic bag lay in the beam of my light, a piece of paper inside. Frowning at the change in routine, I balanced my gun and the flashlight in one hand and scooped up the bag while scanning the field, wondering if anyone watched. Nothing to see so I turned my attention to the paper.

Special instructions at north end of field.

A shiver raced up my spine. Not good. Not good at all. I started northward, questioning my intelligence. What kind of crap were they pulling? A trap — obviously a trap. But why? It didn't make sense, but I had little choice but to follow their rules. Ashley's fate depended on it.

My small light made little difference when I shined it toward the north end of the field — too much darkness too far away. But as I walked in that direction, I saw a large hedge forming. From having reconned the area in daylight, I knew the growth separated the field from the noise-suppression wall along the Sawgrass Expressway. I shuddered again — couldn't help it.

A book I'd quit on recently popped into my mind. It featured a young woman stalked by a vicious serial killer. The story wasn't bad until she woke to strange sounds in the house at two in the morning, noises like a large person moving around. The squeak of a floorboard, followed by soft shuffling. The heroine threw back her covers and crept to the bedroom door. The sounds grew louder, coming from the direction of her downstairs kitchen. Now, any halfway smart person would have barricaded herself in her room, then grabbed the phone and dialed 9-1-1. Not this young woman. She was too spunky. She started down the steps in her sexy, three-inch high heel, pink Marabou bedroom slippers to investigate. I had no idea what happened next because I slammed the book shut before she reached the lower floor.

Now here I was doing the equivalent of the same thing. Following instructions and walking into a probable ambush. I felt like my eyes were bugging out as they alternated between squinting and staring wide-eyed into the darkness. That's all I saw — darkness. I looked up and saw the moon in hiding again. Maybe I should give that book a second chance.

About twenty yards out, I stopped and forced my breathing into a more normal pattern. I couldn't be hyperventilating when I reached my target. Too much at stake. When I had myself under control, I continued at a brisk pace. Since I anticipated danger, there was no point in protracting it. Might as well get it over with.

My light bounced off a package. It appeared to be an envelope, such as the one I found on my first trip to the field. Instructions for Hammonds, or I had to believe it was. It lay on the end line between the uprights of the netless goal. I stopped, my danger antenna sending out a constant beep, beep, beep. Five more yards.

I was there. The envelope lay at my feet. All I had to do was stoop and pick it up. I cradled my flashlight under my armpit, keeping my head up, my eyes peering, scanning, zipping left to right and back, wishing the moon would show itself. My fingers found the package. I curled them to lift it. It didn't move. Something held it down. Damn. I knelt on one knee, my fingers slipping around the edges. It still didn't move. I had to look to discover the reason. With a last sweep of the area, I turned my vision downward.

A hand grabbed the back of my neck and propelled me upward. At the same time, another hand swept down my right arm, jerking my pistol out of my hand. I swung with my left, but I was too slow. The grip on my neck tightened, sucking all the effort out of me. All I could do was cry out in pain.

"Now, bitch," a deep voice said, "we gonna talk. But first, take a look, a good look. Make sure you memorize everything you see."

His hand twisted my neck with my shoulders following until I was face-to-face with him. The moon picked that moment to find a hole in the clouds. What I saw was hideous — a series of oozing sores and scars and all shades of black, blue, and red. A smell of death rose from him.

"Seen enough?" He shoved me back onto my knees, my head into the ground, never letting up on the pressure on my neck.

"The package is for Hammonds. I'm sure you'll deliver it just like the UPS man does — right on time." He chuckled.

The words registered, but I was still in shock at what I'd seen. What had happened to this man? What had turned him into such a grotesque figure? The pain he inflicted didn't help me find an answer. I was more inclined to cry than think clearly.

"This is for you," he said. "Listen and don't forget it. We don't like your interference. We know you been all over town trying to find us. That ain't part of our deal. You best stop right now. You understand? Nod if you do."

He let up with the pressure just enough for me to obey, then the pressure returned.

"If we catch you looking for us again, that little girl gonna pay. Do you understand what I'm saying?"

I nodded as best I could with my face stuffed with grass.

"Good. Make sure you pick up your peashooter before you leave. Don't want no kids stumblin' across it when the sun comes up. And don't forget to deliver that package."

I heard an object hitting the hedge — probably my gun.

"You were told to show up at three a.m. sharp. You didn't follow orders. I seen you cruisin' the area. You gonna work with me, you gonna do what I say. Don't worry. No one will see the bruises except when you want them to."

I cringed as the pressure in my neck increased. I was in for a beating, and there wasn't a darn thing I could do about it. He landed the first blow, a solid shot to my ribs. I'm sure it was a fist, but the pain it produced felt like he used a steel-toed boot. I struggled to breathe and retain consciousness as spears of pain shot through my body.

"Catch your breath. There's more to come."

The only noise for a moment was my gasping, then a new sound filled the air — a screeching somewhere between the call of a banshee and a scream.

Something slammed into my attacker, knocking him off balance. The pressure on my neck lessened briefly, then I was thrown to the side as an enraged howl emerged. I heard another solid thump as if a body had hit the ground.

I reached for my bra gun, intending to even things when a kick sent me flying. Thoughts of retaliation deserted me as blackness descended.

TWENTY-SIX

My eyes opened as a crescendo of pain raced from the top of my head, down my body, and out my toes. It left behind a loud echo of itself, and I folded into a fetal position, not knowing where I was or why my body screamed in pain. Gradually, memory overcame enough of the agony to remind me I was on the ground in a soccer field at the intersection of Royal Springs Drive and Wiles Road. I had come there to . . . Why was I there? That memory strand hadn't recovered yet.

I heard a groan and looked toward the tall hedge. A person, or what I took to be a person, sat there. Although it was too dark for details, I thought he, or maybe she, was holding his or her head.

"Damn som'bitch. I let him git away. He'll be back though. I'll nail his ass next time."

Him. The person said *him* and memory flooded in. I had come to the field to pick up a note from the kidnappers and been accosted by someone. The person on the ground had to be my savior, the one who attacked my assailant. "Hello," I said. "Are you okay?"

"That you, Beth? Yeah, I'm alright. Just too pissed-off to move right now. That som'bitch threw me in this damn bush, and I got scratches all over me. You hang on. I be there in a minute."

Now my head was really spinning and not only from the blows it took. The voice was familiar. Female. "Who are you, and why are you here?"

"I'm here for the same reason you are — to get Linda back, to bring my baby home."

I shook my head — and wished I hadn't. Stars and light streaks of all colors appeared. Her answer didn't make any sense. Who was Linda? I was there for Ashley. Either that or I'd taken a harder hit than I thought.

I raised myself to a sitting position, moving with the speed of a ninety-year-old in a supermarket. "You didn't tell me your name. Who are you?" That seemed a good place to begin. Whys and wherefores could come later.

"It's Dabba. Remember me? Bob's friend? That man has my Linda. I shoulda done better. But I'll get him next time."

Dabba? Linda? My brain clicked and filled in the details. But why was she here in the middle of the night?

After a few minutes, I climbed to my feet and made my way to her. Like she said, she seemed okay, although her mumbling about Linda caused me to wonder.

Remembering my assailant threw my gun into the hedge, I found my flashlight and, with Dabba's help, searched until I located it. Then we spent ten minutes finding Dabba's gun. She saw it first, and it disappeared into a shopping bag. It was a bit scary to think a woman who'd been looking for her kidnapped five-year-old for over forty years walked around with a loaded revolver. In her state of mind, though — mad as hell and making no qualms about it — I wasn't about to argue with her.

I knew I should rush the kidnappers' envelope to Hammonds, but my curiosity about Dabba held me. "What were you doing here? How'd you know about this place?"

"After you come here the first time, I knowed he'd be back. I found his hidey-hole and made one for myself. Tonight when he showed up, I figured I would follow him and find my Linda. But then, he went after you, and I couldn't let him kill you. I couldn't shoot him 'cause I needed him to take me to her, so I jumped on his back, hoping to conk him with my gun." She groaned. "He's a strong som'bitch. Just threw me off like I was a mosquito. Before I could git up, he kicked you and ran like hell. Went thataway."

She pointed in the general direction of the parking lot. "I was still diggin' my way out of that damn hedge when I heard a car start up down the street." She stopped and held her hand out in front of her. "Shine your light over here. My hand feels funny."

I did, and we discovered two broken fingernails.

"How'd that happen?" I asked.

"Don't know. Maybe when I was in that damn bush. 'Course I hope I tore them ripping a hunk of his hide off."

"Possible, but not probable. More like you caught them on something. I've done that. They'll be tender for a few days, but ought to be okay. Does Bob have a doctor you can visit when the sun comes up? Wouldn't hurt to have someone check you over."

"Don't need no doctor. I done worse diggin' in dumpsters. You go on 'bout yo' business. I'm staying here. If he comes back, he gonna get a big surprise. This time I'm shootin' first and jumpin' his ass second."

I turned my attention to the kidnapper's package. He had staked it to the ground by its four corners with long spikes. That explained why I couldn't lift it. He must have guessed I'd relax my vigil enough to bend down to it — and he was right.

I shined my light around the area one last time, wanting to ensure I left nothing behind.

"Put that light over here," Dabba said.

I followed her pointing finger.

She giggled. "Damn. Must be one of them silver-lining things. There's almost a full pack of cigarettes here. Bet that som'bitch dropped it." She stooped to pick them up.

"No. Leave it be. There might be fingerprints."

Dabba gave me an angry look, but backed off.

Digging in my purse, I found a baggie and dropped the cigarette pack into it after shaking a couple out for Dabba. In spite of the pain that still roamed my body, a smile split my face.

After another quick search of the area, I offered Dabba a ride to any place she wanted to go. She'd saved my butt, so I definitely owed her that much. She refused, repeating her mantra that she'd wait for

Linda's kidnapper to return.

Dabba disappeared into the hedge, and I limped toward my car. Loyal as could be, it sat with the headlights blazing and the motor running. After about ten steps, my foot slipped on something that didn't belong. I shined my light down and saw a rubber fright mask in dark colors featuring oozing sores and scars. I felt like an idiot as I scooped it up and put it with the cigarette pack.

My dash to Hammonds' house was uneventful and, as usual, I found it lit up like a football stadium. Media trucks lined the street, but even those pests need sleep. No one bothered me as I parked in the driveway and rushed to the front door.

It opened, and Sargent greeted me. "Did you get the delivery?" He stopped and gave me a once-over. "What the hell happened to you?"

"Yes and long story," I said, stepping into the foyer. "Here it is. Feels like another DVD. But this could be better. Have your people do a check on this cigarette pack and mask fast. It might hold what we need — the kidnappers' fingerprints."

He gave me a quizzical look, but didn't protest. Turning down the hall, he called,

"Campbell. Got another run for you. The lady needs fingerprints like yesterday."

Campbell took my baggie and disappeared. Sargent took the kidnappers' envelope and disappeared. I felt like Cinderella after her ugly sisters left for the ball, hoping the contents of one of my discoveries would be my fairy godmother.

Hammonds came around the corner. "I thought I heard you. Did you —" His voice froze as he stared. "What happened to you? You look like . . . Do you need a doctor?"

"No, but a dozen aspirin would be welcomed. That and a trip to the bathroom to repair myself. From the look on your face and Sargent's reaction, I assume I'm not ready for the pageant."

"Pageant? I don't . . . Oh. Bathroom's down the hall. I'll get the aspirin."

The frizzled hag who stared at me from the mirror explained the reactions I'd gotten — face covered with scratches and dirt, and hair that defied any finger-combing I could give it. The comb I pulled from my purse did no better. It would have to stay wild until I could shampoo and condition it. Even then, a wig might be my best bet. There was no hope for my shirt, but, with lots of soap and water, I might salvage my jeans. In fact, the new tears and stains could enhance their value.

From the hallway, I heard, "Mr. Hammonds, Beth, I have a DVD for you." It was Sargent's voice, dragging me away from my image. It would have to wait. Ashley came first.

I went into Hammonds' office where he and Sargent hovered over the computer. Madeline, Hammonds' sister, stood a respectful distance behind them, close enough to see the screen but far enough away not to intrude.

The DVD was similar to the first. It contained three pictures of Ashley, ostensibly to convince us she was in good health and happy with her life. In each, she wore a different outfit but the same big smile. Had I not known the circumstances, I'd have thought she was a normal, well-adjusted child.

Hammonds fixated on the pictures, touching the computer screen as each came up. He traced Ashley's features and smiled, his tears flowing. Sargent sat mute at the keyboard, and I emulated him, standing to his left. It was Hammonds' show — his daughter.

After several moments, Hammonds took a deep breath. "Let's see what they wrote. Maybe it contains delivery instructions. I want this over and my daughter returned."

I suppose I should say it contained everything we hoped for. But saying that is too difficult because of the chilling words it contained.

Asshole Hammonds!

As before, we have included pictures to assure you that Ashley is enjoying her time with us. If you haven't reviewed them yet, I'm willing to wait. Take a look, then come back to me.☺

Okay, you're back. Let's get serious. But before we move to the more important details, let me fill you in on what will happen if you or anyone else fails to follow instructions exactly as we lay them out. If anything, accidentally or intentionally, looks funny to us, we will simply disappear, taking Ashley with us. We have already made contact with certain business associates and collected bids on her. Such a cute little girl has high value in certain markets. Of course, being blond is an additional advantage. Think about it.

We are guessing that the police are looking over your shoulder, and the PI you employed, Elizabeth Angeline (Beth) Bowman, is reading with the hope our anger will lead us to make a mistake. It will not happen. We are invincible.

Here are the details.

One million dollars in each of four locations. We will service one of those. Whatever happens to the other three million holds no interest for us. If you lose it, our consciences will be clear. We may laugh some though.☺

Put the money in cardboard boxes. Neither the money nor the boxes can be new. Make sure both show the ravages of age and use. Place the cartons as dictated below, walk away, and do not return until after four p.m. two days hence. If the money is still there, you saved a million. If it's gone, c'est la vie.☺

And please don't make the mistake of booby-trapping any aspect of the operation. Such folly would be yours and Ashley's misfortune.

Drop sites.

1. Murder on the Beach Bookstore on NE Second Avenue in Delray Beach, Florida. Place the box in the alley behind the bookstore. Make sure you put it between the dumpster and the back wall of the store.

2. Mizner Park in Boca Raton. The

amphitheater is at the north end of the complex and backs on NE Mizner Boulevard. At the rear, there is a dumpster housed in a U-shaped enclosure. Place the box on the building side of the enclosure.

3. Across from the post office on West Atlantic beyond Route 441 in west Delray Beach. That area is filled with weeds and brush. Stand in the driveway entrance to the post office and look directly across the road. About ten yards in, you'll find the edge of a field suitable for leaving the ransom. Use it.

4. The last site is one you're familiar with — the soccer field at the corner of Royal Springs and Wiles. Facing north, walk the right sideline directly into the deep hedge that separates the field from the Sawgrass Expressway. Look inside the hedge and you will find a hollowed out area, perfect for leaving a large carton.

Have everything in place by midnight tonight. Remember, we will keep Ashley for seven days following the transfer of cash. If all has gone well, the police will find her on the street.

Mr. Hammonds, do not ignore our warnings. Ashley is a delightful and beautiful little girl. She will bring top dollar on the international market.

I pushed down the bile that had risen in my throat as I read. They were threatening to sell Ashley. Sell her? How? Then it hit me. White slavery. I headed for the bathroom, my stomach rolling, nausea threatening me every step of the way. How could anyone be so coldhearted? I hoped John hadn't come to the same conclusion as I. A moment later, I kneeled beside the commode, my stomach rebelling at the evil in the message.

After printing the demands in sufficient copies for everyone, Sargent called up MapQuest and located each site. Other than telling me where they were, there was little more I could gain from the computer. A trip to each was in order.

I was a bit surprised the soccer field was still in play. After what transpired there a couple of hours before — the kidnapper in full retreat from Dabba's attack — I'd have thought they'd shy away from it. Then I remembered they wrote the note before the assault.

The other three sites were in Palm Beach County. Mizner Park was in east Boca Raton, Murder on the Beach was several miles north in the heart of Delray Beach, and the post office was as far west as you could go along Atlantic Avenue.

They seemed strange locations, but as I studied them, I changed my mind and labeled them smart. They crossed police boundaries — three cities, two counties, making for potential communication problems — and far enough apart to cause me to spread my forces. As if I had any.

The last instruction was that the cash had to be in place by midnight. That gave me just over eighteen hours to find Ashley, or John would be out up to four million dollars. More money than I could even dream of. I looked at him, wondering how anyone could accumulate so much.

Hammonds stared at the note, nodded, then turned to Sargent. "I'll need some manpower to help in putting the money in place."

TWENTY-SEVEN

While Sargent and Hammonds discussed the best way to meet the money placement demands, I limped outside for fresh air. The pressure of the night was getting to me, and the pain in my side wasn't helping any. How Hammonds handled such pressure, I had no idea. He had crawled into his attorney shell and shut out the world. He gave me the impression that his only mission was delivering the money as ordered. Perhaps that was his secret to being a successful defense counsel. Ignore the world and concentrate on the sole objective.

I took a deep breath and decided to rest in the gazebo for a bit. It was one of those times when I wanted to be alone, to have a few minutes without interruption, to allow my mind to free-float, to land wherever it chose.

Naturally, it landed on the kidnapping. The logistics still baffled me. Hammonds had to get a million dollars in a used box to each of four locations. The kidnappers would hit one of the sites and pick up the ransom. Or, they'd hit all four and pick the one they wanted. Or, they'd hit all four and take all the money. Or . . . There were so many possibilities, all of them bad, my head threatened to spin off my shoulders.

I stared into the eastern sky, wondering if I saw a crescent of light slipping up. Sunrise? Or the Fort Lauderdale skyline? I eased myself onto a bench in the gazebo and considered the day ahead. Unless they found a clear fingerprint on the cigarette pack and identified it, I was still without any real leads. The case was like one of those dreams where you're pursuing something that only appears as an indistinct shape, just beyond your reach. You're straining, attempting to run faster, attempting to catch up, but making no progress. The image stays beyond your fingertips and unidentifiable. In my situation, it was the kidnappers, and they were as undistinguishable as any nightmare I ever had.

I couldn't expect identification from the mask for several days, perhaps weeks. DNA takes a while to process, no matter how much you might want to speed it along, or how fast TV cops do it. No need wasting my energy on that. By the time it came in, things would be resolved — one way or the other.

I leaned into my hands, elbows on the table. The urge to put my head down and block reality was strong. Hopelessness and helplessness threatened to overwhelm me. Maybe it would have except the front door of the house opened, and Madeline Hammonds exited.

She paused, scanned the area, then headed toward me. I braced, not having a clue what to expect. So far, she'd been more a pain in the ass than anything else. But I couldn't disagree with her argument that I was not qualified to find Ashley. My performance so far did not inspire confidence, even mine.

"May I join you?" she said.

"Of course." What was I to say? It was her brother's gazebo.

"Tough night?" She settled onto the bench a few feet from me.

"I've had better."

"One of the policemen said you were assaulted. Is it true?"

I studied her, wondering if she had a motive behind her interest. Her attitude appeared to be genuine. "Some thug and I had a difference of opinion. Nothing serious."

Silence followed. I had nothing to add,

and, if she did, she kept it to herself.

After what seemed like several minutes, she said, "I love to sit here in the wee hours. It's so restful. Makes me forget the unpleasantness in the world — at least for a few minutes. Some might say the air is hot and humid. For me, it feels good, so different from New York." She looked at me. "I was here earlier tonight, before you arrived. I hope you don't mind, but I said a prayer for Ashley and one for you. Half of it was answered." She ran the back of a finger under her eye.

It was my time to examine her, one might even say stare. I'd sized her up as a hard-boiled businesswoman and no fan of mine. Yet, here she was opening up to me. Should I be wary, or had I found an ally?

She sighed. "I was tough on you when we first met, said some things that were out of line. Since then, I've watched you. I've watched the policemen watching you. I've come to the conclusion that John made the correct decision when he hired you. I might still wish he had more police presence, but you're the right person to lead."

I was so shocked I almost forgot my manners. "Uh . . . thank you . . . I think. I hope your newfound confidence in me isn't misplaced."

"Those messages from the kidnappers," she said, taking a deep breath, "I can't imagine the type of person who'd write them, much less kidnap Ashley. This is your world, isn't it? These are the kind of people you have to associate with." She stood and paced. "I never knew I lived such a sheltered existence. I'm ashamed to say I had no idea that such sub-human forms exist. Who are they? Where do they live? How do they face themselves in the mirror? How do they find others like themselves to associate with? Do they have friends who know what they're doing? It's just too incredible for me to comprehend. I'm not of this world, am I?"

"Ms. Hammonds, you're right. This is not your world. It's not something the vast majority of society knows anything about. For that, we must be thankful. Moreover, although John defends these people in court, this is not his world either. I'm surprised at how well he's coping."

"Yes, I'm very proud of him." She paused. "I'd feel much better if you'd call me Maddy. Ms. Hammonds is so formal, and there's no formal in this situation." She sat down. "Beth, I'm sorry I was hard on you. I didn't know how much I didn't know. I couldn't imagine we'd get to where we are this morning. Do you really think they'll *sell* Ashley?"

I nodded. "Yes. Don't make the mistake of thinking they have any morals. That's one of the things that keeps them on the street. The judicial system will not accept that people so totally devoid of human emotions exist — and prey on society. Instead of putting them away forever, we pat them on the back and give them a second chance."

She looked at me, and I could see a degree of understanding forming in her eyes.

She said, "I feel funny asking, but I'd like to go with you today. Is that possible? I know I asked before, and you said no, but I want to do something . . . anything to help Ashley. I feel so worthless, just sitting and waiting. Can I go?" She held up a hand. "I promise to stay out of the way and do whatever you say."

Maybe I liked her better when she had me labeled as incompetent. This new Maddy was tough to pigeonhole. Did she want to accompany me to look over my shoulder, or was she sincere in her desire to help? Or was this case making me paranoid? Whichever it was, I didn't intend to take her along. But how to weasel out without costing me my newfound *friend*.

It took a moment, then an idea formed. "There is something you can do that's more important than a ride-along. When I picked up the DVD tonight, I found a partial pack of cigarettes and a fright mask. I can't be sure, but they might belong to the kidnapper. Maybe he dropped them while planting the envelope." Telling her about Dabba was not in the equation. I still found Dabba's actions hard to believe. "Anyway, I turned them over to the police, hoping they could lift fingerprints and identify him. It could take a few hours or the rest of the day. What I need is someone here in the house to keep the pressure on. John will most likely be setting up the money drops. I have several stops I need to make and will be moving as fast as I can. I'd appreciate it if you'd stay here and keep reminding the police we need those prints. What do you say?"

She gave me a look of disappointment. "I can do that. And yes, I agree I will probably be more helpful this way than trying to become an instant Wonder Woman." She smiled. "You're pretty sneaky, aren't you?"

So much for fooling her. "Truth. I move fast and loose, and sometimes that puts me in situations any sane woman would stay away from. I don't have time to take care of an amateur. However, that doesn't mean I don't need your help here. I do."

"You're on. I'll harass the police every

hour on the hour until they give us what we need."

We did air kisses, then she rose and headed into the house. I changed my position to ease the ache in my ribs, then checked the skyline again. No evidence of the sun.

I returned to my study of the situation. Unless I received an identification and address from the police, my best bet was to find the right pickup place, follow the kidnappers to Ashley, and whisk her out of harm's way. All I needed was the wisdom of *Dumbledore,* a *Firebolt* for transportation, and the magic of *Harry Potter.* Unfortunately, all I had was me. No, not quite. I also had Bob and his people. The last brought a smile to my face. Maybe I wasn't as lost as I felt. As soon as the sun rose, I knew whom to call. In the meantime, a short nap wouldn't hurt.

An impish sunbeam found its way into my left eye, prying it open. I sat up with a stiff neck and the disappointment of having a hangover without a party-evening to cause it. Also, I discovered that while I slept with my head down on the table in the gazebo, some foul creature had crawled through my mouth, leaving a horrible taste. Too much coffee, not enough dental floss and tooth-paste. After running my tongue over my teeth a couple of times, I arrived at the conclusion I needed to brush them, then find some breakfast. I was hungry.

I went into Hammonds' house and availed myself of the facilities. Using the travel toothbrush and toothpaste I'd packed, I made my mouth taste better. My hair still looked like a fright wig, so I stripped and jumped into the shower. Five minutes later, I toweled myself dry and combed out my wet hair as best I could. After redressing in the clothes I'd taken off, I couldn't see much improvement, but I felt better — all except the hole in my stomach.

I shifted to the kitchen, hoping to find someone with a big breakfast and a willing-ness to share. Nope, only a pot of hot cof-fee. I filled a cup and sat down to sip and plan my day.

Ninety minutes later, I pulled into Bob's parking lot, got out, and entered through the back entrance. Walking in, I saw Bob leave the men's dorm as Dot came from the women's.

"Hey, guys," I said. "Do we have enough people?"

"No problem," Bob said. "As soon as you

called, I put out the word. So far, we have Dot, Ralph, Viaduct, and Blister. There'll probably be others checking in as the day goes by. How many do you need?"

I looked at Dot who wore her homeless attire. In today's outfit, she'd have a hard time getting into Walmart, much less being a Greeter.

She glared at me. "Before you start, don't think you're skipping me, dearie. I'll be with you every step of the way."

"But I need you to keep an eye on a drop site. You —"

"Dearie, anybody can do that. Somebody's got to cover your back. That's me. You tell 'er, Bob."

Bob shrugged. "She is good in the pinch."

"Yeah, I know," I said. "But there are four drops. I need at least one at every location and would prefer to have someone at each place you can get in and out. That's a minimum of eight. Think we can come up with that many *invisible* people? I don't want anyone hurt, so they have to know how to disappear."

Dot cackled. "Only the live ones know how to disappear. The ones that didn't learn ain't with us no more."

"I'll take care of it," Bob said.

The back door opened, and Street walked

in. "Heard y'all need some hep. Ain't much goin' on out there so figgered I'd see what's up."

I wanted to hug him, but decided to save my nasal passages. Street lived up to his homeless tag. He smelled like he'd slept in a dumpster. No, I didn't ask.

"Git in there and take a shower," Dot said. "We got work to do and that stink ain't gonna cut it. Go, *now.*"

Street shrugged and headed into the men's dorm. The rest of us went into the bar where a pot of coffee begged for our attention.

TWENTY-EIGHT

No complications to my plan. I'd post one, preferably two, of my homeless friends at each drop. They'd watch through the night. If the kidnappers showed, my friends would get a license plate number and car description — if they could without endangering themselves. Anything more than that was candy. Once the kidnappers left the area, they would call me with whatever information they had gained.

Simple plan, but I believed simplicity was called for. When the kidnappers claimed their prize, we'd have our best chance to track them. Not apprehend them or get in their way, but track them. That let out anyone in a position of authority. They'd stand out like a camel in a sheep pen. The homeless knew how to not be seen, and that was the secret ingredient. Night after night, they disappeared in plain view. I had faith they could do it once more, and Ashley would benefit.

I laid out my route from north to south so Murder on the Beach Mystery Bookstore was my first stop. It was on Northeast 2nd Avenue in Delray Beach, about three blocks north of West Atlantic Avenue, the main drag through the city center. Dot, Street, and Viaduct were with me. I figured Street for the bookstore and Viaduct for the bandstand at Mizner Park. Back at Bob's place, each had evinced a familiarity with the area. Dot, of course, would stay with me. If Bob came up with other volunteers, I'd get them to their destinations somehow. Maybe my newfound friend, Maddy, would drive them. If she wanted South Florida reality, my homeless friends were it.

At the intersection of Lake Ida Road and Swinton Avenue, a few blocks north and west of the store, I stopped and let Street, Viaduct, and Dot out. If the kidnappers were watching the alley behind the store, I didn't want my accomplices compromised. Viaduct, Dot, and I agreed to meet in an hour. Street would stay and cover the site.

Murder on the Beach Mystery Bookstore was located in a small strip mall containing an Italian restaurant, a U.S. Post Office, the usual Chinese restaurant, a couple of medical offices, and several other small shops. As with most strip malls, some units were vacant. I drove around back and through the alley. It was a narrow, one-lane blacktop without much to distinguish it. As described in the kidnappers' note, a dumpster sat near the rear door of the bookstore. It was far enough from the wall for a large box to fit and be invisible unless you were looking for it. Across the alley was an apartment complex with balconies. I assumed the occupants did not pay extra for the view.

As a drop site, it had negatives and a single positive. The positive was its isolation in the middle of the city. I doubted there was much traffic through the alley after the stores closed. In fact, there was probably little activity when the stores were open. The biggest negative was there were only one way in and one way out. Plus, theoretically, the police could commandeer one of the apartments and watch the alley. But the kidnappers had negated surveillance with their ploy of keeping Ashley for a week after the payment. So overall, it looked pretty good for their purpose.

After learning all I could about the alley, I parked out front and strolled along the sidewalk. The most interesting place was the bookstore, displaying books in the windows along with several posters showing book covers and author pictures. A sign on the door announced a signing by Deborah Sharp, an author whom I'd read. She wrote a humorous series featuring Mama getting into scrapes and her daughter, Mace, rescuing her. Lots of chuckles. In some ways, Ms. Sharp's stories made me mindful of my mother, making me feel bad I wasn't more supportive.

The store was open so I went in. An attractive woman stood behind the counter. I stopped inside the door and looked around at a small room with every available inch packed with bookshelves and books.

"Can I help you find something?" she asked.

"Nice place," I said. "I love the name. Does it have a story?"

"Not really. It's the only bookstore in Florida specializing in mysteries. And every mystery has at least one murder. Thus, I put murder in the title."

"On the beach?" I said. "Not exactly."

"True, but my first store was in Miami Beach, and that one was on the beach. So, when I moved to Delray, I kept the title. Besides, it's Delray *Beach,* right?"

"Touché." I stuck out my hand. "I'm Beth."

"Joanne."

I handed her a business card.

She looked at it. "Beth Bowman, Private Investigator. For real? I have a ton of books in here about you."

I grinned. "I'm sure those PIs lead far more exciting lives than I do. My cases are on the humdrum side. Nothing to write a book about. But I am working today, trying to locate a husband for his wife. He has memory issues and may simply be lost. His wife says he loves to read, mostly mysteries. Have you seen anyone strange around here in the last few days?"

Joanne smiled. "I told you this is a mystery bookstore. You've described half my customers."

"Touché again. Maybe I should reword my question."

"No, I understand." She appeared to think about it. "There was a guy the other day. He was out back near the dumpster when I took out some trash. I thought he might be looking for boxes, so I offered him some. When you receive book shipments almost every day, the boxes pile up. I keep some and donate most of the others to anyone who wants them. Anyway, the man backed up, 'No, no, I have to leave.' Then he quickly walked away."

Bingo, I wanted to scream. That had to be

my guy. "Can you describe him?"

"Oh, my," Joanne said. "Let me see. He was tall, well over six feet — maybe six-three, six-four. He had a paunch, but didn't appear much overweight. No facial hair. Nothing really definite except his height. Sorry, that's as good as I can do."

I thought back to my attacker at the soccer field when he turned me to look at his face. His hand on the nape of my neck had forced my head up. Yes, he was tall, quite tall. "Thanks, but I don't think that's my lost husband. My guy is short and skinny. Anyone else?"

"No. We don't get a lot of extraneous traffic through here. Most of the people I see are regulars."

I thanked her, then checked the shelf labeled *New Releases.* There was an autographed P.J. Parrish I hadn't read, so I bought it, thanked Joanne, and went to my car. Once inside, I reviewed what I had learned — not much. Nothing I didn't expect. The man Joanne saw could have been one of the kidnappers scoping out the area, most likely the same guy who attacked me. It was the first time I felt like I had found a trace. Didn't get me any closer to Ashley, but made me feel a little better.

I took out my notebook and made notes

about what I'd learned. On a scale of one to ten, I gave the alley a six.

After retrieving Dot and Viaduct, we discussed our impressions of the alley as a ransom drop location.

Viaduct said, "If I was in a pinch, I might stay there, but I'd be up and off early. Not the kind of place I'd feel safe."

"I agree," Dot said. "One of the things I learned since I been on the street is always look for the way out. Now, in this case, it's not just out of the alley, but out of the area. Wouldn't they want some place they wouldn't get bogged down in traffic? I mean, most any way you go, you got little city streets with lots of red lights and such."

"Good point. They could get bottled up pretty easy in downtown Delray Beach. Maybe I better lower my grade to a five."

"That's high enough for me," Dot said.

Viaduct nodded.

I crossed to Federal Highway and headed south toward Mizner Park in Boca Raton. Mistake. Although it was only a few miles, there were what seemed like ten-thousand traffic lights, one on almost every corner, giving strength to Dot's words about using the bookstore alley. Of course, heading in the opposite direction to catch I-95 with its bumper-to-bumper traffic probably wouldn't have been any faster.

North of Mizner Park, I pulled into a strip mall and let Dot and Viaduct out. Dot and I agreed to meet at the same place in one hour, as we had in Delray Beach. Then I continued my trip south.

I found a spot in the parking garage and hoofed it back to the amphitheater, then worked my way to its rear. The dumpster was as described in the ransom note. NE Mizner Boulevard bordered it on one side and Federal Highway on another. Ingress and egress offered no problems for the kidnappers — unless the police were ready to pounce on any car that pulled into the driveway. The small turnaround where the dumpster sat had only one way in and the same way out. Again, I assumed the kidnappers thought holding Ashley for seven days after the pickup would keep the police at bay. I gave the location a five on my scale.

I met Dot at our rendezvous, and we headed toward Bob's. Viaduct had disappeared into the scenery — just another homeless victim with no face.

"So?" I said.

"Same as the other one. Maybe even worse. No good way to escape."

Once again, we agreed. I wondered if I should be worried about that. I mean, I was, by definition, the professional. If I only saw the same things as Dot, maybe I wasn't so professional after all.

My plan was to pick up Ralph and Blister and take them to their assignments. I had no reason to examine the soccer field. I'd had quite enough of it. Also, I figured the kidnappers wouldn't go near the place after Dabba's ambush, in spite of its quick access to the Sawgrass Expressway. Again, Dot and I agreed.

I needed to check the West Atlantic site, though. Perhaps it would have obvious advantages for the kidnappers, one demanding they use it.

At Bob's, three surprises occurred. First, several others had answered Bob's call. With a smile I couldn't suppress, I called Maddy Hammonds and asked her to deliver them to their observation points. She agreed, and I could hardly wait to get her impressions later.

The second surprise was that Blister had already taken off for the soccer field. Bob explained that Blister had been my *observer* on my two trips there, so he knew exactly where it was. He was embarrassed he hadn't been close enough to help when the attacker jumped me. By the time he closed the distance, the thug was in hot retreat, so he faded back into the darkness. Bob further explained that Blister had been assaulted a couple of times by punks out for a night of *fun*. After dark, he hid — and hid well. I told Bob I understood and would let Blister know the next time I saw him.

The third surprise was a bit of the good-bad variety. Dabba walked in the back door, her large bag in her hand. "Glad I caught you here. When we gonna git them bastards got my Linda?"

The good — she saved me from a worse beating. The bad — I didn't want her anywhere near me or the kidnappers. She was a loose marble that could roll in any direction, and I couldn't afford any diversions.

"You did your part last night," I said. "I'll take it from here."

Her giggle carried an edge of insanity. "No way, honey. I almost got 'em on that field. Next time, he's mine."

I glanced at Bob, and he gave me one of those *you're on your own* looks. He was right. Dabba was my problem.

"Okay," I said. "You can stick with Dot and me. But, please, don't jump out and do anything unless I tell you to. Remember, Ashley's life is at stake here."

"Oh, I remember, Beth," she said, her eyes

taking on a dreamy look. "I been trying to find her a long time. I ain't about to let them escape agin."

TWENTY-NINE

The site on West Atlantic was tailor-made. It had to be *the* place. It was about two-three hundred yards west of its intersection with Route 441. As stated in the note, there was an entrance to the post office on the left. On the right was a pull-off area that opened into tall brush. Behind that was a weedy field. Perfect for concealing a box.

I drove past and continued another half-mile or so to the end of the road where there was an entrance to West Delray Regional Park. I turned into the park and let Ralph out. As he started to walk away, I stopped him. "Ralph, be careful. My gut says this could be the site. Call me if you get in trouble, and I'll come running."

He shot me a smile. "Don't worry about me. I'm the Invisible Man. I'm only seen when I want to be."

I turned around, then headed toward the proposed drop site, my head swinging as I checked both sides of the narrow road. High brush and trees lined the roadside. There were a couple of buildings and a commercial enterprise or two, but the growth pretty much hid them. It was a perfect location. So many hiding places that anyone could be watching — watching even as I drove through — and no one would ever know. Hiding a car would be more difficult, so that meant any surveillant had to be on foot.

At the designated pull-off, I stopped and got out. Dot and Dabba followed me as we stomped around the area. The most obvious disadvantage was there was only one way in and one way out — West Atlantic Avenue. But, as I'd noted all along the route, there were many places a person could hide if he didn't mind mosquitoes, snakes, and assorted other swamp critters.

Perhaps the biggest advantage was its proximity to Route 441, a major north-south multilane highway, as well as the closeness of the Florida Turnpike. The kidnapper could grab the box and be making a high-speed getaway in less than five minutes. I gave it an eight on my list of the four ransom sites.

"This is one isolated place," Dabba said. "I don't think we gonna find Linda here."

"I don't either," I said. "I just hope Ralph will be okay. This is not like working your way around Boca."

"He'll do fine, dearie," Dot said. "He likes the Everglades. Ralph's got a lot of smarts he don't let on to. He ain't near as dumb as he acts."

I looked at her, thinking that goes for you, too, *dearie.* No, I didn't ask her to explain her remark about the Everglades. I was afraid she would, and I'd know less than I knew before.

We climbed into the car, and I started toward Route 441. Up the road a hundred yards or so, a yellow mobile food truck was parked and open for business. The lettering on the side said it specialized in Mexican food.

"Want to try it?" I asked, stopping on the opposite side of the road.

"Why not?" Dot said. "I'm sure I et worse."

"Ain't got no money," Dabba said. "Waiting for Linda's kidnapper to come back to that field didn't give me no time to work."

I figured work to her was panhandling, but I owed her for saving my cookies at the soccer field the night before. "Lunch, or whatever it is, is on me," I said. "Let's see what they have. I haven't had authentic Tex-

Mex since I left Dallas."

A surprise awaited me. A man and a woman worked in the vehicle, and cooked the orders as they came in. This was not an ordinary *roach coach,* it was a Mexican restaurant on wheels. We waited in line behind several people speaking Spanish and looking like they spent their time in manual labor. An aroma of sweat and freshly mowed grass emanated from them. When we got to the window, I ordered beef tacos with green salsa and sodas all around. The second surprise came with the first bite. They were tasty and the salsa lived up to Texas standards — fiery.

We sat in the shade of the car, ate our tacos, and drank our drinks. By the time we finished, it was almost two o'clock. We had the rest of the day to kill, and I was out of places to check. I called Maddy and asked if she'd heard from the police about the cigarette pack.

"Nothing yet," she said. "I talked to them at one. They said they were working on it. I'll call them again, then go pick up your friends and take them where they need to be. As soon as I squeeze something out of the cops, I'll let you know."

"Thanks, Maddy. I'll be waiting." I closed my phone, trying to come up with something productive to do. Nothing came to mind, so I leaned against the car. "Let's take a break and let those tacos digest."

My phone rang and when I read the caller ID, a smile jumped onto my face — David. "Hello, Doctor. You're just what the doctor ordered."

"Oh, don't you ever tire of bad jokes? Leave those to me. I received a lifetime subscription with my medical license."

I laughed as I rose and walked away from Dot and Dabba. I didn't want my words quoted around Bob's place. David brought out the romantic in me.

"So, my love, how are the lectures? Learning anything you can use on your patients? And by the way, you'd better not be learning anything you can use on me. It's more fun to make it up as we go."

"As a matter of fact, we did have one session on head injuries. I took lots of notes, figuring I would need them if I keep hanging around with you. How's your latest injury?"

"Injury?" I said, wondering if he was psychic. I rubbed my ribs where the thug kicked me, then stopped when I caught myself. "No injuries," I lied. "Things are peaceful here."

"Yeah, I believe that. I also believe I'll

swim home. Let see, hit the Pacific off LA, head south, east through the Panama Canal, then swim north. Shouldn't take more than a couple of days. Right?"

"Okay, you clown, I'm still working the kidnap case. Wish I could say everything is coming together, but I haven't gotten a handle on it. We'll know a lot more after tonight."

"Oh? What does that mean? Are you meeting with kidnappers or something? Stay out of danger. I know you'll do what you have to do, but your getting injured is what I like least about your job."

I chuckled. "Believe it or not, I don't set out to get hurt. But sometimes . . . Do you have some special message for me?"

"You mean like I miss you terribly? Yes, I do. I miss you terribly and can hardly wait to get home. You've gotten so damn important to me in such a short period of time. I'm not accustomed to losing control like this. Unfortunately, I'll be home later than we planned. There's an opportunity Sunday that I want to take advantage of. It's a trip to a lab sponsored by the National Football League. They're studying the impact of concussions and looking for ways to lessen them. Something like this doesn't come along very often. I can't afford to miss it.

With our no-helmet-required law for motor-cycle riders, maybe I'll pick up a few techniques I can use in Florida. It will most assuredly help with you since you insist on sticking your head in front of hard objects."

"So you say," I said, making sure he heard my sigh. It was obvious he'd never let me forget that we met while he fingered my head where I had a huge lump and a minor concussion. "But, be warned, if you're not here on Monday, I may go after you."

"Monday, for sure. And it can't get here fast enough. Good luck with the case. I know you'll find a way. I have faith in you. Gotta run now. Bye, sweetheart." He sent a kiss along the phone line.

I kiss-kissed him back and flipped the phone shut, a feeling of loneliness settling over me. There wasn't any way he could help me recover Ashley, but feeling his arms around my shoulders and his head against mine would go a long way toward making me feel better. I walked back toward where Dot and Dabba sat against the car.

"Hey, dearie. First, you're happy as a blue jay, now you're sadder looking than a manhole cover. What's up?"

"Nothing I can control. David's staying over in Los Angeles for the weekend. That's all." I hesitated, but couldn't keep it back.

"I miss him so damn much. I need him here."

"I know what you mean," Dot said. "I still miss my man."

Dot's words jolted me back to reality. I remembered her man, Bridge. He sacrificed his life to rescue me. I had been caught in a no-win situation, staring down the barrel of a pistol in a hostile fist. The holder left no doubt he intended to leave me as one more body in the room. Bridge came charging through the door and took the bullet meant for me. That gave me enough time to grab a gun and gain the upper hand. I lived, but Bridge died. I squeezed Dot's hand, and she gave me a sad smile.

I thought of David and Mom, then of Bob, Dot, and all those sticking their necks out for me and for Ashley. Life wasn't so bad, after all.

"I miss my Linda," Dabba said and sniffled. "She's such a delight."

I sighed and forced my mind to return to the case where the edge of an idea appeared. "Dot, think you can do your homeless bit in a neighborhood during the day?"

"Of course I can. I do it all the time. What they gonna do, tell me to get lost? Been told worse, much worse. What you got in mind?"

"The more I think about Ralph's idea, the

more I'm inclined to agree it's possible. If I can get the addresses of Mankosky and Simonson, I'd like to swing through their neighborhoods. Both of them died in prison. Maybe one of the wives is seeking revenge."

"Let's do it," Dot said.

"I'll be right there with you," Dabba said. "We can ask 'em if they got Linda."

Oh great, I thought, feeling my eyes roll. Just walk up and ask, "Hey, you been holding Linda for the past forty years?" Simple. Sure. How could I keep Dabba from compromising things even before I had something concrete to compromise?

I debated whom to call. Sargent and Bannon were with John, working out delivery of the ransom boxes. Then I thought, why not start at the top? I dialed the police station, identified myself, and asked to speak to Chief Elston.

"Beth, what can I do for you?" he said when we connected. "Are you ready for tonight?"

"As ready as I can be," I said. "But for now, I need the addresses of the widows of Herbert Lowery Mankosky and Donald Kenneth Simonson. And I need them in a hurry."

"Why? Have you learned something?"

"No. Just tracing every hunch. Trying to

find a key that will unlock this puzzle before we lose Ashley — and Hammonds loses four million bucks. Can you get them for me?"

"Sure." The line went quiet, creating an uncomfortable silence. "Why only those two? Why not all five?"

"We've already checked the three survivors. Now, I'm following a gut feeling. Mankosky and Simonson didn't come home from prison. I'm guessing they have heirs who might blame John Hammonds — blame him enough to think murder and kidnapping are ways to get even. And a million dollars is a powerful argument."

More silence. "Fair enough," Elston said. "Wait while I put you on hold."

The phone went quiet, so I laid it in the grass beside me and turned on the speaker. I leaned my head against the car, willing Elston to find the information I sought. Neither Dot nor Dabba interrupted.

"Beth, you still there?"

I grabbed the phone and said, "Yes, Chief. Do you have them?"

"On a fast search, this is what we came up with." He read off two addresses, both in his jurisdiction, Coral Lakes. "Let me know if you need anything else — anything at all. Either we capture the kidnappers tonight, or we let them make the pickup.

There is simply no other alternative. Well, none as long as Hammonds insists the police keep a low profile."

"I understand. Trust me, I feel the pressure. I will not consider her loss as an option. We will get her back. Thanks for the info. I'm on the run."

I hung up and smiled at Dot and Dabba. "Ladies, it's time to go to work."

I drove down Witherspoon Street, looking at Simonson's house. His wife's status didn't appear to have taken a hit with his death. Since he died of natural causes, she might have collected big time on life insurance. Either that or he left her well-set when his prison term began.

The house was on a large lot with a well-maintained front lawn. Not as grand as John Hammonds' place, but nice. It was three stories in classic Florida masonry with a three-car garage and a roof with several elevations. The windows were dark, either from tinting or closed blinds. Not surprising. All the houses along the street had accordion shutters and opaque windows. I was no realtor, but I placed the Simonson place in the several million dollars range. Of course, in South Florida, a million didn't buy near as much as most places.

I wasn't surprised there were no toys on the lawn. If Ashley were in there, no one would be advertising. I looked at Dot who sat in the front passenger seat. "What do you think? Want to knock on doors?"

"May as well," she said. "Can't go through the garbage during daylight. Go around the corner and drop me off."

"I'll go with you," Dabba said. "We can be a team."

"No," Dot said. "This is a one-person job. If they see two of us at the door, they won't open it."

"Humph. Well, you look good for Linda. Watch for pink. That's her favorite color."

I breathed a soft sigh of relief. Dot had gotten me off the hook with Dabba. I turned the corner and pulled over.

Dot said, "Give me forty-five minutes. I'll work the whole street so it don't look like I'm pickin' on that one. Meet you back here."

"Okay. Dabba and I will make ourselves scarce. My car doesn't live up to this neighborhood. See you in forty-five. Be careful." My real reason for leaving the area was to prevent Dabba from getting any ideas about pounding on the Simonson's door, and demanding *her Linda*.

When I returned, Dot stood under a shade

tree, sipping a cola. I pulled over, and she got in. "Any luck?" I asked.

"Got a free soda and a couple of bucks, but that's about it." She frowned, then continued, "Simonson has a long hallway that leads to the front door so I couldn't really see into the house. A maid opened the door and said *madame* wasn't home. There weren't no evidence of a child in the hall."

"A maid?" I said. "I hadn't considered it, but wouldn't that work against Simonson being the kidnapper? I mean, she'd have to come up with some reason for Ashley being there, some cover story for the maid."

"Don't you reckon she got all that worked out before she stole Ashley? She might be as good a liar as she is a kidnapper."

"That's what I'd say," Dabba threw in from the back seat. "Can't expect no kidnapper to tell the truth."

All I could do was agree.

"If you want, I can check her garbage after everybody goes to bed," Dot said.

"We'll see," I said. "But first we have another address to check. It's on Magnolia."

"I know that street," Dabba said. "Ain't a bit like this one."

Dabba was right. Apparently, Ms. Mankosky hadn't survived as well as Ms. Simonson. The neighborhood had a lower middle-class look about it. Several of the houses needed a fresh coat of paint. The yards were green, but there was a lack of quality shrubs. Most of them needed trimming and shaping. The Mankosky house was one-story, with a zero-lot line. I figured no more than three bedrooms. Again, the windows were dark, and again, I couldn't tell why. Since there were no hurricane shutters, I didn't figure it to be tinting, though. If you couldn't afford shutters in South Florida, why waste money on tinting? My guess was someone pulled the blinds, and that someone could be hiding something — like Ashley.

"What do you think?" I asked Dot.

"I can give it a try, but, neighborhoods like this, folks don't like to open the door."

"Any other ideas?"

"Swing around the corner and lemme see if there's an alley. Maybe that's where the garbage truck makes its run. If so, I can check a few cans."

I did as recommended, but there was no rear access. Apparently, garbage stayed in the garage and only appeared on trash day.

"Okay," Dot said. "Let me out, and I'll bang on the front door. Give me thirty minutes."

"I can do this neighborhood," Dabba said. "Let me take it."

"No, let's stick with the plan," I said. "You stay with me." She didn't appear to like it, but she complied.

I stopped, and Dot climbed out.

Thirty minutes later, Dot was back. "No one answered the door. I thought I heard someone inside, but can't be sure. I walked around the house, but couldn't see a thing. The blinds on all the windows is closed."

"Did you check any other houses?"

She cut her eyes at me. "Of course. You think I'm some kind of rookie at this? Nobody answered on either side."

"Humph," Dabba said. "Anybody could have done that. I'm hungry. Let's find a Mc-Donalds."

THIRTY

An hour later, we sat in a fast food joint, Dot and I watching Dabba eat. Dot had a soda and large fries. I kept it down to a soda, but Dabba went for the biggest combination on the menu. It had only been about three hours since our Mexican feast, but Dabba went at it like it was her last meal. I smiled at her gluttony, assuming the life she lived taught her to eat when she could because there might not be more for a while. No way I could argue with her.

My phone rang. The caller ID showed an area code I didn't recognize at first, then it clicked — New York — Maddy.

After my hello, she said, "Call Chief Elston. They pulled a print off the cigarette pack. He wants to talk to you about it."

"Couldn't he tell you who it is?"

"He said it's more complicated than a simple ID. He's still uncovering information on the man. Give him a call at his office."

"Okay," I said. "Thanks for hounding him."

"Before I let you go, I have to ask. Where did you find those friends I dropped off for you? I swear, we have *homeless* in New York that dress better than they do. And they sure didn't major in communication. When I tried to talk to them, all they did was grunt."

I wanted to laugh, but held it. "Yeah, they're pretty special. But you'd be amazed at the skill set they bring to the game." No lie in that. The homeless know things normal citizens never consider.

"Call if there's anything else I can do," Maddy said. "I'll be at the house." She hesitated. "Even pick up those people." Her distaste dripped off each word.

I killed the call, then punched in Chief Elston's number. "What's up?" I asked when he answered.

"We ID'd the guy who assaulted you. His name is Larry Lawrence." He chuckled. "Actually, it's Lawrence Lawrence. Guess his parents had a sense of humor."

"Yeah, sick one," I said.

"We got a solid match from the cigarette pack. This guy's a big, mean SOB who has spent more time in stir than on the street since he turned eighteen."

My ribs must have heard what he said

because they slapped me with a pain to say they agreed.

"But that's not the interesting part." He paused, then finished with a flourish. "He was Mankosky's cellmate for two years. Rumor has it he was either Mankosky's boyfriend or his bodyguard. Either way, nobody messed with Mankosky when Lawrence was around."

"What happened? Mankosky took a knife, didn't he?"

"Yeah. I wondered the same thing. Took me a couple of hours to make contact with the warden. Turns out Lawrence was in the infirmary with the flu when Mankosky bought it. Of further interest, though, is Mankosky's killer hanged himself in his cell. The warden said they classified it as suicide since he was all alone, and they couldn't prove anything different."

"You're thinking Lawrence evened the score?"

"It's one possibility. Most of his crimes had to do with assault — sometimes during commission of another crime, but more often, because he felt like it. Be careful, Beth. As I said, he's a mean SOB with no qualms about hurting people."

I remembered his attack the previous night. "I believe you. But bear in mind, I'm not a piece of pink fluff, either. Now, where is he? Where does he live?"

"That's a problem. He got out of prison about a year ago. For six months, he checked in with his parole officer like clockwork. Then he quit. The P.O. went to the address Lawrence had given, and it was a blind. He called the phone number and —"

"Dummy number, right?"

"You're right again. The natural thing is to jump all over the P.O., but these people have so many parolees to keep up with I'm surprised they do as well as they do."

"I'm guessing your bottom line is the department has no idea where Lawrence is."

"Sorry, but that's it."

I looked at Dot and thought of closed windows with drawn blinds. I thought of a widow whose living status had dropped since her husband went to prison, never to return. I thought of a lower middleclass neighborhood on Magnolia Street, where she lived. I thought of an alliance that might appear ordinary on the surface — the grieving widow and the best friend of her husband. Then I remembered the ranking of suspects Hammonds put together at my urging. Number one on that list was Herbert Lowery Mankosky. Maybe his wife was filling in for him after his death. An image of the house re-formed. I pictured Ashley in one of those rooms, waiting for her parents to come after her.

"I know where he is," I said. "And tonight, your people will capture him." I paused, my mind racing, looking for a plan to end this thing without Ashley being hurt. "I'll get back to you, Chief. I gotta do some hard thinking."

"Oh no you don't. Where is he? Is he the kidnapper? Talk to me, Beth. You're still just a PI. I'm still Chief of Police."

"Sorry, Chief. I have to sort this out. You've dropped a load on me, and I need to get everything in order. Hang tight. I promise to get back to you."

"Okay. Just don't go vigilante on me. This is still a criminal matter. Don't make me arrest you."

I chuckled. "Now, you sound like Sargent. You know I'm a team player."

"Like hell," he said as I punched off.

I leaned forward in the booth. "Finally a break, Dot. We have work to do."

"Me, too," Dabba said through a mouthful of burger. "Gonna git my Linda back."

"Yeah, you, too," I said, wishing I could say anything except that. Somehow, I had to ditch Dabba before the witching hour. I felt sorry for her, but having her around, waving that gun of hers, was far from number one on my list of favorite things.

When Dabba finished her meal, we moved outside and sat at a table in the shade. I soon realized what a smart selection I'd made. We were beside a screened and covered children's playground. Dabba left us for a chair beside the enclosure where she could watch the kids play. She looked so sad, I almost reached out to her — almost.

"Okay, Dot, here's the situation." I filled her in on what the chief told me and my supposition that Ms. Mankosky had Ashley and was in an alliance with Larry Lawrence. I finished by saying, "We're getting Ashley back tonight. Then we're saving John Hammonds four million dollars."

"I like it," Dot said, smiling. "What's your plan? What's my part?" She looked around. "And, uh, what you doing with Dabba?"

I pushed the hair off my forehead, sighing in the process. "The first answer is I don't have one yet, the second is I'm not sure, and the third is I don't have a clue."

"Hot dang. The way we work best. Don't know what the hell we're goin' to do."

I took a notebook from my purse, flipped

it open, and began to doodle. "Here's what I'm thinking. Lawrence should be gone from the house by eleven. I figure he'll want to be in his hole so he can watch the money delivery. That'll leave Mankosky and Ashley. We —"

"And any other members of the gang," Dot said.

I thought about it and the threats in the ransom notes. She was right. "Yes. And any others. But if you were running the show, wouldn't you have your people keeping an eye on as many of the drop sites as possible? I'd want to know what the police were doing, how they were handling it."

"Yeah, makes sense."

"And if I'm wrong, I'll have to take my chances."

"You? What am I, roadkill?"

"No. You're my diversion. While you're getting someone to answer the front door, I'll be slipping in the back. Once I'm in the house, I'll have the element of surprise. And my Walther is a powerful persuader."

"And me?"

"You come busting through the front door and grab whoever opens it. You still have my .38, don't you?"

"One of the things I love about you, dearie. You don't complicate things. Can't get much simpler than that. I like it." She pulled at the straw in her soda, and a slurping sound was her reward. "But . . ."

"Yeah?"

"You ain't told me what you're doin' with Dabba."

"You're a pain in the ass, Dot."

"I know, dearie. But you love me for it. So?"

I looked at Dabba, who appeared mesmerized by the children. "I can't get rid of her, so I'll keep her with me. We can make it work."

"I hope you're right, dearie. I sho' hope you're right."

We sat for a moment without speaking. I don't know what Dot was thinking, but my mind was picturing the break-in at Mankosky's. If it went right, we'd leave there with Ashley. But — that was the nasty word I couldn't shake — if it went wrong, what would Ashley's fate be?

A woman left the enclosure where the children were playing and spoke to Dabba in a loud voice, "You're scaring my little girl. Why are you staring at her? You just quit it — *now.*"

Dabba opened her mouth, but I jumped in. "Sorry, ma'am. She just likes to watch children play. We're about to leave." I switched to Dabba. "Come on. It's time to go."

Dabba looked at me, then at the woman. "You got a pretty little girl. I used to have one, too. Somebody kidnapped her, and I never got her back."

She stood and shuffled away, leaving the woman with an embarrassed look wrapped around a gaping mouth.

We shifted our location to a Starbucks where I called Chief Elston and told him my plan. He was not happy, but gave in when I threatened to call John Hammonds. He agreed to arrange for a four-man team to cover each drop site, from at least four blocks away. They would do nothing until he gave them a go-ahead, then they would swoop in, secure the money, and detain everybody in sight. The idea was to grab a bunch and shake out the guilty later. I hoped Bob had spread the word that none of his homeless should be in the four areas — except my watchers. I was confident they would be so well hidden, not even another homeless person could find them.

My part, other than rescuing Ashley and capturing Ms. Mankosky, was to let the chief know when I had physical control of Ashley. I also told him my priority was Ashley. If I had to let the woman go, she could run. Then she'd be his responsibility.

He was adamant he needed to have someone with me, and I was just as adamant I had all the help I needed. Finally, to throw him a bone, I agreed he could have a team no closer than four blocks away from Mankosky's house, and they could take over once I secured Ashley.

"Beth, there's one thing you better be aware of. I don't know how you're planning to get into the Mankosky house or how you plan to grab Ashley, and I probably don't want to know. But, if it goes south, and you have broken any laws, you'll be treated like any other citizen. No favors. Understand?"

I exhaled a puff of air. "Yeah, I get it. But I don't think Mankosky will be pressing charges. She'll be too busy ducking."

"Fine. That's settled, then. Now, who do you have working with you?"

I looked at Dot and Dabba and winked. "Some real pros. They could teach your boys some lessons."

"So, who —"

"Dropped call," I said and closed my phone. When it rang almost immediately, I turned it off.

I leaned back, reviewing the *plan.* A nagging point leapt to the front. Suppose I couldn't get in the back door. Maybe they had deadbolts. Maybe they had a chain on the door. Not getting that door open fast enough was the difference between success and failure.

I activated my phone and called a friend who ran a cop supply store. He and I had done business in the past when I needed something slightly out of the ordinary for normal citizens. In return, I ran down a couple of deadbeats who owed him money.

When he answered, I said, "Mo, Beth here. I need something."

"So do I — a million dollars so I can retire. You got it for me?"

"If I had that much money, I'd retire and not have to do business with your shady operation."

"Hey, it's not shady. I sell cop supplies to our law enforcement officers. Nothing illegal with that."

"I know," I said. "That's through the front door. What about that back entrance?"

"Enough, enough. You're on a cell phone, aren't you? What do you need?"

I told him, and he only groused for a minute or so before giving in. We agreed I'd pick it up within the hour.

THIRTY-ONE

At eleven P.M., I parked two blocks away from Mankosky's house on a cross street. "Okay, ladies, it's the witching hour. Dot, give Dabba and me ten minutes, then head for the front door. We'll get around back and be ready to break in. You hit that doorbell and don't let it stop ringing until someone shows up. As soon as it opens, cry rape or anything you can think of to keep the person engaged. With luck, it'll bring everyone else in the house running to the door."

I patted Dot on the shoulder. "I know you can make a ruckus. I've heard you do it. Dabba and I will be alert for your signal. When I hear you screaming, I'll count to ten, then I'm going in. I would prefer to do it without a lot of noise, but I can't take the chance with a deadbolt or a chain. I'll make as much racket as necessary to get through that door. Once inside, I'll increase the uproar, which should draw attention away from you. That'll be your clue to come through that front door, moving like a cat with a tin can tied to its tail. Be ready to neutralize anyone who tries to stop you. Don't kill 'em, though — unless you have to."

Dabba said, "What about —"

"I'll get to your part in a minute. Let me finish with Dot first." I stopped and thought through the actions I laid out. "That's about it. Dot, once you're inside, we'll team up, secure everyone we meet, and search for Ashley. Do you have the duct tape?"

"Got it," Dot said, patting her purse. "Uh, one question, though. What if it's not the right house?"

"Not something I want to consider. But if it's not, you and Dabba run like there are Dobermans nipping at your butts. I'll wait for the police."

Dot's mouth opened, but I turned away from her. "Now, Dabba, I need you for my backup. You'll help me with the break-in, then remain outside the door, covering me in case someone comes running. Be careful, though. It could be an innocent neighbor, someone who thinks we're burglars. Stop them. Don't shoot them."

"But I got to find Linda. She won't know

who you are. She'll be scared. I can't stay outside."

"Please, Dabba," I said. "I really need you there. I can't afford to have someone surprise me from behind. I need you to protect my back. Without you, this cannot work and we'll never recover . . . uh, Linda."

Dabba appeared to think about it. "Okay, but make sure you tell Linda her mama's waiting for her. And you bring her to me fast. If you don't, I'm bustin' in that house."

I exhaled the lungful of air I'd been holding, while hoping Dabba would agree to stay where I wouldn't have to worry about her. "I promise. I'll bring Linda to you."

"I don't like it, but I'll do it. If you ain't out with Linda fast, I'm goin' in."

I figured that was as much control over her as I'd ever have. "Is everyone ready?"

"Dearie, I was born ready," Dot said. "Seems like I spend all my time waitin' for you."

"Ready to git my Linda," Dabba said.

We did fist bumps, then got out of the car.

Dot said, "Wait up a minute, dearie." She took me by the elbow and steered me toward the back of the car. Over her shoulder, she said, "Dabba, I just got something I need to tell Beth."

"I'll be right back." I made a motion for

Dabba to stay where she was.

When we were a few feet away, Dot said, "You know you can't trust Dabba. If she does what you say, I'll be one surprised ol' woman."

"I know. But I don't have many options. Telling her to stay with the car is a loser. It's better to give her a job to do. I'm hoping she won't come crashing in until after we have things under control."

Dot sighed. "Good luck, but watch your back. She's your joker in the deck."

I stared at Dot, wondering if I would ever have a better friend. Life sure deals some strange hands. A homeless woman, almost twice my age, with a terrible track record and me — a misplaced Texan with a private eye license — on the way to becoming best friends. Didn't make much sense. I pulled her to me in a hug. "Thank you."

"Humph. Don't git all squishy on me, now." She squeezed me in return. "Now, let's do it."

I let her go. "Yeah. Okay, let me gather our stuff, then we're on our way. Remember, ten minutes."

A moment later, Dabba and I skulked from shadow to shadow as we worked our way toward Mankosky's house. I wanted to approach from the rear, not taking a chance someone would spot us coming down the sidewalk. During our afternoon reconnaissance, I noticed that the house behind it, facing Elmendorf Street, had an open back yard that joined with Mankosky's. That was the direction Dabba and I headed, down Elmendorf Street. The three-feet-long package we carried might have made us obvious to anyone looking through a window, but I couldn't worry about that. Even if they called the police, things should be over by the time they arrived.

I was in the lead with Dabba behind. "Move a little faster," I said. "We have to be in position before Dot gets there."

"I'm movin', I'm movin'. What is this thang? Weighs a damn ton, it does."

"It's our passport into the house holding Linda. That's why we have to move fast."

She grumped, but picked up her step, and soon we were creeping alongside the house facing Elmendorf. The windows were dark, making me hope either no one was home, or they were sound asleep. So far, our luck held.

I whispered, "We have to get across the open yard between the houses. Can you make the run?"

"Humph. Don't go slow, or I'll be passin' you, and pullin' you along with this thang."

I smiled. "Let's go."

True to her words, Dabba pushed me all the way.

At the back of Mankosky's house, we pressed up against the siding, the package at my feet. I knelt and pulled the covering off, revealing a battering ram. It was solid steel with a flat head and straps so it could be swung by one person. In the backroom of Mo's store, I had hefted it and let it swing. Mo said it weighed about thirty-five pounds and would crush its way through any standard lock and doorframe it hit. According to him, it was a favorite of SWAT teams around the country. I hoped he was right. I figured one smash at the door would bring everyone running, and I had to be inside before they arrived. I counted on surprise to give me an upper hand.

I whispered to Dabba, "Remember, once I get inside, you keep your eyes open for anyone coming behind us. Don't hurt them though — unless you have to. Make sure before you jump anyone."

"What, you think I'm crazy or sumthin'? I knows how to git things done."

Squinting at her in the dark, I let my eyes roll, then decided to believe her. I took a deep breath before saying, "I trust you. I'm nervous. That's all."

"Then let me do it. It's my Linda in there."

There went my newfound confidence in her.

The faint sound of a ringing doorbell saved me from having to answer. The house had the old-fashioned kind that actually rang, rather than dinging or chiming. It must have been Dot, and she was riding that button like it was a fire alarm in a high rise.

I took my Walther from my purse, then handed the purse to Dabba. "Hold this for me, please." I lifted the battering ram and got into position beside the door. It was awkward because I was trying to hold my pistol and one of the straps in the same hand, but I wasn't about to give up either one. The doorbell went quiet, and I stepped around and let the ram swing. The door crashed inward, just as Mo said it would. I dropped the ram and raced inside, finding myself in the kitchen.

Something slammed into the middle of my back as a hand reached around and grabbed my right arm. That sent me into an out of control spin which brought me face to chest with a huge man who could only be Lawrence Lawrence.

Another mistake, making me wonder if I was doomed to set a new record in this case

— my third biggie. My first was jumping to the conclusion John killed his wife and the maid. Then there was the soccer field, resulting in a trouncing I still felt. And now, I'd made another. I had assumed Lawrence would be at one of the ransom drop sites by now. Apparently not.

When I tilted my head up, I saw that he looked just like the chief described him — one big, mean son of a bitch.

My right hand hurt, and I realized it was because Lawrence had it crushed in a death grip. My pistol clattered to the floor.

"Well, Ms. Bowman, we meet again. Guess you didn't learn anything last night. You've made yourself a pest. Hasn't she, Edith?" He looked toward the entryway into the kitchen and I groaned. A woman stood there, holding Dot in front of her. From the look on Dot's face — pure outrage — I guessed the woman was in control.

"Ms. Mankosky, I presume?" I had to give credit to the police sketch artist. He'd done a good job of capturing her. I looked at her left hand, the one squeezing Dot's arm. She wore a large marquise-cut green stone on her third finger. My guess was it was an emerald, and as described, surrounded by diamonds. It didn't help my situation any, but I applauded Ms. Dimitri, the school secretary. She had nailed it.

Edith Mankosky smiled, a small one. "Nice to meet you, Beth Bowman. Who's your friend here? She's not very talkative."

"You just take that damn gun outa my back, and I'll show you talkin'. I'll spell out some words all over your ugly face. What you say to that, you fat bitch?"

Dot was wound up, and I had no doubts she would do just what she threatened.

"Feisty, isn't she?" Lawrence said, laughing. "You might need a bigger gun to handle her."

I gave a quick shake of my head to Dot, hoping she'd get the message to *cool it.* If she did, she didn't show it.

"Well, you gon' put down that peashooter and go toe-to-toe with me? Or, ain't you got the guts? Hell, I'm twice your age, and you damn sure outweigh me. Shit, I bet you got forty pounds on me. But I'll still kick your fat ass all over this place."

Edith shoved her toward me and took a step to the side. "Shut your mouth, you old hag, or I'll drop you right here. I can do it now just as good as later." She waved her pistol around Al Capone style. "You do know both of you have to die, don't you? But you'll do it at my convenience — when and where your bodies won't turn up too soon. Larry, lock them in my bedroom closet. We'll leave them there until Joe gets back with the ransom. Then we'll take them to the Glades and get rid of them."

Joe? Another miscalculation? No, I forgave myself for that one. Having another person covering a drop site didn't surprise me. The emails had said the writer had enough people to keep things covered at all times. "Just a minute," I said. "You at least owe me an explanation. How'd you know I'd come busting through your back door while my partner rung the front doorbell?"

"Because you're so transparent, that's how."

"Sorry," I said, "I must be more dense than you think. How does my being transparent answer my question?" From the serious look on Edith's face, I assumed she didn't get my poor attempt at a joke.

"I saw you this afternoon," she said, "creeping up the street in your car, casing my house. Then your friend comes around the corner where you turned and starts knocking on doors. She didn't know that everybody in the neighborhood works. When she banged on my door, I got a real good look at her." She glanced at Dot. "Not someone I'd be likely to forget — ugly as a manatee. Tonight when the doorbell rang, I peered through the peephole, and there she was. Your plan was just too easy. If she was at the front, you had to be at the back. I sent Larry to take care of you, and I took care of your friend."

"How in hell did you get a PI license?" Larry said. "You're too stupid to live. Now, move your butt that way." He nodded toward the doorway through which Edith had entered. "It's time for you to disappear for a while."

It wasn't exactly *He who runs away lives to fight another day,* but it was close enough. As long as I was breathing and my heart was beating, fate could deal me a winning hand. And the same went for Dot.

"Don't be in such a rush," I said, raising my voice as much as I dared. "You can tell me why you did all this. Ashley's never done anything to you." I was stalling, hoping Dot was right about Dabba, that she wouldn't do anything I asked her to do. In fact, I was wishing Dabba would ignore my instructions and come crashing in, looking for Linda. I inched myself toward the back door.

"Oh, funny girl," Larry said. "You think —"

"Why not?" Edith said. "She thinks she's so damn smart. No problem in her knowing

356

the whole story as long as she's going to die anyway. It'll be fun to watch her face when she finds out how dumb these rich farts are."

"Yeah," Dot said. "Why'd you do it?"

Edith laughed, then sneered at Dot. "Why the hell do you think? Look at this dump I'm living in. That damn Hammonds took most of our money to defend Herb, then let him rot in jail. That left me with a pittance. I had to sell the house and most of the furnishings. I even had to sell a lot of my jewelry. You ever tried to sell something fast? You get a few pennies on the dollar. I was lucky to get enough to buy this crap of a house.

"And, can you imagine what it did to a gentle person like Herb to go to prison? The cretins he faced every day? The people he had to share life with? It was hell. Every time I saw him, he blubbered about the way the guards and the other prisoners treated him. The guards didn't miss a chance to abuse him, calling him all kinds of vile names. And the prisoners beat the shit out of him at every opportunity. He was terrified of taking a shower. The guards didn't care. They watched and laughed. I expected a message any day he was dead. When it finally came, I was not surprised at all."

She looked at Larry. "The only good part was Larry moving into Herb's cell. He befriended Herb, became his friend. Herb told me he could never repay Larry for what he did. I will though. He gets a third of the ransom. That'll buy him a new identity in Mexico."

She paused. "Now you know why. Won't keep you alive any longer, but you'll die knowing I have good reasons for what I'm doing. Hammonds is suffering, and he deserves it. And you're powerless to stop any of it."

I nodded. "You've had a tough time of it. I can understand your grudge against John Hammonds, but why his daughter? She's done nothing to you. Will you live up to your promise and return her?"

"Not sure yet. At first, it was all about getting even with that lawyer-bastard. But now . . . well, I don't know. It's amazing how much some people are willing to pay for a young blond girl with good genes. Her mother was beautiful, you know. Her old man ain't bad looking, either. Larry and I are still talking about it. We might turn her loose on the street and let some cop find her. Or, maybe we'll just sell her to the highest bidder, and let someone else take the risk. They'll probably have their ways of getting her out of the country." She paused, obviously satisfied with herself. "It won't matter to you what happens to her, though. You won't be around to see. Nope, you and your buddy will be alligator shit before then. Now, let's move."

"Give me a minute," I said. "There's one more thing I don't understand. If all you wanted was to kidnap Ashley, why did you kill Ms. Hammonds and the maid? That took you from thirty-forty years in the pen to death row. I don't get it."

Edith grinned. "They have to catch us first, and that's not going to happen. We'll be long gone before the police have any trail to follow. Seven days, remember?"

"Yeah," I said, wondering where the hell Dabba was. "What about Ms. Hammonds and Carmina, the maid?"

Edith glared at Larry, then at me. "Mistake. Simple mistake. It was our only screwup. We didn't know Ashley was in school. We thought we'd find her at home. Then we'd grab the kid and her mother. But, dear mummy decided to play heroine and try to escape. I had to kill her. That left us with the maid as a witness to murder instead of being the messenger to spread the word about the kidnapping. She had to go. Larry took care of her. Satisfied?"

"No, not satisfied. I won't be satisfied until I see you get the needle."

Edith's smug look infuriated me, but I couldn't think of anything else to ask — or any way to swing the pendulum my way. As long as we were alive, though, there was a chance. "Okay, Dot," I shouted, as if Dot were hard of hearing. "They have the winning hands. We're helpless here. Time to do what they say."

Dabba had had plenty of time to act. She might have wandered off to find her next meal, or maybe she saw a little girl in pink and was following her. In either case, Dot and I were in deep trouble. However, I had a hunch there was no room, closet or not, that could keep Dot contained. She had too many street smarts to stay locked in. With her by my side, I had faith we'd prevail.

Dot had been staring at Edith during her dissertation, but now, her eyes popped over to me, saying, *You gotta be kidding.* But, as quickly as that happened, the look disappeared and she assumed an expression of defeat. "Guess you're right. This fat bitch won't fight me and they got the guns. Ain't nothing we can do but go along. C'mon Larry, baby, move that big ass and let's git it over with."

That sealed it. Dot gave in too easy. No

way. I knew she had an ace up her sleeve. I might not have known what it was, but I was sure it was there. Then the obvious sunk in. Dot had a clear view of the back door.

"You bitch, you took my Linda," I heard before a shot sounded.

Edith dropped her gun and grabbed her chest. Larry spun toward the doorway and fired.

THIRTY-TWO

I went to my chest and came up with my bra gun. I snapped off a shot and got lucky, catching Lawrence in the upper arm on his shooting side. His pistol clattered to the floor. He reached for it with his left hand, but Dot was faster, kicking it out of his reach.

"Hold it right there, asshole," I snarled in my tough gal voice. "This derringer has a round left, and I'll be more accurate with the next one. I'll put it right between your eyes. Dot, hand me my Walther, please."

That's when I noticed Dot held two guns, one in each hand. An image of Faye Dunaway as Bonnie Parker came to mind — well, a much older version of Ms. Dunaway.

"Can I shoot this bastard first?"

"No, not yet. Just grab my Walther. It's there, inside the door."

Dot did as I asked, and I felt much better armed as I slipped my derringer back into its holster.

Lawrence squeezed his shoulder, blood oozing between his fingers. "Gotta hand it to you, bitch. I'd never have expected you to be armed there, other than the weapons nature gave you, I mean."

I looked at him, trying to decide if that was his version of funny.

Edith moaned, proving she was alive. That disappointed me. I'd have been more than happy if she were dead. "Dot, keep an eye on her. Lawrence, move over and sit beside Edith. Trust me when I say Dot will blow you to hell if you blink wrong. Don't get the sniffles or dust in your eye."

I remembered Dabba. She had to be the one who shot Edith. Where was she? I walked to the back door and looked. Dabba lay in a pool of blood. "Oh, damn, Dabba is down," I said, yanking my phone from my pocket. I hit the speed dial to Chief Elston.

He answered halfway through the first ring. "Beth, you okay?"

"Yes, get your men in here to take over and call the EMTs. I have three wounded, two I don't give a shit about and one that I do. I want someone here to patch Dabba up now. The others can wait a few hours."

"You heard her, Mike. Get your ass in gear."

He had me on speakerphone. If I'd known . . . Hell, I'd have probably said the same thing.

"Do you have Ashley?"

"Not yet, but I'm searching as soon as I get you off the phone. Tell your site watchers to move in and grab anyone that moves. There is at least one of the kidnappers at one of the sites, name of Joe."

"Find Ashley. I'm moving now."

I started to close the phone, but yelled, "Hold on. Tell your men to enter easy. The one holding the guns is a friend. Don't spook her, or she might shoot the wrong target."

"Gotcha."

Flipping the phone shut, I said, "Dot, hold these two slugs. I'll check Dabba, then search the house."

"Can I shoot them?"

I looked at Edith and Lawrence. Edith was in pain and scared. It showed all over her. Lawrence held his shoulder and sneered.

"Only if they move, Dot. Watch the big asshole. He thinks he's tough."

"Don't I hope?" Dot said.

I went outside and knelt over Dabba. She was unconscious, her breath ragged, but steady. The blood came from a head wound. They always bleed a lot. When I looked

closer, it appeared to be superficial. I hoped
so. The flow had slowed to a trickle, which
gave me hope.

Since David is the only one with medical
knowledge in our two-some, all I knew to
do was make her comfortable. I folded her
bag and stuffed it under her head. "Hang
on. Help's on the way." In case she could
hear me, I added, "I'm going after Linda."

I returned to the inside of the house where
Dot was doing a great impression of a
mercenary on guard duty, lips twisted into
a snarl. "I think Dabba will be okay. I'm going to search for Ashley."

"Go on, dearie. We ain't gonna have no
problems here. Are we, crumb and crumb-
ess?"

Edith moaned.

Lawrence glared.

I moved into the main part of the house,
knowing Dot had things well under control.
My fear was she might have them so well
under control she'd decide to use Lawrence
for target practice. No time to worry about
that, though. If she did, I'd come up with a
story later.

A dining room opened into the living
room with a hallway branching off to the
left. I took it, moving slow and cautious. I
didn't expect to meet any more of the gang,

but I hadn't expected Lawrence to be at the back door either.

A door on the right opened when I turned the knob. Woman's bedroom. Neat, the bed made with throw pillows all over. Edith's. No Ashley. I moved on.

A second bedroom. Messy. Men's stuff thrown around. Unmade bed. Lawrence's. No Ashley.

A third door. Locked. I examined the doorknob and discovered a keyhole. Somebody had installed a regular lock in place of the kind one usually finds in a bedroom. I pushed on the door. It didn't move at all. Tight fit. Accidental or modified?

I considered retrieving the battering ram or trying to kick the door open. I was sure my adrenalin flow was so fierce, I could not only kick it open, but sail it across the room. No, couldn't take that chance. If Ashley was in there, she was probably terrified and hiding under the bed from the noise of the gunshots. Slamming into the door would only scare her worse.

I forced myself to slow down and count to ten, then did it a second time. What I needed was a simple solution, and the simplest was the key. The answer was in the kitchen — Edith. I'd pound on her until she told me where it was.

As I turned, the obvious came into view. A small hook protruded from the doorframe with a key dangling from it. I wondered why I always think complicated, when simple is such a better approach.

I lifted the key, slipped it into the lock, and opened the door. There were two night-lights, one on each side of the room. On the bed lay the most beautiful blond-headed girl I'd ever seen in my life — Ashley. I scooted over to her and stared. I could hear her breathing, soft and regular. I wanted to scream hallelujah, but backed out of the room instead. She'd never seen me before. If I woke her, she'd probably be terrified.

In the hall, I called Chief Elston again. "I have Ashley. Get Hammonds here as fast as you can. She's asleep, and I want him to be the first thing she sees when she awakens."

"Is she okay?"

"As far as I can tell. Her breathing sounds right, and she has a smile on her face."

"Her dad's on the way."

"I'll stand guard until he arrives."

I heard noises from the direction of the kitchen and realized the police had checked in. A moment later, Dot came down the hall, followed by Sargent. I held my finger to my lips in the traditional shushing sign.

When they were close, Dot said, "Medicos say Dabba will be okay. She'll have a new part in her hair for a while, but that should go away."

Sargent said, "Body count's smaller this time. Or do you have some others hidden in corners we haven't checked yet? We have things under control now. You can back down."

"Step off a tall cliff," I said, "but be quiet about it. Ashley's asleep in there, and I'm not moving until Hammonds has her in his arms."

"Agreed," he said, surprising me. "Mind if I stay with you? I'm not needed out there."

"Suit yourself." I softened my tone. "Actually, I'd welcome it. Suddenly, I'm bone-tired."

"Oh, my," Dot said, giving me the eye. "Is this what y'all call bonding? I liked it better when you two were spittin' at one another."

THIRTY-THREE

Sunrise found me sitting in Hammonds' kitchen, a fresh cup of coffee in front of me. Hammonds and Maddy sat across from me.

Ashley slept in her own bed, surrounded by her favorite stuffed animals. The doctor had given her a thorough check and pronounced her fine. He guessed she might have been given some kind of sedative, but he wouldn't know for sure until results of the blood test came in — later that day, the next, or it could be a couple of days. He put the rush on them, but some things can't be hurried. In the meantime, he suggested Hammonds let Ashley sleep as much as possible. The rest would help her get through the trauma of discovering her *mommy* was gone.

I was still bone-tired, but the combination of caffeine and adrenalin kept me awake. That, plus the smile I knew owned my face. It felt like it was wrapping my mouth around my ears.

"Beth, I'll never be able to thank you enough," Hammonds said. "Without you, Ashley might be dead now."

"Not to mention saving four-million dollars," Maddy said.

"The money's not important," Hammonds said. "Only Ashley counts. I can always defend a couple of scumbags to recover the funds." He smiled, but it was obvious it was forced.

"How about your friends?" Maddy said. "Are they all right?"

"Not sure about Dabba. The EMTs said they thought the worst for her would be a superficial scalp wound and a minor concussion. But they wanted a doctor to look her over. They bundled her off to the hospital. I'll check in with her later."

"And . . . what's her name, Dorothy?"

I laughed. "Not sure she'd ever answer to that, although that's probably her proper name. Dot. She calls herself Dot. She's fine, just doesn't like the bright lights. As soon as they took Dabba away, Dot gave me a hug and melted into the night. I hope I can find her tomor— uh, later today."

"Chief Elston said you had people at each of the ransom sites," Hammonds said. "Hope none of them got swept up when the police descended."

"Not my friends," I said. "They're like light-colored smoke. The slightest breeze makes them disappear. But, even if any got picked up, I'm pretty sure they're back on the street by now. I gave Bannon and Sargent a rundown on each of them." I looked at Maddy and smiled. "If Maddy goes driving today, she will probably see some of her *taxi passengers* from yesterday working intersections. Be kind to them."

Maddy laughed, actually laughed — first time I'd heard it. I was surprised it wasn't some kind of cackle. Maybe she wasn't the witch I'd pictured her to be.

"You could have warned me," she said. "I didn't know what to think when they came pouring out of that bar, headed for my car."

"Nope. My only regret is I wasn't there to see your expression. I'll ask them about it later. Should be some good stories." I chuckled, thinking about this super-straight woman from NYC getting close to her first real homeless people.

From a baby video monitor sitting on the counter, we heard sounds of Ashley turning over.

"Look," Hammonds said. "Before Ashley wakes up, I want to pay you."

"No rush. I'll send a bill."

"No," he said. "You can't itemize what you did for me. That's impossible. Here." He slid a check across the table to me. The payee was Beth Bowman, and he had signed it. The rest was blank. "Fill in any amount up to the four-million you saved me. Ashley is worth that and much, much more. Money will never express how strongly I feel about you, but it's all I have."

"I can't —" That's as far as I got before his hand gripped mine.

"You can, and you will. Be generous to yourself. I owe you."

Maddy sat beside him, beaming. "When you're next in New York, everything is on me — and I do mean everything."

"But —"

"Hush," Hammonds said. "I don't have much time, and we have other business." He pushed a second check toward me.

I picked it up. This time, the payee line was blank, but it was signed and made out in the amount of fifty thousand dollars.

"That's for your friends," John said. "I don't know their names, so I'll leave it up to you to spread it around as you see fit." He stood. "Now, if you'll excuse me, I'm going back to sit beside my daughter until she wakes up." He offered his right hand.

Tears threatened to overwhelm me as I

remembered my first meeting with this man. I had suspected him of killing his wife and maid. How wrong could I have been? I shook his hand, then moved around the table. "A handshake is not enough. I need a hug."

He complied, which was almost too much for my overloaded tear ducts. As he left the kitchen, he stopped, and turned back to me. "If you ever need anything, and there are no limits on that, you'd better come to me first. I'd offer you a well-paying job, but I don't think you'd enjoy working my side of the street. I'll tell your boss, Sly Bergstrom, though. He'd better treat you right."

"I do have one other small thing, if you don't mind."

He stopped and came back to me. "Name it."

"The woman who was wounded at the house, the one they found outside. Her name is Dabba. She's a friend and was instrumental in rescuing Ashley. She has no money for hospital bills and no defense against the police — if they decide to charge her with anything." I was thinking about the gun she'd been carrying — the one I didn't grab because my mind was wrapped around searching for Ashley. My last recollection was it had fallen by her side. "Can you help her?"

"Consider it done. I'll take care of her. Anything else?"

"No." I tried to smile, but my face refused. Instead, I cracked, and the tears ran as he headed back to be with Ashley. Maddy took me into her arms, and I heard her sniffling, too. "He means it, and so do I. You're the kid sister we never had."

When I entered Dabba's room at the hospital, I wasn't surprised to find Dot sitting beside her bed. Dot looked clean and refreshed and wore her *damn greeter* outfit. Dabba appeared to be sleeping.

"How's she doing?" I asked.

"Nurse says fine. The bullet gave her a new part in her hair, then the doctor shaved most of her head so he could do some sewing. She won't be happy when she looks in a mirror."

"Somehow, I don't think she was all that vain about her appearance. She'll probably just jam on a hat until it grows out. In fact, that could improve her looks." I smiled to reinforce the joke.

"Hey, can't a girl get no rest in this place?" Dabba said. "I'm trying to sleep here. And I ain't got no hat. Gonna buy me one?"

"Any kind you want," I said. "If you hadn't taken that bitch out, Dot and I would be alligator wrestling — or being digested. Now explain why you've been listening to every word we said without letting on you're awake. How do you feel?"

"Good. They got some mighty fine happy-juice here. You oughta try it. In fact, you look like you need it more than I do. Did you get Ashley back?"

I started. It was the first time she'd said Ashley instead of Linda. Whatever, I wasn't going there. "Yes. She's fine. Her father took her home. She was asleep in her own bed when I left his house." I looked hard at Dabba. Her eyes were clear. If she was drugged, it didn't show.

"I'm glad." A tear slithered from her eye, and disappeared into the pillow. "I ain't never gonna see Linda again, am I?"

I looked at Dot, who leaned forward and took Dabba's hand. "Dearie, she's gone. It's been too long. She ain't never coming back."

Dabba turned her eyes on me.

I nodded.

"I s'pose I knew that," she said. "But I been dreamin' so long, it's hard to stop. Do you reckon it's alright if I just keep thinkin' she's alive, still out there somewhere? As long as I keep lookin', I got a reason to live. It won't hurt nobody, will it?"

"No one can take away our dreams," I said.

Dot kissed her on the cheek.

My next stop was Bobby's Bar. En route, I called and Judy said he was on his corner, peddling newspapers. I asked her to have him meet me at the bar. She was reluctant until I explained that I had something for him — something he'd want.

When he came through the door, and I handed him the check Hammonds gave me, his eyes almost bugged out. "I can't take this. It's . . . it's . . ."

"Preposterous?" I said.

"Yes," he said. "That's an excellent word for it."

"Doesn't matter. John Hammonds is a rich man who takes care of those he cares about. You and your people now fall under that umbrella. Use the money to help them. He'll feel like he's paying a portion of a debt. Make us all feel better."

I went home and slept eighteen straight hours. I may have smiled the whole time. I had made mistakes in the Ashley Hammonds case, but none that affected the outcome. I was one proud private investigator. In the shower, I sang so loud my neighbors might have thought I'd lost my sanity.

David made it home Monday afternoon, and we celebrated being together again, celebrated several times that night. For reasons I couldn't understand, he seemed surprised I wasn't injured — not even a single lump on my head.

On Tuesday, David and I headed for Orlando where I introduced him to Mom and Ike.

Ike shook his hand while eyeing him like a father checking out his daughter's first date. Apparently, he still had his protective wings spread over me.

David passed Mom's inspection without a hitch. After all, he was a doctor.

ABOUT THE AUTHOR

Randy Rawls is a retired U.S. Army officer and Department of Defense civilian. He is the multi-published author of the Ace Edwards, Dallas PI series, as well as of short stories in various anthologies and *Thorns on Roses,* a South Florida thriller. Living in South Florida, where fact and fiction run together, gives him a rich environment in which to harvest plots. He smiles because life is fun.